Fog o

S J Richards

FOG OF SILENCE

Published worldwide by Apple Loft Press

This edition published in 2024

www.sjrichardsauthor.com

For Harry, Tabby, Immy and Heidi

The Luke Sackville Crime Thriller Series

Taken to the Hills

Black Money

Fog of Silence

The Corruption Code

Lethal Odds

Chapter 1

Alfie reached for the mousse and applied some to his left hand and then onto his hair. He smoothed it back and looked in the mirror, turning his head first to the left and then to the right. He added a smile but that made him look like a Chucky doll, so he toned it down from a gurn to a gentle upturn of his mouth. Much better.

His clothes were cool. They weren't too fancy that his Mum and Dad would wonder what he was up to, but sick nonetheless. He was wearing his dark navy jeans and a plain white t-shirt with an unbuttoned navy and white check shirt over the top. He pulled on his white Nike trainers and stood back.

He looked wicked! Older than sixteen he thought, more like eighteen, perhaps even older. That was important. He was going to be mixing with some awesome guys in their twenties and even thirties and he didn't want to come across as a little kid.

Hopefully, Owen would look the part too. He had a habit of wearing the same black hoodie to everything and if he did that he'd come across as a complete tool.

After a final admiring glance at himself in the mirror, Alfie turned to go downstairs. He glanced in the lounge to see his Mum, Dad and older sister ensconced in their favourite chairs, eyes glued to the television.

"I'm off now," he said.

"Do you want a lift?" his Dad asked without turning around, his gaze fixed on whatever loser trash it was they were watching.

"No, I'm fine. I'm meeting Owen and then we're getting the bus."

"Have a good time at the party," his Mum added

absent-mindedly. "Be back by twelve."

"Sure, Mum."

No way was he going to be back that early, but they'd never know. They were in bed long before eleven and they'd be snoring their socks off by the time he got in.

His sister was the only one to wrestle her eyes from the TV. She turned around and looked him up and down. "Looking cool, little bro," she said. "Feeling lucky?"

Alfie hated it when she called him 'little bro', and he certainly wasn't going to answer her question. She meant would he pull a girl but that wasn't what this evening was about. Not by a long shot.

She was only three years older than him and, like his Mum and Dad, hadn't any idea where he was going. He'd said he was off to a mate's birthday party but the truth was much more exciting. It would have been cool to tell them where he was really going, and the names of the people he'd be spending the evening with, but something told him they'd think it was wrong. More fool them - they didn't know how to live.

"Enjoy Love Island or whatever," he said, but she wasn't listening, her eyes already back on the screen.

Alfie shrugged, checked he had his front door key and then headed out. The sky was cloudless and it was a warm June evening. Where he was going had a pool, which was real cool, and he was wearing his swim shorts under his jeans.

He was ready for anything!

Owen was already at the bus stop when he got there and he was pleased to see the hoodie hadn't made an appearance. Okay, he wasn't quite as cool-looking as him, but he had scrubbed up pretty well in a tight black t-shirt over black chinos. The beanie looked out of place but that was Owen for you.

They fist-bumped.

"Hi bro," Owen said, all teeth and smiles. "Gonna be

slammin' tonight."

Alfie agreed and they spent the journey speculating as to who they might meet.

They got off the bus halfway up Lansdown Road and it took a moment or two to get their bearings. When they did find the turning into Lansdown Park, they were immediately struck by how humungous the houses were.

"Got to be upwards of, like, two or three mill each," Owen said.

"Yeah, got to be." Alfie looked around and pointed over the road at a sign that read 'Whistler House'. "That's the one," he said.

They crossed and walked between two stone pillars and up a gravelled drive. It swept around to the left and after a few yards emerged onto a parking area in front of a large ultra-modern house. It had a flat roof and was dominated by windows. A few people were visible through one of them, though Alfie suspected the majority would be around the back by the pool. He heard the sound of some great R'n'B but it was the parked cars that drew his attention.

"Look at the cool Lambo," he said, pointing at a low-slung sportscar. "And isn't that a Ferrari?"

The other five or six vehicles weren't quite in the same league, but they were all Jaguars and Mercedes at a minimum, any one of them a zillion times better than his Dad's Volkswagen.

"Here we go," Alfie said, and they fist-bumped again before walking to the front door.

It was opened before they could ring the bell and a drop-dead gorgeous blonde in a low-cut dress pulled it wide and flashed her pearly-whites at them.

"Good evening, guys," she said. "I'm Eve."

"Hi, Eve," Alfie said, momentarily taken aback. "I'm Alfie and this is Owen. You said it was okay to bring a friend?"

"Of course it is." She turned her attention to Owen.

"Nice to meet you, Owen."

There was no response and Alfie became conscious that his friend was staring at her with his mouth open.

"Come on in," she continued, apparently oblivious to his gawping. "I'll introduce you to Baz later. Why don't you mingle and enjoy yourselves? Most people are out the back and there's a bar there too. Just ask for whatever you want." She hesitated before adding in a whisper, "Don't tell anyone, but there's a rumour that Wally Zee is coming later."

"Amazing," Alfie said.

"Isn't it?" Eve flashed her smile again. "Anyway, you two go right on through and make yourselves at home." She gestured down the corridor towards an open door, beyond which Alfie could see fairy lights twinkling from the branches of a tree.

They started down the corridor while Eve took a different route towards what looked like a large open-plan kitchen come dining room. After a couple of steps, Alfie turned to his friend. "Baz Hartman is one thing," he whispered, "but Wally Zee!"

"I know," Owen said. "It's, like, amazing!"

They stepped through into a paved area enveloped on three sides by the house and fronting a large rectangular pool which was lit from underneath. The music was a lot louder now.

Alfie cast his eyes around. There were upwards of thirty people, a few who looked about their own age while the rest stretched from their thirties through to their forties or perhaps even fifties. They were standing in small groups of anything from two to half a dozen and, almost without exception, turned to eye up the newcomers as they made their way to the bar area.

Behind the counter was a man in full evening dress. He handed them each a flute of champagne and winked. "This'll set you up for the evening," he said.

They took their drinks and turned around. Owen pointed to a group of four men standing on the opposite side of the pool. "Isn't that Damon Prendergast?"

Alfie nodded but his thoughts were elsewhere. "Have you noticed?" he said.

"What?" Owen said, taking a sip of his bubbly and flinching at the taste.

"Aside from Eve," Alfie went on, "there are no women."

Chapter 2

Owen was still focused on Damon Prendergast's group. "Perhaps the women will be along later," he said absent-mindedly. He nudged Alfie with his elbow. "Hey, look! Ozzy Vaughan's joining them. Here, hold this." He passed his glass over and removed his iPhone from his pocket. "I've got to get a photo."

He raised his phone and an arm stretched from behind and snatched it from his grasp. "Sorry, sir," the barman said. He was smiling as he added, "No photos. These people need their privacy. I'm sure you understand."

"Oh yeah. I guess so," Owen said.

"You should have been asked for your smartphone when you came in." The barman turned to Alfie. "I'll need yours as well please, sir."

Alfie handed it over. "When will we get them back?"

"Don't worry. I'll pop them in our safe and they'll be returned when you leave." He put the phones in his pocket. "Can I fetch you both another drink?"

"I'm fine, thanks," Alfie said.

"Have you got a Peroni?" Owen asked.

"Sure. I'll be back with it in a second."

The waiter left and Alfie was about to speak but realised someone was looking at them and gesturing. He smiled back and said to Owen, "I think that guy with the monster goggles is calling us over. I'm sure I know him from somewhere. Come on, let's see what he wants."

They walked over.

"Hello, lads," the man said. He was tall but very thin and his over-sized glasses made him look like a double-headed lamp post. "We took pity on you," he went on. "Didn't we, Reggie?"

"We did indeed, Marvin," Reggie said, his voice seeming to issue from his nose rather than his mouth. He was as tall as Marvin but very overweight and wore a white t-shirt that did his figure no favours. The corners of his mouth turned up as he spoke and he raised both eyebrows at the same time. It was an odd, and more than a little creepy, thing to do and it dawned on Alfie that he'd seen him do the same thing on television.

"Hey," he said, "Aren't you both on 'Hall of Flame'?" He turned to Marvin. "I thought I recognised you."

"That's the price of fame," Reggie said, and his smile moved from weird to smug. He looked Owen up and down and licked his lips, turning the creep factor up to eleven. "So," he went on, "what brings you two handsome fellows here?"

"Eve invited us," Alfie said. "I applied to be in the audience for Baz Hartman's show…"

Marvin interrupted before he could finish the sentence. "Our show," he said.

"Sorry, yeah, your show. Anyway, I was unsuccessful but she emailed me with some questions. After I'd sent them back she asked if I wanted to bring a friend to this party as a kind of consolation prize."

"Epic consolation prize," Owen said. He was looking around at the other guests. "Look, there's that news presenter who was on Strictly."

"Cool, isn't it?" Reggie said, following his gaze. "So, are you two in the entertainment business?"

"No we're, ah, we're at University," Alfie said. "Bath University. Just finished our first year. Isn't that right, Owen?"

Owen nodded his head vigorously. "Yeah, that's right."

"That's nice," Reggie said. He and Marvin exchanged a glance before he went on, "So you're Owen, and you're…?"

"Alfie," Alfie said. He felt his cheeks flush but he wasn't sure why.

"So, what's it like being on the show?" Owen asked.

"Tiring," Reggie said. "And when you're in the limelight all week it's really important to make the most of the weekends. We all have to take advantage of the opportunities life offers us." His eyebrows met the top of his head again. "Don't you agree?"

Alfie was about to reply when there was a loud crash and a scream behind him. He turned to see someone topple backwards out of the corridor they had come through. The man's arms were flailing and he was unable to stop himself from falling onto the floor. A second man, much larger and clearly very angry, stormed after him and leaned down as the other man twisted onto his back and tried to get up.

"Don't you fucking move, you moron!" he screamed as he put his foot onto the first man's chest to hold him down.

Alfie was conscious of movement in his peripheral vision and turned back to see Damon Prendergast, Ozzy Vaughan and two other men he didn't recognise being ushered into the house by another entrance. One of the two men doing the ushering was the barman who had given them their drinks.

The music was still playing but all conversation had ceased. Without exception, everyone's eyes were on the drama being played out in front of them.

After a few seconds had passed, the larger man took his foot off the prone man's back and stood back, allowing him to clamber to his feet. He leaned forward and grabbed him by the shoulder and half-shoved him back to the corridor.

"Someone deal with him," he said. "I never want to see his fucking face again."

With a start, Alfie realised that the big man was Baz Hartman, the host of 'Hall of Flame' and all-round nice guy. His actions in the previous few minutes were so at odds with his smiling TV persona that he hadn't recognised him.

The two men in dinner jackets emerged from the

house, grabbed the smaller man by the arms and ushered him out. Baz Hartman followed a few paces behind.

A minute passed and a couple of people started talking quietly, then the barman came out again and said, "Sorry, everyone. The party's over." He stood to one side and gestured for everyone to leave.

There were a few muted comments as everyone moved towards the house.

Alfie grabbed Owen's arm and held him back. "We need our phones," he whispered. "Let's stay at the back. Perhaps we can ask someone for them."

They slowed and were the last into the corridor at the back of the house. There was a door to the right which Alfie thought might be a cloakroom. He decided it was worth a try anyway.

"Hang on, Owen," he said. "I'm going to look in here."

He pressed the handle down and stepped into a room which looked to be a large study or office of some sort. His attention was immediately drawn to an ultra-modern metal-legged crimson sofa against the wall facing the door, and to the right of it a sleek white desk and chair. It was all very elegant.

He turned his head to the left and his heart leapt into his mouth.

Sitting on the floor, his back to the wall and his head bent forwards over his chest, was a completely naked man. There was blood covering his front and flowing down into his groin. It was also falling down the sides of his body onto the floor, staining the pale cream rug he was perched on.

The figure was unmoving and Alfie realised that he was looking at a dead body. Something about his haircut and build told him this was a teenager rather than an older man, perhaps his own age or possibly even younger.

He swallowed and backed out of the room. He had to tell someone and get them to call the police. And to check he was definitely dead. It could be he was just unconscious and the wound wasn't as bad as it appeared.

Once he was out of the room he shut the door, took a deep breath, and said, "You'll never believe…" before realising the person waiting for him in the corridor wasn't Owen.

"What are you doing?" the man asked, and Alfie recognised him as the taller of the two men who had escorted Damon Prendergast and his group away earlier.

"I was looking for my phone," Alfie said, "and I saw someone on the floor in there." He swallowed. "I think he's dead. You need to call the police."

The man grabbed him by the arm. "Come with me."

He pulled Alfie down the corridor and through another door into what appeared to be a cinema room. He pushed Alfie onto the nearest seat.

"Where's Owen?" Alfie asked.

"Your friend's gone. What's your name?"

"Alfie. Aren't you going to ring the police?"

"Where's your phone, Alfie?"

"It was taken from me earlier."

"Right. Wait here a minute."

The man left and reappeared a couple of minutes later. "Is it one of these?" he asked, holding two iPhones in the air.

"It's that one," Alfie said, indicating the blue phone in the man's left hand.

"What's the passcode?"

"It's okay, I can use my finger to…"

"Didn't you hear me?" The man took in a deep breath and seemed to be trying to calm himself. "What's the fucking passcode?"

Alfie told him and he entered it, giving a little nod of satisfaction when it was accepted.

"Are you going to call the police?" Alfie asked.

"Leave it with us. We'll handle it. You need to forget

you saw anything."

"What?" Alfie was taken aback. He gulped and held his hand out. "Can I have my phone back?"

The man ignored him and started pressing keys on the iPhone. "I see you've got your Mum and Dad's contact details on here," he said. "Also Owen, your friend. And this girl…" He pressed a few more keys. "Oh, she's pretty." A couple more keys. "I see her name's Milly. Is she your sister?"

"What are you doing?"

The man put Alfie's phone back into his pocket. "I'm keeping this. Call it insurance."

"What do you mean?"

"When I said you have to forget you saw anything I meant it." He sneered. "You don't tell anyone about this evening. Do you understand? Not Owen, not Mummy and Daddy and not the gorgeous Milly. They seem like really nice people. I'd hate for them to be involved in an accident."

"What?"

The man grabbed Alfie by the arm and pulled him out of the chair, then shoved him back out of the room and down the corridor to the front door. With a final push, he was catapulted out, and only just managed to stop himself from falling over. He turned in time to see the door closing with a resounding thunk.

Chapter 3

The Executive Conference had morphed into a self-indulgent, back-slapping, sales-oriented horror show and Luke Sackville was hating every moment.

"I think our sector will hit the target," the short bespectacled man next to him was saying, but for the life of him Luke couldn't remember his name, let alone what sector he was in. Wilbert, was it?

"That's good," he said and spotted James standing alone a few yards away. This was a possible escape route.

"Hey, James," he called. "Why don't you come and join us?"

James walked over and shook the other man's hand. "I'm James McDonald, Head of HR," he said, smiling.

"William Longsmith," the man said, his face serious. He grasped James' hand and shook it vigorously. "I'm the GNE Client Director."

Of course he is, Luke thought. He really must remember it this time. He was hopeless at mixing and making small talk.

He had been Head of Ethics for a few months now but the team had not yet worked in Filchers' Media Sector. However, he was well aware of the importance of William Longsmith's account. Global News and Entertainment, known to everyone as GNE, was a major player on the world stage and wrestling the outsourcing contract from IBM five years ago had been a major coup. Since then, the Media Sector had grown to be Filchers' second largest revenue earner after Central Government.

"Did I hear you organised this?" William went on.

"With my team, yes," James said.

"Well done. It's been very good and our customers have

loved it."

That was hardly surprising. Free food and drink from dawn to dusk, and what passed for entertainment in the evenings. Luke looked at his watch. It was only ten o'clock and Edward Filcher had made it clear he expected his direct reports to linger until midnight.

"Excuse me, gents," he said, pointing vaguely across the hall. "There's someone I need to speak to."

He left James and William and headed for the opposite side of the room, then out and onto the patio at the back of the hotel. To his relief, it was deserted. He stood by one of the benches overlooking the garden, shook his head and muttered, "Two more bloody hours."

"I know what you mean."

Luke turned to see Fred Tanner, the Head of Marketing, standing beside him. He had only been with Filchers a couple of months, having taken over from the disgraced previous incumbent, but Luke had already grown to like the man. He had been poached from a Marketing Consultancy and was a very down-to-earth Yorkshireman.

Fred was a couple of years older than Luke, perhaps forty-five, and at six foot one was above average height, even though that did mean Luke had a good five inches on him. He kept himself in good shape and the two of them had played squash together a couple of times and every game had been close.

"Did I see you with William Longsmith?" Fred asked. "Reet asswipe, that 'un."

Luke chuckled. "I wasn't with him for long, fortunately."

"He's had my team doing all sorts for GNE. Seems to think we have an endless budget and sticks his nose in all over the place too."

Luke knew that the GNE contract was coming up for renewal, and that was why the Client Director and his top team had lobbied to extend the Executive Conference to customers. It was doubtless the reason they were hassling Fred to do more marketing.

"Roll on 1 pm tomorrow," Luke said.

"Amen to that. At least it doesn't start until eleven to give that lot," Fred gestured behind them at the hall, "the chance to get over their hangovers. What's the agenda? Is our illustrious superior speaking?"

"Fortunately not. There's a guest speaker, but it's a surprise. A celebrity of some sort I suspect. Then there's a talk from Francois Lausanne."

"Who's he?"

Luke shrugged. "He's the boss of FNCM," he said. "They're a large French logistics company, and he's just joined the Board. I expect it'll be full of motivational tosh. Last to speak will be Ambrose."

He didn't have to explain who Ambrose Filcher, the charismatic founder of Filchers, was.

Luke heard the sound of footsteps and turned to see a portly man of fifty or so staggering towards them. He had a ruddy face and was carrying an almost full brandy glass which he was unsuccessfully trying to keep level, with the result that his pale green polo shirt was covered in cognac.

"Hello," he said as he pulled up beside them. He almost fell backwards when he stopped and Luke had to resist the urge to put his hand behind his back to hold him up.

His glass was in his right hand and he tried but failed to transfer it to his left in an attempt to shake hands. After a few tries he gave up and nodded at each of them in turn.

"Peter Feiffer," he said, which sounded like the start of a tongue twister to Luke. "Are you…?" He paused and hiccupped, then tried again. "Are you friend or foe?" He bent forward to stare at both of their faces in turn before straightening up again and adding, "I'm foe."

"Foe?" Luke asked.

"I'm a customer, not…" He waved one hand in front of both of them. "…not Filchers. I'm Head of

Informshun…Inforation…bugger." He giggled. "I-T."

"You're Head of IT?" Fred asked.

Peter nodded and poked his finger in Fred's chest. "Got it in one. At Genie."

"Genie?"

"No." Peter sucked in his breath and tried again, speaking more slowly this time. "Genie. I work for Genie. Head of IT."

It dawned on Luke what he meant. "Oh," he said. You mean GNE?"

"Exactly. Gi' the man a cigar." Another hiccup. "Whass you two do?"

"Fred's Head of Marketing," Luke said, "and I'm Head of Ethics."

Peter tapped the side of his nose. "Two Heads are better than one." He giggled again and then tried to compose his face into a more serious pose. "Juss a minute." He tried to focus on Luke, though his eyes were wavering around a fair bit. "Did you say Ethics?"

"Yes, I'm Head of Ethics."

"And not ethics as in the county?"

"No, ethics as in moral principles."

"Got you." He nodded his head up and down. "Ought to have a word. Something I need to ask."

"Go ahead."

"Tomorrow. When I'm less…" He waved his hands around indicating the surrounds of his body.

"Good idea," Luke said, though he was fairly certain Peter Feiffer would have forgotten the whole conversation come morning.

"I'll come and find you." Peter looked down at his glass which was now empty, though this was because he'd been waving his hands around rather than because he'd drunk any of it. "Need 'nother cognac." He turned and staggered back towards the hotel.

Chapter 4

Luke wasn't sure why he'd felt the need to hang on until midnight but he'd done it. Spending most of the last couple of hours chatting to Fred Tanner had helped. However, dot on pumpkin-time he had gone to his room and fallen asleep almost instantly.

It was 7:30 when he went down for breakfast and he was pleased on two counts. First, the place was practically deserted, and second, the man behind the counter agreed to rustle up steak, egg and chips. He grabbed himself a double espresso and an orange juice, took them to a table in the corner and returned a few minutes later to pick up his meal, grabbing some English mustard on the way back.

Luke cut into his sirloin and was delighted to see it was rare as requested. He popped the first piece in his mouth, savoured it for a second and looked up to see Peter Feiffer walking towards him. To his astonishment he looked bright and cheery, no sign of the appalling hangover his drunken state the night before seemed certain to deliver.

"Good morning," Peter said. He gestured to the seat opposite Luke. "Do you mind?"

"Not at all," Luke said, though he had been relishing the thought of a solitary meal.

Peter put his phone and reading glasses down on the table. "That looks good," he said. "I might try that for myself."

He returned a few minutes later with a meal matching Luke's and sat down. "It's Luke, isn't it?"

"That's right. Luke Sackville."

"Thought I ought to make sure. I don't know if you noticed, but I was a bit the worse for wear last night."

Luke smiled. "To be honest, I'm surprised you can

remember my name."

Peter returned his smile and filled his fork with a large piece of steak and some chips before answering. "More than that," he said, "I remember you said you were Head of Ethics." He put his food in his mouth and started chewing. "Mmm, this is good." He finished his mouthful before continuing. "I've never heard of anyone being Head of Ethics before. What does it involve?"

Luke gave him a summary of what the job entailed, leaving out any mention of standing in at post-mortems or working alongside MI6.

"Interesting," Peter said and then continued with his meal. When they had both finished, he said, "I wonder if you could give me some advice."

"If it's anything to do with IT I doubt it," Luke said smiling. "Will you excuse me a minute? I want to grab another coffee. Do you want one?"

Peter confirmed that he did and Luke returned a minute later with one black and one white coffee.

"No, it's nothing to do with IT," Peter said. He looked around to make sure no one could overhear. "I was having lunch in our canteen last week, I think it was Tuesday, and a friend of mine who's in television production joined me."

Luke took a sip of his espresso and sighed inwardly, anticipating a boring and probably long-winded anecdote.

"He had heard a rumour," Peter went on, "that one of the presenters of a programme he's working on is, well…" He paused for a moment to get his thoughts straight. "I guess you could say he's mislaid his moral compass."

"That's a bit general," Luke said. "And by the sound of it, it's third-hand information at best."

"I suppose so."

"Do you know any more? You said 'he' so I presume it's a male presenter. But do you know what it is he's supposed to have done?"

"My friend didn't say, and he didn't feel he had enough

information to report it to anyone. But the thing is, what if it's true and it's serious? It would be terrible if there was some kind of Jimmy Saville thing going on and no one said anything."

Luke sat back in his seat and gave it a few moments thought. "Do you mind if I ask a few questions?"

"Not at all. Fire away."

"You said last night that you're Head of IT at GNE but my understanding is that Information Technology hasn't been outsourced to Filchers. So how come you're here this weekend?"

"You're right. The only areas outsourced at the moment are Finance, Administrative Support and the Contact Centre. However, we're looking to outsource IT and Security in the near future."

"So you were invited because you're a prospect?"

"Exactly. As was my colleague who's Head of Security."

"Do you know where your producer friend heard the rumour?"

"It was from another of the presenters."

"But you don't know which one?"

"Sorry, no." Peter paused for a second. "I don't know why I thought you might be able to help. Stupid really. It's just a rumour and you don't even work for or with GNE in any capacity. It's been worrying my friend a lot, that's the thing."

"I think you're right, Peter. I'd love to say there's a simple solution, but…" Luke shrugged.

"Thanks for listening anyway."

"No problem."

Peter stood up. "Maybe catch you later." He left and headed for the lifts.

Luke decided a third coffee would go down well. He got up and went to fetch another double espresso only to find one of his least favourite people sitting at the table when he returned. He would have done an immediate Uturn had he not left his phone on the table.

"Good morning, Glen," he said as he shuffled in opposite Filchers' Head of Security.

"Morning," Glen said, his head in his hands and a thick black coffee in front of him.

"Feeling rough?"

Glen pulled his hands away from his face to reveal bloodshot eyes under which were deep rings of puckered skin. He had little hair, just a greying buzz cut, but Luke suspected that if he had it would have been all over the place. As ever, his shirt was skintight against his steroid-enhanced six-pack, but it was stained and he looked as though he'd slept in it.

Luke raised his voice. "Heavy night?"

"Don't!" Glen said in a near-whisper. He put his head back in his hands.

"I didn't see you all evening. Were you mixing and mingling?"

Glen removed his hands again and picked up his coffee. "I can't remember much," he said before taking a sip of his drink, pulling a disgusted face and putting the cup back on the table. "She was attractive. Nancy or Nina or something."

"Who was attractive?"

"A client or prospect I think." Luke could almost see the cogs trying to engage as he tried to recall the events of the night before. "Shit!" Glen exclaimed. "I've just remembered."

"Remembered what?"

"I rubbed her up."

"What?"

"I rubbed her up. It was gone midnight."

Luke shook his head. This was too much information.

"Oh god," Glen said. "That's her."

Luke turned to see a woman with a bob of blonde hair looking around for a table. She saw him looking at her, smiled and headed towards them, then spotted Glen and hesitated for a second before continuing.

"Good morning Glen," she said when she reached them. It was clear from her accent that she hailed from somewhere in the south of Ireland. She pointed to one of the two vacant seats and looked at Luke. "Do you mind?"

"Not at all."

Glen had his head back in his hands, and Luke was left wondering what exactly these two had been up to.

"I'm Luke Sackville," he said. "I work for Filchers."

"Hi," she said and smiled. "I'm Niamh O'Dare. GNE." She was a big woman, not overweight but tall and well-built. Her ruddy cheeks and full lips reminded Luke of a stereotypical farm girl.

She gestured across to Glen. "Last night he and I had a bit of a…"

She hesitated and for one horrendous moment, Luke thought she was going to give him all the excruciating details.

"…fling?" he suggested, wanting to end her description before it had begun.

"Heavens, no," she said and laughed. "Me and him?" She gestured to Glen. "You have got to be joking."

"Sorry," Luke said. "It's just that Glen said…"

She poked Glen in the arm. "What exactly have you been saying?"

Glen removed his hands from his face. "Nothing. Only that we argued."

"You said you rubbed her up," Luke said.

"I did."

Niamh's cheeks grew even redder. "You did nothing of the sort!" she said.

"But you said it yourself."

Luke held his hand up and smiled. "Hang on," he said.

"This is nothing to smile about," Niamh said.

"Oh, it is." He bent to Niamh's ear and whispered, "I

think he meant to say he'd rubbed you up the wrong way."

She sat back and laughed, and it was a real belly laugh that attracted looks from people at neighbouring tables. "He certainly did," she said. "I was wearing something a wee bit more revealing and he asked if this," she pointed to the centre of her chest, "was Silicon Valley." She then pointed at each of her breasts in turn. "Do they look false to you?"

Luke shook his head, trying to hide his smile. "No," he said.

"Oh god, did I?" Glen whimpered.

Despite himself, Luke felt he had to come to his colleague's rescue and change the subject. "I'm Head of Ethics at Filchers," he said. "What's your role at GNE?"

"I'm Head of Security."

"Really?" This was getting better and better. "Peter Feiffer was here earlier and he said you were going out to tender soon." She nodded. "Obviously Filchers will be bidding, so I guess you'll need to work closely with our Head of Security."

"Probably," she said. "I haven't met him yet but people tell me he's got an all-male team and refuses to recruit women. Sounds like a real eejit."

Luke raised one eyebrow and gestured with his head to Glen.

"He isn't?" she said.

"I'm afraid so."

Niamh looked at Glen who tried to smile but the result had all the sincerity of Shere Kahn. "Sorry," he said. "Can we start again, Nina?"

She shook her head in despair. "It's Niamh," she said.

"Of course. Sorry." He paused. "Is that spelt N-e-e-v-e?"

"No, it's…" She sighed and shook her head. "Never mind."

Chapter 5

"You realise we can't tell Baz?" Kieran said as they were walking to the mobile cafe. "He'd hit the roof."

"Of course," Nat said. This was as much as he'd said since they left the house. He was normally chatty and Kieran had never seen him as quiet as this. But then the last twelve hours had been very draining and it had clearly had an impact on him.

Kieran perused the handwritten menu resting against the side of the trailer and looked up at the man behind the counter. "Bacon roll and a flat white please," he said. "Same for you, Nat?" Nat nodded and Kieran passed his order on and paid. Once they had their food and drinks they returned to the other end of the lay-by and climbed into his Isuzu 4x4.

He sat behind the wheel and took a bite of his roll. It was excellent, with exactly the right amount of tomato sauce, and he was surprised to find he was enjoying it despite everything.

Nat, on the other hand, was staring out of the windscreen, his breakfast as yet untouched.

Kieran waited until he had finished his food before speaking. "We had no choice, Nat," he said. "It's not as if it was us that killed him."

"What we did seems so wrong though. And the poor kid's family…"

Kieran pointed to Nat's roll. "Are you going to eat that?"

"I can't face it."

"Give it here then."

Nat passed it over and Kieran took a bite. "I'm starving."

"I don't know how you can eat," Nat said.

"I've seen worse. I was on riot duty in Bristol a few years ago and we charged a mob of climate protesters, shields raised, full-on aggressive."

"What happened?"

"A young woman fell down and got trodden on. She didn't stand a chance. Died instantly. You should have seen the state of her face."

"That must have been awful."

Kieran took another bite. "Yeah, well these things happen." He grinned and licked the corner of his mouth where some ketchup had lingered. "It's all in the line of duty."

Nat shook his head. "Whoever killed that boy is going to get off scot-free, isn't he?"

Kieran swallowed his mouthful before replying. "It can't be helped," he said. "Baz pays our wages and our job is to protect him. End of."

"Are we going to tell him?"

"You have to be fucking joking. He'd blow his top. It's just you and me who saw the body. Let's keep it that way."

"What about the other kid? The one you booted out."

Kieran pulled a blue iPhone from his pocket. "I've got this," he said, "and young Alfie was practically pooing his pants when he left. He's not going to tell anyone."

"What did you say?"

"I may have suggested I'd hurt one of his family if he told anyone," Kieran said and smirked. "Stupid tosser believed me too."

"He and his mate Owen seemed like nice kids. I gave them their drinks when they arrived. How come they were at the party?"

"That was Eve. She's a tremendous fixer." He wiped a piece of bacon from the corner of his mouth, licked it off his finger and smiled. "A real looker too. Shame she's out of bounds." He finished his roll, belched, wiped his hands on his jeans and started the engine. "Right," he said. "Let's go back and face the music."

Fifteen minutes later they arrived at Whistler House and Kieran pulled up next to the Lamborghini. "Let me do the talking," he said.

"Fine with me," Nat replied.

Baz was waiting for them in the lounge when they entered the house. He was seated on the red sofa, legs curled up beside him. As usual, he was flamboyantly dressed, on this occasion in a full-length Indian kaftan decorated with flamingos.

"Where have you two been?" he said, and yawned.

"Throwing away some of the rubbish from the party," Kieran said. "Syringes, condoms, that kind of thing. Stuff we don't want to go in the household bins."

Baz's mouth puckered. "Too much detail," he said. "What happened to that arsehole Mountfield?"

"He was very apologetic and promised he'd never do it again. Said he was tempted because they were so pretty."

Baz snorted. "Pretty valuable, that's what he fucking meant. I paid through the nose for that cruet set. Did you know it's 24-carat gold?"

"Yes, you've told me before," Kieran said and shuddered inwardly. Baz's treasured salt and pepper set was truly revolting, designed as it was to represent two men in the act of sex.

"He ruined everything and I was really looking forward to the evening," Baz said sulkily. "Make sure he's kept out in future, will you? And that includes anyone else's parties. Spread the word that he's a thief. Okay?"

"Will do, Baz."

"Good. Now fetch Eve in."

"Shall we go?"

"No, stay."

"I'll fetch her," Nat said.

He left the room and returned a few minutes later with

Eve. She was wearing an all-white outfit, a boob tube and tight shorts, and Kieran had to fight to stop himself from staring.

"Shame about last night, Baz," she said.

"It's unfortunate, but what's done is done. However, I can't have it getting around that I'm a poor host. I know it's short notice but can you arrange a rerun for next weekend?"

"You're at the GNE Awards ceremony next Saturday."

"Oh yes, I forgot."

"We could do the Saturday after, though."

"Great. Can you fix it? The usual people. And can I rely on you to ensure there are a few of our young fans?"

"Of course, Baz." She smiled. "No problem."

Chapter 6

The celebrity speaker turned out to be a man Luke had never heard of.

Ivor Reynolds had won 'I'm a Celebrity' and gone on to host a successful television series on how to escape from the jungle. He turned out to be nothing but a pale imitation of Bear Grylls, completely lacking in personality and without the ability to deliver what was supposed to be a motivational speech. His attempts at humour failed too, and at the end there was sporadic applause and no questions.

Ambrose Filcher, the septuagenarian founder of the company and now the Chairman and CEO, joined Ivor on stage.

"Thank you, Ivor," he said graciously. "I appreciate you taking the time to be with us today."

He turned to face the audience as Ivor Reynolds left the stage.

"And now," he went on, "please welcome Francois Lausanne. He has been central to the growth of FNCM and I am delighted he has agreed to join the Board." He gestured to the front row and there was polite applause as Lausanne mounted the steps and approached the microphone. He shook Ambrose's hand vigorously before turning to the audience.

He was in his early fifties, handsome with a chiselled face and matt black hair that Luke felt sure was dyed. Ambrose returned to his seat and Francois grasped the microphone, his face serious. He cast his eyes around the audience before he started speaking.

"Lass year," he said, speaking slowly, "zee profits of Feelchurs…" He paused for effect, "Zay wier terri-bill." He glared at people in the front, then at those further back.

"Ah was offally dis-app-oyn-ted."

There was mumbling in the audience as they struggled to understand what he was saying, his accent somewhere between that of Raymond Blanc and Gerard Depardieu. There were a few giggles too.

"Pleez lissenn to may." Lausanne glared at the audience. "What ah am say-ing eez virry am-port-awnt."

"Zis year," he went on, raising his voice to emphasise the importance of his words, "we must fuck-us."

The audience went silent and Lausanne realised that he had finally got their attention. He waved his hand along the front row, pleased that his message was hitting home. "You must all fuck-us. If you fuck-us you will come…"

He had a coughing fit at this point and was only vaguely aware that laughter had broken out in different corners of the room. "Saw-ree," he said when he had managed to compose himself. "Az ah was say-ing, if you fuck-us you will come-plitt a good year. Feelchurs' profits, zay weel be hay."

Someone started applauding and soon others joined in. A few people even stood up. Francois smiled and bowed. "I zank you," he said. "Az they say een Ang-land, I zank you from zee heart of mah, ah…" He paused, struggling to remember the correct phrasing, then smiled as it came to him. "From zee heart of ma bottom."

More people stood up and Francois bowed again. He was about to resume speaking when Ambrose Filcher rushed to his side. "That was excellent," he said. "Why not end now, Francois? While you're on a high."

"Baht ah have more."

"Please can we have more," some wag called.

"No really, Francois," Ambrose said hastily. "What you said was very motivational but we're already running late."

"Aw, o-kay." He turned to the audience. "Zank you for attending me."

He returned to his seat and Ambrose remained at the

microphone. He kept his speech short, starting with a subtle and amusing reference to Francois's unintended humour that was delivered effortlessly. Not for the first time, Luke was struck by the charm and charisma of the man. Ambrose finished by thanking everyone for giving up their precious weekends to attend, assuring them of the confidence he had in each and every one of Filchers' staff.

As Luke left the hall he looked around for Peter Feiffer and eventually spotted him talking to Edward Filcher. He made his way over.

"Ah, Luke," Filcher said as he approached. He gestured to the man by his side. "This is Peter Feiffer. Important man. Head of IT at GNE." He winked.

"Are you okay, Edward?" Peter said. "Is there something in your eye?"

"Fine. Ah, something in my eye? Yes. Must be." He rubbed his eye. "There. Gone."

"We've met," Luke said.

"Right. So you know Peter's…"

"Important?"

"Indeed." Filcher turned to Peter, grasped his hand and shook it up and down vigorously. "Excellent to meet you, Peter. Hopefully, we'll see much more of each other when," he tapped the side of his nose, "we've won. Hah!"

"I'll be looking forward to Filchers' proposal," Peter said.

"Yes. Definitely. Rest assured it will be innovative," Filcher said. "Out-of-the-box thinking. Pushing the envelope."

"We'll be looking for stability."

"Of course. Of course. That too. Equally important. Keep the rudder straight and make sure we stay on the road." He smiled. "Anyway." He realised he was still pumping the other man's hand up and down and let go. "Ah, must go."

He turned and marched away.

"Is he always…" Peter started to say.

"Always," Luke said. "I'm glad I caught you, Peter. I've been thinking about what you said earlier and I'd like to try to help. Is your friend based in London?"

"Yes, he's based in Head Office."

"I've got a light day tomorrow and I could get the train in. Could you ring him and see if he can meet me?"

"Definitely."

Peter took out his phone.

"Hi, Victor," he said when the call was answered. "I've found someone who might be able to help with the Baz thing." He paused, and after listening for a few seconds said, "Could you see him tomorrow?" He waited for the answer, then turned to Luke, "He's busy most of the day but could see you at 9. Is that too early?"

"No, that's fine," Luke said.

Peter confirmed arrangements, hung up and gave Luke his friend's contact details. "I should warn you," he said. "Victor's pretty full on."

"Full on?"

Peter smiled. "You'll understand when you meet him."

Chapter 7

Josh was enjoying working in the Ethics Team. Luke was a great boss and the work was challenging and varied.

He was also delighted that there had been a significant step up in his and Leanne's relationship. They had been seeing each other for three months and were growing more and more fond of each other. While they both still lived at home, they had very accepting parents and were spending four or five nights a week at either his house or hers. The idea of them moving in together was very much on the agenda.

The problem was that Leanne didn't know any of this.

Well not yet anyway.

They had their disagreements of course, but no more than any other couple and most of the time they got on brilliantly. And when they did argue it was usually because he had put his foot in it in some way. Or sometimes it was because he was daydreaming when she was speaking, but he was getting better at that all the time.

"I said, are you listening to me?"

He looked up from his plate. "Pardon?"

"Have you heard a single word I've said?"

"Eh, uh… Yes, of course."

"So what did I ask you?" Leanne had her head cocked to one side and he turned away, trying to remember. She'd been talking about her sister's fiancee…

Buggery-shit-shit.

"Um, uh." Josh racked his brains. "Was it about us living together?" She furrowed her eyebrows. "No, no," he added hastily. "Your sister. She's getting married. You asked me, uh…whether…um…"

"I asked if you wanted an extra sausage."

"Right. Yes, that was it."

"Well?"

"Uh?" She pointed at his plate. "Oh. Yes please."

Leanne shook her head and went back into her mother's kitchen, returning a few seconds later and placing a sausage on his plate.

"Thanks."

She sat down opposite him and put some butter and marmalade on her toast while he continued with his fry-up. She was about to take a bite when she realised what he had said.

"What did you mean about us living together?" she asked.

Josh stopped mid-chew, still looking down at his brunch. "I, ah…" He finished chewing, swallowed his mouthful and raised his head to look across at his girlfriend. "I think we should perhaps give it a try."

"Where?"

"I thought we could rent a flat together. Something small, obviously, just one bedroom, but we're both earning. I've done the sums and I'm sure we could afford it."

She was smiling now. "You've given this a lot of thought, haven't you?"

"If you don't want to…"

She reached across the table and put her hand on his. "I'd love to, Joshy."

"Wowza." His smile stretched from ear to ear. "Marvelissimo!"

"Perhaps we can look online after we've eaten," she said. "See if there's anything suitable."

"I've been on Rightmove and I've got a few saved."

"You have been busy."

"Who's been busy?'

Josh looked up to see Leanne's mother walking into the dining room with a carrier bag full of shopping.

"Hi," Josh said.

Leanne turned around. "We're thinking of renting a flat together."

"That's fantastic." Her mother took the carrier bag into the kitchen and returned a few seconds later. "Are you sure you're both ready to take that step?"

"I know what you mean, Mum," Leanne said. "He can be pretty hard work at times."

"I'm sitting right here, you know," Josh said. His phone rang and he looked down at the screen to see it was Luke calling. He mouthed 'It's the guv' to Leanne and then accepted the call.

"Hi," he said.

"Hi Josh," Luke said. "I'm sorry to bother you at the weekend. I hope I'm not interrupting anything."

"Not at all. I was just telling Leanne I'm sitting right here."

"Why? Has she gone away?"

"No."

"Then…" There was a pause. "Look, never mind. Are you okay to come with me to London tomorrow?"

"Of course, guv. Where are we going?"

"GNE's Head Office."

"Gucci."

"Pardon?"

"Gucci," Josh repeated as if everyone used the expression. "That's dead cool. Are we meeting anyone famous?"

Luke ignored the question. "We need to be there by nine," he said. "Are you okay to meet me at Bath Spa at seven?"

"Sure."

"Great, I'll see you in the morning."

Chapter 8

Luke was pleased to see Josh waiting for him when he got to the station at just before seven. He picked up their tickets and they made their way to platform 2 for the train to Paddington.

"Are we having breakfast on the train, guv?" Josh asked while they were waiting.

"Yes, that makes sense."

"Great. I'm starving. Leanne got up early and made me a bacon sandwich but that was nearly an hour ago."

Once on board, they found their reserved seats, which were opposite each other next to the window, and Luke dispatched Josh to fetch their breakfast.

The train was full. Next to Luke was a middle-aged man in a dark pin-stripe suit, while next to Josh's seat was a woman of thirty-five or so who was also dressed for the office.

"Excuse me," Josh said when he returned. "Sorry to disturb you."

"No problem," she said.

Josh passed Luke his sausage roll and double espresso and placed his own bacon roll and flat white on the table in front of him. "So, what's the deal, guv?" he asked. "Who are we meeting and why?"

Luke was conscious that everything they said could be heard by their table companions. "Best I tell you once we're off the train."

"Gotcha, guv." Josh pulled his phone out of his pocket and retrieved some earpods from his briefcase.

Luke was pleased. He didn't think he could bear over an hour of Josh wittering on about something and nothing. He pulled his own headphones out and connected them to his iPhone. He was about to put them on his head when Josh spoke.

"Leanne and I are moving in together."

The man in the pin-stripe was immersed in his Daily Telegraph but Luke sensed the woman's ears prick up when she heard this.

"That's nice," Luke said.

"I found a few belting apartments yesterday. Maj helped me draw up a shortlist and warned me that anywhere near the centre is pricey. Weston's not too bad though."

"Mmm." Luke put his headphones on.

"I'd love to know what you think."

Luke sighed, took his headphones off and put them on the table. The woman looked up from her paperback and smiled sympathetically.

"There are eight," Josh said. "I've got a couple of favourites, but I'd appreciate your views on the pros and cons of each." He clicked a couple of times on his phone and then passed it over.

"What's your budget?" Luke asked.

"£900 a month plus bills." Josh gestured to the phone. "It seems plenty. There's one there that's only £580."

Luke flicked through the eight properties and Josh watched with interest. When he saw that Luke had reached the last property he couldn't contain himself any longer. "Well, guv," he said, "which one do you think is the best?"

"They're all student properties."

"I noticed they all mention students but Leanne and I aren't much older so I'm sure they'd accept us."

"No, Josh. What I mean is that they're shared. All you would get is a bedroom of your own."

"What?" Josh held out his hand and took his phone back.

"I couldn't help overhearing," the woman next to Josh said. She smiled again and Luke noticed a dimple appear in her left cheek. "May I?" She held her hand out to Josh and he passed his phone over. She clicked a couple of times. "I heard you say your friend Maj looked at this. Did she check the filters?"

"Maj is a man," Josh said. "He's Somalian and it's short for Majid. He and I work for the guv." He indicated Luke with his hand.

She raised one eyebrow. "The guv?"

"Yes." There was pride in his voice as he added, "I call Luke that because he used to be a Detective Chief Inspector. He runs the Ethics Team at Filchers now."

"Oh, I see." She pointed at the screen. "I don't think your colleague Maj can have checked the filters." She clicked twice more and then passed the phone back. "I've adjusted them. I recently moved to a new flat and made the same mistake."

"Thanks." Josh took the phone and Luke saw his face drop.

"I know," she said. "Prices in Bath seem to be shooting through the roof. I had to pay £1300 a month for my place and it's not very big. One bedroom, a kitchen-diner and a small bathroom."

"I don't think Leanne and I could afford that."

"Mine's in Milsom Street though. There will be cheaper ones outside the centre. Pass it back."

Luke decided to leave it to them and reached for his headphones again.

Five chapters later a voice over the speakers announced that they were approaching Paddington and Luke paused his audiobook.

"Rachel's been really helpful," Josh said once Luke's headphones were off. "And would you believe it, she works for GNE."

"At Head Office?" Luke asked.

"No," Rachel said. "I work from home, but I go to London once or twice a week. I'm a content designer."

"That must be fascinating."

She laughed. "You haven't the faintest what a content designer does, have you?"

He held his hand up. "Got me." He paused. "Sorry, I'm Luke."

She gave him a little wave, said, "Hi, Luke," and the dimple made a reappearance.

"What's the best way to GNE?" he asked.

"The Bakerloo Line. It probably makes sense to travel in together."

"That would be helpful. We've got a meeting at nine and I don't want to be late."

Rachel looked at her watch. "It's just gone 8:30 so we should just about do it."

"Lead the way."

She had been right about the journey time and it was about five to nine when they reached GNE's Head Office. It was a massive contrast to Filchers' headquarters, a ten-storey cube of glass that was just as ugly but with very much a 70's feel. On the roof was a single communications mast that was almost as tall as the building itself.

They said their goodbyes and Luke asked for Victor Robertson at reception. They were told to wait and walked over to a couple of uncomfortable-looking seats that were a definite case of style over substance. He decided not to risk sinking his large frame into them.

"I'm conscious you don't know why we're here, Josh," Luke said. He paused to collect his thoughts and was about to summarise the situation when there was a voice behind him.

"I'm guessing you're Luke."

Luke turned to see a man wearing what he could only describe as rainbow clothes smiling up at him. His open-necked shirt had all the stripes from red to violet while the left leg of his trousers was green and the right side blue. The whole concoction almost brought tears to his eyes.

He looked Luke up and down. "My word, you're a big

boy," he said, his voice outrageously camp. "Don't worry about this ensemble," he went on, gesturing to his outfit. "It's be-as-flamboyant-as-you-can day."

"Is it really?" Josh asked.

"No, dear, it's just me." He cupped his hand around his mouth and put it to Josh's ear before saying in a stage whisper, "I'm the resident eccentric."

"Oh, uh, right."

"I assume you're Victor?" Luke asked.

"The very man." He smiled. "I've got a room booked. Walk this way."

He sashayed off and Josh started to say something but Luke held his hand up to stop him. "Don't."

"Right, guv," Josh said. He dropped his voice to a whisper. "He's a little unusual, isn't he?"

Luke was pleased to find there was decent coffee waiting for them in the meeting room. Great Western Railway's attempt had all the flavour of a soggy envelope.

"Thanks for coming in," Victor said once they had all sat down around the table and introductions had been made. "This is really sensitive but as I'm sure Peter told you, I'm very concerned."

Luke was pleased to see Josh had taken out his notebook. "Is it okay if Josh takes notes?" he asked.

"Of course." Victor paused to collect his thoughts. "Oh my, I suppose I'm a whistleblower of sorts. Rather exciting actually. Where should I start?"

"Peter told me you have concerns about a presenter on a programme you're working on. Can you explain what those are?"

"Of course. The programme is 'Hall of Flame'."

"Magnifico," Josh said, looking up from his pad. "I love that series."

"I'm sorry," Luke said, "but I've never heard of it."

"You should watch it, guv. It's dead cool. There are eight celebrities and they have to…"

Luke held his hand up. "Hold your horses, Josh. I'm sure it's a great programme but I'm not sure the format is relevant."

"Oh but it is," Victor said. "I have concerns about a couple of the guest celebrities too. Let me explain. The host is Baz Hartman…"

"Guc…" Josh started but Luke stilled him with a glance.

"As Josh said, there are eight celebrities." Victor smiled as he continued, "Well we call them that, but they're hardly A-list. They have to complete several tasks, all involving fire but also demonstrating strength of character and teamwork. They start as teams and then work as individuals until only the winner remains."

"It sounds fascinating," Luke lied.

"It certainly has excellent ratings."

"And is it the host Baz Hartman who you believe has, to quote Peter, mislaid his moral compass?"

"It is, yes." Victor sighed. "And also two of the so-called celebrities on his show. Marvin Winespottle…"

"He's a real character," Josh said.

I'm not surprised with a name like that, Luke thought.

"…and Reggie Dowden," Victor continued. "I know for a fact they've become regulars at Baz's parties." He paused. "Now, you may not believe this, but I'm gay." Luke nodded, trying to keep his eyes from Josh who was keeping his head down. "And Baz and I were in a relationship last year."

Josh looked up. "Baz Hartman's gay?" he squeaked.

"Oh yes, dear. It's an open secret within GNE although he's never officially come out."

"Wowza. I mean he's so, uh, well he's not," Josh waved his hand in Victor's general direction, "I mean, uh…"

"Please continue, Victor," Luke said, deciding it was time to help Josh out of the hole he was digging for himself.

"Baz has always been one for parties," Victor went on, "and I used to go, obviously when we were, you know, but for a while afterwards as well. Our break-up wasn't at all acrimonious which is just as well given we have to work so closely together. Anyway, I stopped going because the parties changed."

"In what way?" Luke prompted.

"They became all-male affairs. Nothing wrong with that in itself of course, and I went to the first one where women weren't invited and it was fine. I only went to one though. To be honest it didn't have the sparkle when it became all-male. Anyway, recently I heard that they were inviting special guests." He swallowed. "Young guests."

"How young?"

"Fifteen, sixteen, that kind of age."

"For what reason?"

"Well, that's the question, isn't it?"

"So you have no evidence that these special guests are being mistreated or abused in any way?"

"None. It could be innocent of course, but what if they're being groomed or worse?"

"Mmm." Luke turned his head to look at Josh.

"What is it guv?" Josh said.

"I've had an idea. Can you stand up?"

Josh stood up.

Victor eyed him up and down and nodded. "Yes, it might work," he said.

Josh looked from one man to the other. "What might work?" he asked, his voice an octave higher than normal.

Chapter 9

Josh was slouched in his chair when the meeting started.

"What's wrong with him?" Helen asked. "Does he think a wee seagull's going to shite all over him?"

Luke smiled. "I've given him an assignment, and he's none too pleased about it." Josh grunted and shuffled deeper into his chair. "Let's deal with your current projects," Luke went on, "and I'll tell you at the end of the meeting."

Sam summed up progress on the investigation she and Maj were conducting following an accusation of sexual harassment in one of the admin teams. "We've still got a few people to talk to next week," she concluded, "but should be able to wrap it up after that."

"How's it looking?"

"We've got two statements which suggest the accusation is genuine, but the harassment was relatively minor in both." Sam looked down at her notes. "He asked Elly Grant out four times even though she said 'no' immediately each time and," she turned the page, "he put his hand on Rhianna Plunkett's shoulder on at least five separate occasions despite her asking him not to. Both women said they feel very uneasy around him."

"Mmm," Luke mused. "Not enough there to take action."

"No," Maj said, "but we're hoping to get more from the women we see next week, especially the one who made the initial accusation."

"I think the man's a danger," Sam said. "He may do something a lot worse if he's allowed to remain in Filchers. Would you agree, Maj?"

Maj nodded. "Definitely. He's a bad sort."

"Sounds like it," Luke said. "Good work, guys. Let me know if you need me to do anything." He turned to Helen. "What about you, Helen? How's it going with the Home Office contract?"

"Nay so bad. I've added a few clauses in and it's off for review. I should have it wrapped up this week or next."

"Excellent." He looked at Josh. "Josh, do you want to tell them about your GNE assignment?"

"No," Josh said. "You tell them."

"He sounds like a grumpy thirteen-year-old," Helen said.

"Funny you should say that," Luke said, and there was another grunt from Josh.

Luke outlined what had happened in their meeting with Victor Robertson the previous day, and what they had agreed to do.

"How old's your brother, Josh?" he asked when he'd finished.

"Thirteen."

"And how tall is he?"

"About five foot and nothing else."

"His clothes won't fit you then." Luke reflected for a minute. "I wonder if the three of you would be prepared to take Josh on a little shopping trip. Find something suitable for him to wear."

"I'm up for that," Helen said. "Something for the party that makes him look like a fifteen or sixteen-year-old."

"I'm not wearing gay clothes," Josh squealed.

"There's no such thing," Sam said.

"No, but…"

"I'll bring Sabrina," Maj said. "She's just turned fourteen and she loves clothes. She'd love nothing more than finding you an outfit or two."

"Shall we say the day after tomorrow?" Sam asked. "There's late-night shopping in Bath on a Thursday."

"Sounds good," Maj said. "If we say five, that'll give

Sabrina a chance to get back from school and have a bite to eat."

"Do you want to ask Leanne to come?" Helen asked.

Josh shook his head vigorously. "Crumbs, no." He sat up straight as something occurred to him. "Oh shittedy-shit-shit. I'm going to have to tell her about this, aren't I?"

Helen smiled. "Hard to avoid it. Still, I'm sure she'll love having a wee toy boy."

"Will his clothes go on expenses?" Sam asked.

"Of course," Luke said. "Filcher won't have any problem with that."

As soon as the meeting ended Luke made his way to the Executive Floor where Edward Filcher was deep in conversation with Gloria, his secretary.

"No more salesmen," he was saying. "Pass them to Fred. Or James. Or someone. Not me."

"Okay, Mr Filcher," she said. "What about the lady from Solid Doors? You met her last month if you remember."

"Oh yes, the young…" Filcher looked up to see the towering presence of his Head of Ethics nearing the desk. "Ah, yes, the Solid Doors, uh, professional salesperson. Yes, uh, yes, she can see me. No others though, unless…" He glanced at Luke before adding, "We'll talk about this later, Gloria."

He turned his attention to Luke. "What do you want, Luke? You weren't at my meeting yesterday. Why not?"

"I had to go to London, Mr Filcher. Sorry about that. It was a GNE meeting."

"Was it?" Filcher raised one eyebrow. "GNE, eh? Important prospect. Come into my office." Luke followed him in and Filcher sat behind his desk and gestured for him to sit opposite. "I assume you were seeing Peter Feiffer? Excellent. Vital we build bonds."

Luke decided a little white lie would be useful. "He said to thank you for inviting him last weekend."

"Did he? Of course he did. Yes, I'm pleased with what I did. Excellent conference. Had help from James of course."

"Our Deputy Chairman certainly went down well."

"Mmm. Best forgotten that one. But well done, Luke." He tapped his nose. "Good to get into bed with someone like Peter."

Luke wasn't quite sure how to respond. "Ah, yes," he said.

"Right. Good." Filcher looked at his watch.

"Peter did put in a request."

Filcher looked up again, his interest rekindled. "Did he indeed? Does he want to meet me?"

"No. It's an odd one actually. One of the waiters knocked red wine over his suit and it's completely ruined. His shirt as well."

"Well buy him a new outfit. Put it on expenses. Need to take action. Could be new business. Potential big contract."

"Thanks for the advice, Mr Filcher."

"Any time. My door's always open."

"I'll ring for his measurements and buy him something this week."

"Very good. Tell him I sanctioned it."

"I will, Mr Filcher." Luke stood up ready to leave.

"Close the door on your way out."

Chapter 10

He put the mug down on the coffee table and chewed on his bottom lip. As far as he knew there were only two people who knew about the murder. It was too many, but the body had been disposed of so perhaps that would be the end of it.

He had been fucking stupid.

Should he take action to make sure no one else found out? He reflected for a moment and decided that on balance he shouldn't. If someone else died then that might bring the police into it and at the moment they weren't even aware anyone had been killed.

That was what was so good about the fixer, Eve. She got these young boys along in such a way that they didn't tell anyone where they were going. He smiled. It was almost like she was setting them up for him.

But then to all intents and purposes, she was.

The boy had told him he'd travelled down from Birmingham, which meant connecting his disappearance with the party would be really hard given he had travelled a fair distance from home. The dumb kid had tarted himself up, anticipating that his looks and charms would earn him the night at someone's place. He'd certainly looked pretty, but his appearance had earned him a lot more than he'd bargained for.

He picked his coffee up again, took a lengthy slurp and sighed. He was determined not to make the same mistake again. It had been an enormous risk to kill the lad when there were almost forty people at the party. The urge had taken him, that was the problem.

But it had been worth it. He smiled again as he recalled how delicious the moment had been. When the knife had sliced through his neck he had felt a deep inner satisfaction and a sense of triumph. It had been over all too quickly but there had been no choice. He couldn't afford to be overheard and keeping it quiet, even with the boy gagged, would have been hard if he had drawn it out.

He should have waited until afterwards, taken the kid somewhere private and had his fun there. He could have taken his time, taken all night if he wanted to. Yes, that would have been so much more satisfying.

Next time he would be more careful.

Next time his victim wouldn't be so fortunate.

He savoured the thought.

Chapter 11

Josh decided he wasn't going to tell Leanne. Well, not yet anyway. She would rib him endlessly and the less time he had to endure her taking the mickey out of him the better.

He also wanted more time to get to grips with the concept before she found out. How was he going to be able to pretend he was fifteen or sixteen? He was a grown man, for goodness sake.

Josh looked over at his little brother Noah, who was thirteen and a half and ridiculously childish and immature. How on earth could anyone think that he, Josh Ogden, was only two years older? He was cultured, sophisticated, a man of the world.

His brother reached for the remaining bar of Josh's Kit Kat.

"Stay away, half-pint," he snapped. He picked the bar up, licked the end and smirked before putting it back on the coffee table. "I bet you don't want it now."

"Are you off to see your lover this evening?" Noah said, before adding, in a poor imitation of Leanne, "Joshy."

"She's not my lover. She's my girlfriend."

"So you haven't…"

"Leave him alone, Noah," their Mum said without looking up from her copy of Good Housekeeping.

"Thanks, Mum," Josh said. He looked back at his brother. "You're so immature."

"No, I'm not.'

"Yes, you are."

"Not."

"Are."

She looked up then. "For goodness sake, stop it boys," she said. "Are you going to Leanne's tonight, Josh?"

"Possibly later," Josh said. "I'm going shopping first."

"New clothes for work?"

"Ah, kind of, yes."

Noah's ears pricked up at this. "What does 'kind of' mean?"

"I'm going to be, well, uh…" Josh considered how best to reply. After a moment's thought, he sat upright in his armchair. "I'm going undercover."

"Liar, liar, pants on fire!"

Josh smiled. "I'm going to be working with celebrities."

"Oh yeah. Name them then."

Josh tapped the side of his nose. "I can't, can I, dumbass. It's a secret because I'll be undercover."

"How do I know it's true then?"

Josh drew his thumb and index finger across his lips in a zipping-it gesture, then picked his Kit Kat up and took a bite.

"What clothes are you buying?" Noah asked.

The little bugger was like a dog with a bone sometimes. Josh decided to ignore the question and took a second bite.

"Are you buying women's clothes? I bet you're going undercover as a girl. I'm right, aren't I?"

Josh continued to stay silent, though the temptation to reply was almost overwhelming. He took the third and final bite of his Kit Kat before screwing the foil wrapper up and flinging it at his brother. It had no weight and fluttered to the floor halfway between them.

"Pick that up and put it in the bin," his Mum said absent-mindedly, her attention fully on the magazine again.

Josh stood up, retrieved the wrapper and put it in the bin in the corner of the room.

"I'm off then, Mum," he said. "I'm meeting the guys at five and I'll ring you afterwards to let you know if I'm home this evening or staying at Leanne's."

"Okay, darling."

Thirty minutes later Josh found himself standing

outside Urban Outfitters. He felt like a wildebeest calf, with four hungry lions encircling him and deciding how best to devour him.

"His hair's fine," Helen said.

"Definitely," Maj's daughter Sabrina said. "If anything, that style is too young for a fifteen or sixteen-year-old."

"Hey!" Josh, said, putting his hand to his head.

"So, ladies," Maj said. "What do you think he should wear?"

"Do you reckon something bright would work, Sabrina?" Sam asked.

"Not pink," Josh said hastily.

"Yes, bright is cool," Sabrina said. "Red might be good."

"Hoops would work well," Helen said. "They'd stretch his body out, make him look even skinnier."

"What do you mean 'even' skinnier?" Josh said.

"Do you think jeans or chinos?" Sam asked, ignoring his question.

"Faded jeans are back in," Sabrina said. "The ones he's wearing now are very old man-ish."

"I see what you mean," Helen said. "Very flabby and ill-fitting."

Josh sighed. God, please let this be over with soon.

Sabrina pointed at Josh's feet and laughed. "And those Adidas trainers!" she said. "I mean, they're so, like, last century."

The discussion continued for another five minutes, though to Josh it felt like five hours. Eventually, they led him into Urban Outfitters where, after much to-ing and fro-ing and multiple visits to the changing room, they were able to buy his complete outfit.

Josh left the store with a carrier bag containing a Nascar multi-coloured t-shirt, faded blue jeans and Vans blue and white trainers.

"And now," Helen said, "all we've got to do is get your

nose pierced."

Josh looked across at her in shock but the broad smile on her face gave the game away. He sighed with relief. "Right," he said. "Uh, thanks, everyone. Especially you, Sabrina. I'll see the rest of you tomorrow."

They all heard the sound of 'when the red, red robin' and Maj retrieved his phone from his pocket. "It's Luke," he said as he clicked to accept the call.

A minute or so later, he hung up.

"What did he want?" Helen asked.

"He was asking how we were getting on with clothes for our teeny-bopper over there," Maj said, gesturing to Josh, "but also, he asked if we could buy some clothes for me."

Helen snorted. "There's no way we're making you look fifteen."

Maj smiled. "Don't worry, we're not trying to achieve the impossible. Do any of you know where Moss Bros is?"

Chapter 12

"My, my," Victor said, looking Maj up and down. "All eyes are going to be on my plus one tonight."

Luke thought this unlikely given what Victor was wearing. His trousers, shirt, waistcoat and jacket had all been fashioned from the same material, a pattern of large pink and red flowers on a cream base that was reminiscent of the Library curtains at Borrowham Hall.

"Sit down, Maj," Luke said, trying not to smile at the expression of abject horror on Maj's face.

"Yes, please do, dear," Victor said. "I don't bite." He paused and then looked Maj in the eyes before adding, "Though in your case I might make an exception."

Maj sat down opposite Victor, and Luke took their orders and went to fetch drinks. When he returned there was complete silence at the table.

"I'm glad you're back, Luke," Victor said. "I think I may have frightened Maj."

Maj started to protest but Victor held his hand up to stop him. "What you have to appreciate," he said, toning the campness down from 10 to 4 or 5, "is that I am an eccentric and, dare I say it, an extrovert. I was jesting with you a moment ago, and the truth is I'm very grateful to you for agreeing to accompany me this evening."

"When Victor told me about the awards ceremony," Luke said, "I realised it would be an excellent opportunity for someone in our team to meet the key people in advance of Josh going to the party. You'll be able to get a feel for what they're like and we'll be better placed to brief him ahead of next Saturday."

Maj reached for his lime and lemonade and took a sip. "It makes sense," he said.

"You look absolutely scrumptious, by the way," Victor said, turning camp back to 10 again.

"Thanks." Maj found himself smiling now. "Was a dinner jacket the right thing to wear?"

"Oh yes. Most people will be in evening dress so you'll fit right in. I, on the other hand, will stand out somewhat in my little ensemble, but then that's my intention."

"I suggested we meet before the awards, Maj," Luke said, "so that you know each other in advance, and for Victor to give you background on the people you're going to meet." He turned to Victor. "Please, fire away."

Victor spent the next fifteen minutes running through a set of names that Maj had never heard of. Maj made a few notes on a piece of A4 paper and, when Victor had finished, folded it and put it into the inside pocket of his dinner jacket.

"Thanks for that, Victor," he said.

"No problem," Victor said. "By the way, since we'll be going as a couple you should call me Vicky. Now, tell me a little about yourself."

Maj started to answer but Luke put his hand up to stop him. "Let me," he said. "Maj is Somalian by birth, having moved here when he was nine."

Maj wondered why he wasn't being allowed to tell his own story, but realised why when Luke continued. "As far as people tonight are concerned, he is single and lives alone in Brixton, having moved here from Bristol last year. He's a systems programmer for a software house, and you met each other at the Ku Bar in Soho a few weeks ago."

"I've never been to an awards ceremony," Maj said. "Is there anything I need to know?"

"Not really," Victor said. "The whole evening is a rattlingly good piss-up." He gestured to Maj's drink. "Though I guess you're teetotal."

Maj nodded. "I am, yes."

"Not to worry. It's also a tremendous opportunity for

people-watching. The ones who are shortlisted but don't win can be the most entertaining. You wouldn't believe the look of pure hatred that appears on their faces." He gave a little chuckle and then looked at his watch. "But anyway, dear, it's time we headed off."

"Okay," Maj said. He looked at Luke. "I'll ring you afterwards with an update."

"Thanks, Maj," Luke said. "And good luck."

Victor hailed a cab outside the pub and he and Maj sat in companionable silence as they made their way to the Savoy.

Maj found himself warming to Victor. Yes, he was eccentric, but he was also caring and it had been brave of him to highlight what he feared might be happening behind closed doors.

They were dropped off at the entrance and several journalists and photographers immediately rushed to the taxi doors, only to retreat disappointed when no A-list celebrity emerged from inside.

"You might not partake," Victor said, "But for me, the first stop is always the bar. Follow me."

They walked through the reception area and upstairs where a burly guard checked them off on his clipboard before letting them proceed to the ballroom. Maj guessed there were two or three hundred people inside, most of the men in black evening dress, while the women wore a variety of what he assumed were one-off designer outfits.

"Ah, there's Baz," Victor said. He pointed to a handsome man who Maj vaguely recognised. "Would you mind fetching our drinks and bringing them over so that I can introduce you?"

"Sure," Maj said. "What will you have?"

"A porn star martini."

"A what?"

"It's a passion fruit cocktail. You should try one. Oh, I forgot, no alcohol." Victor giggled. "I'm not sure a virgin porn star exists, but I'm sure you'll think of something." He waved his hand in the air vaguely and then made a beeline for his friend, saying as he approached, "Baz, my love, you look simply gorgeous."

Maj made his way to the bar and found himself standing next to a woman in an elegant black cocktail dress. She was about to order but stopped when she saw him.

"You go first," she said smiling. "I'm in a party of eight and it'll take ages."

"Thanks," Maj said. "I'm only getting two." He turned back to the woman behind the bar. "Is there such a thing as…" He swallowed, uncertain as to whether Victor had been having him on, "…a porn star martini?"

"Yes, of course, sir."

"Great." He sighed with relief. "And a lime and lemonade please."

The woman next to him gave a little laugh. "Don't be embarrassed. It could have been worse."

"Worse?"

"There's a cocktail called Sex on the Beach."

"You're joking?"

She shook her head. "No, I'm serious."

"I'm pretty ignorant as far as alcohol is concerned," he went on. "I've heard of a gin and tonic and it doesn't get much further than that." He paused. "I'm Maj by the way. Short for Majid."

"Hi, Maj. I'm Rachel. Are you up for any awards?"

"I'm not even in the industry. I'm a software engineer and I've come tonight as someone's guest. What about you?"

"Do you watch 'Rock-n-Roll-n-Rap'?"

"My wife does. Are you on it?"

"Oh no." She laughed again. "I'm a content designer and we developed a YouTube short to promote the series. It was popular and we're up for 'Best Campaign'. It's one of the minor awards."

"Good for you."

"Your drinks, sir," the barwoman said as she placed two glasses down on the bar.

"Come over to our table if you get the chance," Rachel said. "I'll introduce you to our team."

"I'll try to do that," he said and picked up the drinks, squash for himself and a peach-coloured concoction with a slice of fruit on the top for Victor.

"Thank you, darling," Victor said when Maj handed him his drink. "Maj," he went on, "this is Baz and this darling lady is Eve."

Baz Hartman shook hands with Maj perfunctorily before returning his attention to Victor. Eve, on the other hand, presented her most dazzling smile and gestured for Maj to stand to one side with her.

"Delighted to meet you, Maj," she said. "Don't mind Baz. He's somewhat preoccupied."

"No worries." He took a sip of his drink and recalled that Victor had said Baz had a 'fixer' called Eve. This had to be her and he was intrigued to find out how she would describe her job. "So what do you do, Eve?" he asked.

"I'm Baz's Personal Assistant." She smiled again. "He's the creative one and I'm his admin lady. I look after his diary, organise events, that kind of thing."

"That must be exciting."

"It's certainly challenging." She lowered her voice. "Baz is hard work but some of his friends…"

"They can be difficult?"

She nodded. "And some. They seem to forget Baz is the one paying me. As soon as they hear I'm organising a party they're straight on the phone making their demands. Wally Zee is the worst."

"Music demands?"

"Oh no." She laughed again but there was no humour in it. "People demands. Telling me who I should and shouldn't invite. Damon and Ozzy are nearly as bad."

Maj raised his eyebrow. "Damon and Ozzy?"

"You haven't seen 'Rock-n-Roll-n-Rap'?"

Maj was about to answer 'my wife does' for the second time that evening when he remembered he was supposed to be gay. He shot a look over at Rachel. He would have to try to nab her later before she said something.

"No, I haven't," he said.

"Damon Prendergast and Ozzy Vaughan are two of the presenters."

"Got you."

"That's them over there," she said, gesturing to Rachel's table. "Damon's the tall bearded guy and Ozzy's the black man with the bald head. He's a rapper."

"Right."

"Do you want me to introduce you?"

"No, it's okay." The last thing he wanted was to be introduced to Rachel's table as Victor's plus one. "I'll maybe wander over and say hello later."

"I wouldn't leave it too long. They'll be pissed as newts in an hour or so." This time her laugh was genuine.

They continued talking for a few more minutes and Maj found himself growing to like Eve. He found it hard to believe she was involved in anything immoral or illicit but knew he had to keep an open mind.

It occurred to him that he might learn more from guests at the ceremony after a few drinks had been consumed. First, though, he needed to try and rescue the situation with Rachel before she gave him away.

Maj waited for a natural break in the conversation, excused himself and made his way over to her table. She was sitting alone, staring at a half-full glass of white wine on the table in front of her.

"Mind if I sit here," Maj said, gesturing to the chair next to her.

"Not at all," Rachel said. She gestured to the deserted table. "It's nice to have someone to talk to. The others are all off mingling."

Maj edged a little closer to ensure they couldn't be overheard. "Earlier," he said, "I told you my wife watches 'Rock-n-Roll-n-Rap'."

"I remember."

"The thing is, I'm here as Victor Robertson's plus one."

"Oh, I see." She smiled. "Don't worry, your secret's safe with me."

"Thanks. I'd rather you didn't tell anyone I'm married if that's okay?"

"Don't worry, I won't." She hesitated before continuing. "Tell me, Maj, do you believe in coincidences?"

Maj laughed. "You sound like my boss."

She looked him in the eyes. "Would that be Luke Sackville, Head of Ethics at Filchers?"

Maj gulped. "What?" he said. He looked around and lowered his voice to a whisper. "How did you know?"

"I met Luke and Josh on the train last Monday and Josh mentioned you. Meeting two people within a week called Maj short for Majid felt a little unlikely." She paused. "Am I right in assuming you being here is connected to their visit to GNE's Head Office?

Maj nodded. "Can I trust you, Rachel?"

"Of course."

"I'm here because we've been asked to look into Baz Hartman's parties."

"By Vicky?" she asked.

"Yes." Maj paused. "Vicky suspects young guests at his parties are being groomed or worse. Have you heard anything?"

"No, I haven't, but I'd be happy to ask around if that would help."

"That would be brilliant. Are you around on Monday?"

"I'll be working from home."

"That's great. I'll be in touch. Thanks, Rachel."

"No problem."

Chapter 13

It was gone ten when Luke reached Borrowham Hall. The house was shrouded in darkness and he decided to ring his brother rather than risk waking people up.

Mark opened the door and put his fingers to his lips before gesturing for Luke to follow him. He led him into the Library, shut the door and sighed deeply.

"What's up, Mark?" Luke asked.

"You had better sit down."

Luke sat in one of the armchairs but his brother remained standing. He walked to the window, then turned.

"It's been one hell of an evening," he said.

"Is it Mother?"

Mark snorted. "No. Mother's much the same."

"Erica, then?"

Mark walked to the sofa next to Luke and slumped into it. He wiped his hand across his brow and gave an ironic chuckle. "You guessed it." He leaned forward. "She's known about this for months. Why she didn't tell me earlier I can't fathom."

"You're losing me, Mark. Known about what?"

They both turned as the door opened and Erica wafted in. She was wearing a sheer silk nightdress that was much too revealing.

"What are you doing in here, Mark?" she demanded and then noticed Luke. "Oh, it's you! Has he told you?"

"I was just about to," Mark said.

Luke's phone rang and he looked down to see it was Maj calling. He declined the call.

Erica wafted over to the other armchair and descended slowly into it.

Mark swallowed. "We're going to be parents."

"Isn't that good news?" Luke said.

"It should be, except…"

Luke's phone rang again. He pressed the red button and put it on silent.

"Bloody typical," Erica said.

"He can hardly help it if his phone rings," Mark said.

"I've switched it to silent," Luke said. "You were saying, Mark, that Erica is pregnant."

Mark gave a mirthless laugh. "No, she isn't."

"But you said…"

"We're going to be parents because Marion's coming to live with us," Mark said. He saw Luke's eyebrow go up. "Sorry, I forgot. You don't know her name, do you?" He swallowed before continuing. "Marion is Erica's daughter."

"She's your daughter too," Erica snapped.

"No, she isn't. I've never even met her."

"You need to welcome her, make her feel part of the family."

"Well, you've hardly made it easy."

Luke decided it was time to intervene before their disagreement escalated into a blazing row. "My understanding was that your daughter had been adopted, Erica. What's happened?"

"I wanted to check she was doing well," Erica began, "and about twelve months ago I hired private investigators to locate her."

"Without telling me," Mark said huffily.

Erica ignored him. "They discovered that she had been taken from her adoptive parents and placed into foster care."

"Why was that?" Luke asked.

"They were drug addicts. Worse, actually. The father was a dealer. Anyway, when they told me that, I looked into it and discovered I could apply for reinstatement of my parental rights." She smiled then, a rare occurrence in Luke's experience. "They granted me custody yesterday."

The smile disappeared as she turned to her husband. "You need to be fully behind this, instead of which all you've done is moan all evening."

"It's hardly surprising, throwing this at me and expecting me to act immediately."

"Whoa," Luke said, his tone firm. They both turned to look at him. "You have to realise, Erica," he went on, "that Mark needs time to absorb everything he's learned today." He turned to Mark. "And for your part, Mark, you have to accept that Erica has been through a lot, and that what she's told you this evening is tremendous news. It's life-changing but in an incredibly positive way."

"She could have…"

Luke held his hand up. "As I said, you need time to think things through."

"I'm not going to have much of that, am I?"

"Why not?"

It was Erica who answered. "We're travelling to Los Angeles tomorrow afternoon," she said. "I booked the flights this morning. Two tickets out and three coming back in a week's time."

"That's another thing she did without telling me," Mark said grumpily. He turned his attention to Erica. "You know what things are like here. Mother is seeing the consultant on Wednesday, and Father wants me to take her. I can't leave them for a week."

Oh no, Luke thought, but then what option did he have? "I can cover for you, Mark," he said through gritted teeth.

He looked down at his phone to see a message had come in.

"I think that right now," he went on, "you need to talk to each other, at length, about exactly how you're going to take this forward." They started to speak but he shushed them with a glance. "Above all, you need to talk through what's best for the both of you and for Marion, not just for you as individuals. You're a team and you need to behave like one."

They were both silent.

"I'm going to the kitchen," Luke went on. "I'll give you an hour and when I return I want some sense out of both of you." He was being bossy he knew, but they were their own worst enemies and needed someone to set them straight.

When he got to the kitchen he put the kettle on and read Maj's message. Then he read it for a second time but it still didn't make sense.

I MADE CONTACT WITH SOMEONE YOU KNOW
WHO'S ON THE INSIDE AT GNE AND WILL HELP
US.
I NEED ADVICE ON DRUNKS.
RING ME.

He took his phone off silent and rang Maj's number.

"Hi, Luke," Maj said when he answered, though Luke could hardly make out his words, there was such a cacophony in the background. "Give me a minute."

Luke waited.

"I can talk now," Maj said, the background noise now reduced to a mild hum. "I'm in the toilets. If I stop talking it's because someone's come in."

"Are you still at the ceremony?"

"Yes. The awards are over but a lot of people are still here."

"Your text said there's someone I know who's going to help us."

"Rachel Adams. She's a content designer. You and Josh met her on the train."

"And she's going to help?"

"Yes. We'll need to follow up with her next week."

"Okay. What did you mean about needing advice on drunks?"

"I'm the only sober one here, and it's a great

opportunity to get information out of people while their guard is low. And believe me, their guard is very, very low. Some of the things I've heard would make my hair stand on end." He laughed. "If I had any hair."

"So what's the problem?"

"How far can I push it, Luke? When people get drunk do they forget everything they say? Or do I still have to be careful?"

Luke thought about this for a moment. "Unfortunately, there's not a clear answer. I've known some people who forget absolutely everything, even where they've been, let alone what they've said. Others can remember much more."

"That's a shame. I thought it would be more black and white than that."

"But the thing is, Maj, if they do tell you anything there'll be no comeback. You're along for this evening but that's the end of it. They'll never see you again, and as far as they know you're a software engineer."

"That's true. Thanks for the advice, Luke. I'd better get back. I'll see you next week."

"You won't actually. I'll be working from my parents' house."

"Is one of them ill?"

"Yes, but it's a little more complex than that. I'll explain on Monday."

Chapter 14

"Are Baz's parties worth going to?" Maj asked.

"Too fuckin' right." Damon Prendergast took a glug of his whisky, managing to spill some down his shirt as he did so. "You're with Vicky, aren't you?"

"Yes."

Damon winked, or at least attempted to wink, though it was more like a slow blink of first his left and then his right eye. "You like 'em older then?"

"Not exclusively."

"Ah."

"Do you like younger men?" Maj prompted.

"Me?" Damon smiled lasciviously. "I like 'em all ages, but young and firm is good, yeah."

Maj had to fight to hide his disgust. "I heard there are young men at Baz's parties."

Damon raised an eyebrow and nodded. "Certainly are." His grin returned. "Very young." A gentle tap on his shoulder almost caused him to fall over. He turned his head slowly. "Ah, Ozzy. How ya doin'?"

"This and that, Dame-oh." Ozzy flicked his fingers and waggled his head from left to right. "Bobbin' and divin'. Workin' the room, sure thang." He noticed Maj. "Watcha, bro'." He looked him up and down. "Like your style. What's your moniker?"

Maj held out his hand. "Maj. I'm here with Vicky."

Ozzy grasped Maj's hand with both of his and jerked it up and down. "Nice to meet you, man. Not many brothers here tonight. Bussin' gig though." He lifted his glass to his lips and downed it in one. "Free-flowing booze. Gotta be good, innit?"

Maj was taken aback by the man's complete mish-mash

of accents as his voice veered from cockney to US deep south and back via the Midlands. He suspected Ozzy's real accent was none of those.

"Maj was asking…" Damon paused mid-sentence and belched. "…'bout Baz's parties."

"Really good, innit," Ozzy said. "Lots of spring chickens, know what I mean?" He looked down at his empty glass, then turned to the group standing next to them and tapped the nearest man on the shoulder. "Need a drink," he said.

The man turned and it was clear he recognised the rapper. "Hi, Ozzy," he said. "Nice to meet you. I'm…"

Ozzy waved his hand to cut him off mid-sentence. "Whatever." He grabbed the man's hand and pressed his glass into it. "Rum, no ice." He turned back to Maj and Damon, his order issued and the man forgotten. "What was I…?" He flicked his fingers again.

"We were talking about Baz's parties," Maj said.

"Right, bro. Buzzin' gigs. Trouble last time, wannit Dame-oh?"

"Oh yeah, Ozzy," Damon said.

"What happened?" Maj asked.

"Baz gave a man some kickin'," Ozzy said.

"There was worse," Damon said. He attempted to tap the side of his nose but missed. "A lot worse. Heard someone was hurt real bad."

"Heard that too, Dame-oh," Ozzy said. "One of the spring chickens."

"Kids?" Maj prompted.

"Yeah. The ones Eve invites. Fit young talent and trim. Know what I mean, bro?" Ozzy smiled in a way that made Maj's stomach turn.

"And one of them was hurt?"

"Right on. Real bad."

"Do you know who hurt her?"

"Wan't no 'her', man." Ozzy chuckled. "No femmes at

Baz's gigs."

"I heard it was Marvin," Damon said.

"Nah," Ozzy said. "It was Reggie. Sure thang." He flicked his fingers yet again. It was almost a tic, Maj thought.

"Marvin and Reggie?" Maj prompted.

"They're on Baz's show," Ozzy said.

"Celebrity guests?"

Damon snorted. "Neither of 'em are fuckin' celebs," he said. "Z-list."

"True that," Ozzy said.

"Are they here tonight?" Maj asked.

It was Damon who answered. "There," he said, almost losing his balance as he gestured to a group of four men sitting at a table.

"Marvin's the goggles," Ozzy said, pointing to the youngest in the group. He was sitting to the right of the others and wore large aviator glasses. "Reggie's the fatty next to him."

"Right," Maj said.

The man in the group next to them returned with Ozzy's drink and he took the offered glass of rum without acknowledgement.

"How often does Baz hold his parties?" Maj asked.

"There's one next week," Damon said.

"Yeah," Ozzy added. "We're goin', man, You wanna go?"

"No, I'm busy next week," Maj said.

"Vicky could get you in," Damon said.

Maj smiled. "I'd love to but, as I said, I'm busy. Maybe the one after."

"Cool, bro," Ozzy said, and there was that flicking again.

Maj raised his head and waved at no one in particular. "There's someone I need to speak to," he said. "Will you excuse me, guys?"

"Sure thang," Ozzy said, while Damon merely nodded.

Maj walked away in the direction he had waved and then veered off to the toilet to collect his thoughts.

Chapter 15

Once he was locked in a cubicle, Maj ran through who he had met and what he had learned.

First, there were Baz Hartman, the presenter of 'Hall of Flame', and his Personal Assistant, Eve. He'd had too little time with Baz to develop an opinion of him, but Eve had been a genuine surprise. Supposedly the fixer for whatever was going on at Baz's parties, she had come across as pleasant and genuine.

Damon Prendergast and Ozzy Vaughan had confirmed that Baz's parties were all male affairs and that Eve invited young men to them. How young hadn't been clear, although from what Ozzy had said they hadn't sounded like they were very old. Of course, it could be that all that was happening was that young gay men aged eighteen to their early twenties were going to Baz's get-togethers. If that was the case then it was possible that there was nothing wrong or amoral going on, and that Victor's suspicions were unfounded.

Then there was the reported incident at Baz's last party where one of the younger men had been hurt badly. Neither Damon nor Ozzy had witnessed anything, but Damon had heard Marvin was responsible while Ozzy had been told it was Reggie. Ozzy had said that both of them were minor celebrities on Baz's show.

Maj looked at his watch. It was nearly eleven and he needed to make the most of what remaining time he had. He was about to stand up when someone banged on the cubicle door.

"Gonna be long?"

It was clear from the slurring that the man was very drunk. Maj was about to answer when he heard the sound of vomiting and then a second voice.

"Fuck, Marvin. What's wrong with the sink?"

"I couldn't, Reggie. I…"

Marvin broke off to be sick again.

Maj pulled the chain, opened the door and stepped over the mess on the floor to one of the sinks. He turned the tap on, put his hands under the running water and said, "Is your friend okay?"

"Fucking blotto," Reggie said, his chins waggling as he spoke. It was clear he'd had a few drinks but also that he was considerably less affected than Marvin. Perhaps it was his size that reduced the impact of the alcohol, Maj thought. Reggie had to be twenty-two stone if he was a day, none of it muscle, while his friend was half that.

"I told him to take it easy," Reggie went on. "But he doesn't fucking listen."

Marvin was bent over one of the sinks now, his chest heaving. "Had too much," he said.

"No shit, Sherlock," Reggie said. "Have you stopped up-chucking?"

"Yeah."

"Let's get you to a taxi then."

"Do you want me to help?" Maj asked. He lifted one of Marvin's arms without waiting for an answer and wrapped it behind his neck. Reggie grabbed the other side and they manhandled Marvin out of the bathroom and into the corridor.

Once there, they propped Marvin against the wall, and he slowly slid down to a sitting position.

"I'll wait with him," Maj said.

"All right," Reggie said. He reached for his phone. "No fucking signal. Back in a minute."

He headed out.

"Where's he gone?" Marvin asked, his eyes blinking as he tried to focus on Maj's face.

"To arrange a taxi."

Marvin nodded and Maj decided to take advantage of the situation. The man was blind drunk, almost paralytic, but it was worth a try.

"Did you beat someone at Baz's party, Marvin?" he asked.

"What?" Marvin looked at Maj, trying to take in his features. "Were you there?"

"I heard you hurt a young man. Hurt him badly."

"Reggie."

"What about Reggie?" Maj sighed. This was hard work. "Did Reggie beat him?"

"Worse."

"Worse than beat him?"

"Yeah." Marvin belched and for a second Maj feared he was going to be sick again.

"What did he do?" Maj asked.

"Forced him."

"Forced him to do what?"

"Very young."

It was proving impossible to keep Marvin on track and Maj decided to go with the flow.

"Are you saying the man who was hurt was very young?"

This was greeted with silence and Maj realised that the sentence was too complex for Marvin to process.

"How old was he?" Maj asked.

"Who?"

This was getting harder and harder.

"The young man."

"Don't know." Marvin thought for a moment before adding, "Young."

"And he was forced by Reggie?"

"What the fuck?" said Reggie from behind Maj who turned to see the big man staring at him, one eyebrow raised. "What are you two talking about?"

Maj swallowed, hoping that Reggie had only that

moment returned. "Nothing," he said, before hastily adding, "Did you manage to get a taxi?"

"Yeah. Can you give me a hand to get him up?"

"Sure." Maj helped Reggie lift Marvin to a standing position. "Do you want help taking him to the car?"

"Nah. I can manage."

Reggie pulled Marvin's arm around his shoulder and then half-dragged, half-shuffled him down the corridor and away.

Maj breathed a sigh of relief, waited for a couple of minutes to ensure they were out of the way, and then headed for the exit.

Chapter 16

Maj was relieved when Helen walked into the Ethics Room.

'My brain's full," he said. "I met a lot of people on Saturday night. Do you think you could create an investigation board so that I can get everything straight in my head?"

"Nae problem," Helen said. Josh and Sam walked in as she was wheeling the whiteboard out and she explained what she was doing.

"Crazy wall," Josh said. "Gucci."

"Any idea where Luke is?" Sam asked. "He's usually in by now."

"I spoke to him on Saturday," Maj said. "He's having to stay with his parents this week. Why don't we have a crack at the board and then give him a ring?"

They agreed that was a good idea and stared at the board.

And then stared at it a bit more.

It was Helen who broke the silence. "It's a wee bit hard without a crime," she said.

"Why not put 'Suspected Assault' to be going on with?" Sam suggested.

"Aye, that'll work." Helen wrote 'Suspected Assault' on a Post-it and stuck it in the middle of the board.

"We know it's something to do with Baz Hartmann's parties," Josh suggested.

"Great," Helen said. "Now we're getting somewhere."

"And I met some of the key people on Saturday," Maj said. "Most of them are celebrities, or at least semi-celebrities. Do you think you could find images and print them off, Josh?"

"Cool."

They spent the next hour adding people and their photographs and what they knew or suspected to the list. When they'd finished they stood back.

"There's a lot there," Maj said.

Helen chuckled. "There sure is, especially given we don't even know if anything criminal or untoward has happened."

"It's not pretty," Sam said. She held her hand up when she saw Helen was about to defend herself. "I don't mean you've done a bad job, Helen. What I mean is that the whole picture is very sordid. My instinct is that there's something bad going on at Baz Hartmann's parties."

"Aye, I'm of the same view. Why don't we ring Luke and see what he thinks?"

Helen took a photo of the board, WhatsApp'ed it to Luke and then rang him on the conference phone.

"Good morning, everyone," Luke said. "Well done, Maj. You seem to have met a few of the key people. There are eight on the whiteboard, including Victor, who's our whistleblower, and Rachel, who works at GNE and has offered to help. Can you give us an assessment of where we're at please?"

"Sure." Maj paused to collect his thoughts. "Most of the people I met were very drunk, but there was a common theme to what they were telling me. It seems clear that Baz Hartman's parties are all male affairs with young men, possibly under eighteen, invited to attend by Eve, his Personal Assistant and 'fixer'. I believe it's also likely that one of those young men was badly hurt at the last one just over a week ago."

"Any thoughts on who might have done it?" Luke asked.

"It could have been Baz himself," Maj said. "He certainly attacked someone at the party but I was left with the impression that there were two separate victims." He looked up at the right-hand side of the board. "The other four possibles are Damon and Ozzy, who host 'Rock-n-Roll-n-Rap', the show Rachel works on, and Reggie and Marvin who are Reality TV stars and contestants on Baz's show 'Hall of Flame'.

"Did you form any views on which of the five most likely to be the offender?" Luke asked.

"From what I heard on Saturday, Reggie seems the most likely," Maj said. "Though to be honest, it could have been any of them. Or for that matter one of the thirty or so other guests at Baz's party." He looked at Josh. "You've got your work cut out on Saturday, Josh."

"Geez, thanks," Josh said.

"We need more intelligence before the weekend," Luke said. "Was Rachel serious about helping us?"

"Definitely," Maj said. "She seemed quite excited by the idea."

"Does she know all the people you've put on the whiteboard?"

"All bar Eve, though of course neither her nor Victor are on our suspect list."

"Great. Helen and Sam, please can you arrange to meet her, bring her up to speed and get her to do some digging?"

"She told me she's working from home today," Maj said.

"We'll get onto it," Sam said.

"Aye," Helen added. "We'll see if we can meet her this afternoon."

*

It was just after two when Rachel let Helen and Sam into her apartment.

"Sorry about the stairs," she said as she showed them into her lounge.

"No problem," Sam said. She walked over to the window which faced out onto Milsom Street, looked out and then turned back. "It's worth it for the view."

"Yes, I was really pleased to get this place," Rachel said and smiled. "I split from my boyfriend a few months ago and was desperate to find somewhere quickly. My timing was lucky."

"How long have you been in?

"Only three weeks."

Sam looked around the lounge. It retained some of what she guessed were the original features but had a modern twist. The room had high ceilings with an elegant light fitting hanging from an ornate plaster rose in the centre of the ceiling. The carpet was deep red, the leather three piece suite cream, and the pictures colourful and abstract.

"It looks lovely," she said.

"Thanks."

"Are these by Jonathan Oakes?" Helen asked, looking at the two paintings over the fireplace.

"Yes. I love his work," Rachel said. "Are you a fan?"

"No, but my son was. He loved his stuff."

"Doesn't he like him any more?" Rachel asked.

Sam knew this was a sensitive subject for Helen and decided to cut the conversation off. "Shall we get on, Rachel? We don't want to keep you for too long."

"Of course. Please take a seat. Can I get you a drink?"

"I'm fine, thanks," Sam said.

"I'd love a wee cup of tea," Helen said.

"Right," Rachel said. "Back in a mo'." She left for the kitchen.

"Thanks for changing the subject," Helen whispered to Sam once they had seated themselves on either end of the sofa. "That conversation could have gone to the dark side."

Rachel returned a few minutes later with Helen's tea, placed it on the coffee table in front of her and then sat on the armchair nearest Sam.

"To be honest," Rachel said, "I'm thrilled to be involved in this. It makes a change and your boss Luke is nice."

"And you've met Maj and Josh as well," Helen said.

"Yes, of course," Rachel said hastily, and Helen noted a tinge of pink appear in her cheeks. "They're both nice as well."

Sam opened her laptop and twisted it around so that Rachel could see the screen.

"This is a photo of our investigation board. I guess you know most of this from talking to Maj on Saturday."

Rachel inspected it for a few minutes. "Nice to see I'm not a suspect," she said at one point, pointing to the Post-it in the bottom left with her name on it. When she'd finished she gestured to Reggie's and Marvin's names. "I didn't expect them to be on there."

Helen explained what they had said when Maj had encountered them in the bathroom at the awards ceremony. "Victor has wangled it so that Josh is invited to Baz Hartman's party this Saturday," she went on. "He's going to pretend to be a teenager so that he'll blend in."

"Not too much of a stretch," Rachel said with a smile.

"So what we need," Sam said, "is as much information as possible before the weekend so that Josh can make the most of it. Would you be able to ask around, find out more about the attendees and whether there are rumours about anything untoward?"

"Definitely. I'm in Head Office tomorrow and Thursday and I'll see what I can uncover. I could meet Luke to update him on Friday."

"Unfortunately, Luke's not around this week," Helen said.

"Oh, right."

Helen noticed a hint of disappointment in her voice and had to fight to stop herself smiling. "Would you be able to come to our office on Friday morning?" she said. "It's on the Lower Bristol Road and it might be easier given we'd like Maj and Josh to be in on the meeting."

"Yes, that would be fine." Rachel paused for a second. "Have you got a number for Luke? I'd, um, like to give him a ring to, um, thank him for letting me help."

"Of course," Helen said and passed his contact details over. "Thanks again, Rachel. This is really good of you."

Rachel showed them out and they said their farewells then started down the stairs.

"I liked her," Sam said.

"She fancies the pants off our Luke," Helen said with a chuckle.

Sam stopped dead in her tracks. "You think so," she said, looking back at the door to Rachel's apartment.

"I know so, lassie," Helen said. "Why do you think she asked for his number?"

"She said she wanted to thank him."

"Oh Sam, you can be so naive sometimes."

Chapter 17

Rachel was in a buoyant mood as she walked from the underground to GNE's Head Office. She was happy for two reasons. First, she was looking forward to doing some secret squirrel work, and second, she had Luke Sackville's number.

And it was this last point that excited her. She didn't believe in love at first sight but there was something about him that attracted her. It wasn't his looks especially, though he did have the rugged look and build that she typically went for, and the scar on the side of his face added a sense of intrigue. No, it was his personality. He was confident but modest at the same time. She'd love to get to know him better.

She decided she would ring him at the end of the day to update him on how she'd got on. If she did that she'd be able to assess whether her interest was reciprocated. With her luck, it probably wouldn't be. Doubtless he liked short women with big breasts, not tall willowy women. Mind you, he was well over six foot so perhaps…

Even if he liked her looks could she be too outgoing for him? Had he been offended when she'd broken into the conversation he and Josh had been having on the train? He'd seemed perfectly okay about it, but had she been over the top? She shook her head. No point in worrying about what might never happen. First things first.

She walked in through the revolving doors, nodded hello to the woman on reception and swiped her card to open the glass door to the building proper. Once in, she headed for the bank of hot desks on the first floor that was her usual domicile and took her laptop, notebook and pen out and placed them down to reserve her space.

It had been a stroke of luck that both Damon and Ozzy were in and had agreed to meet her for a coffee, Damon at 10:30 and Ozzy at 11:30. Ostensibly, she was meeting them to discuss her plans for taking the 'Rock-n-Roll-n-Rap' graphics to the next level.

At 10:30 she was in the canteen cradling a coffee and preparing her spiel when both men appeared beside her.

"Hi girl," Ozzy said. "No need for us to meet at 11:30 when you're seeing Dame-oh, innit?"

"You might as well tell us both at once," Damon said, taking a seat opposite her.

"We was in a meet," Ozzy said. He turned the chair next to Rachel's so that the back faced her and then sat on it the wrong way round. "Dame-oh says you're telling him plans, and I says same, so we thought two birds. Is that okay, Ray-O?" He flicked his fingers. "Makes sense, girl. Don't waste your time, don't waste ours. Sure thang."

"Yes, that's fine, Ozzy."

She spent the next ten minutes telling them what she envisaged for the graphics for the next series and how she would create a supporting YouTube video."

"Cool," Ozzy said when she'd finished.

"Yeah, sounds fucking ace," Damon said.

"That's great. I'm pleased you like it," Rachel said. "It makes it easier for me if I know you two are on board."

She swallowed. Here goes.

"I'm going to try to work on it over the weekend," she went on. "I've got friends coming around though, so that might get in the way. Are you two up to anything special?"

"Ducking and divin'," Ozzy said and flicked his fingers.

"One of Baz's parties on Saturday," Damon said. "They're fucking brilliant."

"I heard they were good," Rachel said. "Any chance I could come along?"

"I thought you were seeing friends?" Damon asked.

"Oh yes, I am. But I meant to a later party, his next one

perhaps."

"Not your scene, baby girl," Ozzy said.

"You think I'm too dull?"

Ozzy smiled, his single gold tooth catching the light from the overhead fluorescent. "Ain't the fact you is dull. Is the fact you got those." He pointed at her breasts and clicked the fingers of both hands.

"What?"

"It's men only," Damon said.

"Oh." Rachel feigned ignorance. "Why's that?"

'We has fun," Ozzy said, "and it's only man fun. You know what I is sayin'?"

"I heard rumours of bad things at Baz's parties, but I didn't realise it was men only. Someone said women were being hurt at them."

"Not possible if there ain't any, innit?" Ozzy said.

"So are there men being hurt?" She noticed that Damon was looking at her in a peculiar way. "What is it, Damon?"

"Why are you asking these questions?"

"I'm interested in what you're up to at the weekend, that's all."

"So you've heard women are being hurt at Baz's parties but you ask us to snag you an invitation. What's that about, for fuck's sake?"

"Well, um, they were only rumours." Rachel could feel colour coming to her cheeks. "I thought they were probably untrue, but I wanted to check with you."

"Leave her, Dame-oh," Ozzy said. "She was only like askin', innit."

Damon leaned forward and wagged his index finger up and down. "You want to keep your trap shut, Rachel. Don't interfere, you got me?"

"Of course, Damon." She tried to smile but it was a weak attempt. "Anyway, thanks for meeting me, guys. It's great to have your support for my plans."

"Yeah," Ozzy said. He stood up. "Got some bro's to see, girl. Be catchin' you."

"See you, Ozzy," Rachel said.

"I've got to go too," Damon said. He was still scowling as he turned to follow Ozzy out of the canteen.

Rachel took a sip of her coffee. Her questioning had gone badly and she wondered if she should go through with the second part of her plan.

She gave a half chuckle. Calling it a 'plan' was overstating it somewhat. She had found out that they were filming 'Hall of Flame' and she was going to approach Reggie and Marvin when there was a break. And that was her 'plan'.

Ah well, what did she have to lose apart from a bagful of pride? She decided to head straight to Studio 2 and see when the next break was scheduled.

When she got there there were two men outside beneath a sign that read 'Filming in Progress - Quiet on Set'.

They were deep in conversation but stopped when they saw her hesitation. The taller of the two gave her a quick and obvious up and down before smiling.

"Can I help you?" he asked.

"I'm looking for Victor. Am I in the right place?"

"Sure." He held his hand out. "I'm Kieran."

She shook his hand. "Rachel."

He held her hand a little longer than necessary and the smile never left his face. "Here, let me show you where he is." He turned to the other man. "Be back in a moment, Nat," he said, and Rachel could swear she saw him wink as he said it. He was starting to creep her out.

"Thanks," she said, and he opened the door and gestured for her to go in first. Once in, it was clear that they were mid-scene. A young woman wearing headphones turned and put her finger over her lips before returning her attention to the set. It was designed, Rachel guessed, to simulate a room in a castle, with eight people seated around a blazing brazier while Baz Hartman paced around them.

Kieran tapped her on the shoulder and pointed to a dark corner of the room where Victor Robertson was sitting. She had met him briefly on two occasions and now knew from what Helen and Sam had told her that he was on her side.

Rachel nodded thanks to Kieran who gave her another broad smile before turning to go back outside.

She approached Victor whose eyes were fixed on the set. Baz Hartman was pacing around the seated contestants, occasionally stopping to ask them a question.

Victor turned when she was a yard away and whispered, "Good to see you, Rachel."

"Is there a break soon?" she said as quietly as she could.

"In five, dear." He gestured to the seat next to him and she sat down.

Ten minutes later the Director called "Cut" before the woman who had shushed Rachel shouted, "Lunch everyone. Back at one on the dot."

The silence was immediately broken as contestants stood up and conversations started. A heavily overweight man headed for the exit.

"That's Reggie," Victor said. "The man with glasses talking to the woman in blue is Marvin."

"Ah yes, I recognise him now. Thanks."

She decided to grasp the opportunity to speak to Marvin while Reggie wasn't there. She didn't want to ask both at once and run into the same problem as earlier.

She stood and walked over to Marvin.

"Sorry to interrupt," she said. She looked at the woman in blue. "I need a word with Marvin. Do you mind?"

"Not at all." She stepped away.

"Hi," Marvin said. He raised an eyebrow. "Have we met?"

"Very briefly on Saturday." She smiled. "I doubt you

would remember. You were pretty out of it. My name's Rachel."

"Hi, Rachel." He shrugged. "Yeah, I was a bit of an embarrassment. How can I help?"

"It's a bit sensitive." She paused. "I believe you're a regular at Baz's parties."

"Yes. Why?"

"The son of a friend of mine is interested in going."

"Really? How old is he?"

This struck Rachel as an odd question and she decided to ignore it. "I wondered if you could get him an invitation."

Marvin's chest visibly inflated. "I could probably do that, yes."

"The thing is, there are rumours the parties aren't safe. Have you found they're okay?"

Marvin cocked his head to one side. "Where have you heard that?"

"Oh, I don't know. Just around and about."

"Mmm. You didn't answer my question. How old is he?"

"Ah, he's sixteen. Does that make him too young?"

"Make who too young?" Rachel turned to see Baz Hartman standing beside them. "Who are you talking about?"

"A friend," Rachel said. "He's interested in your parties."

"They're fucking great do's," Reggie said from behind her.

So much for trying to conduct her questioning one-on-one. There were three men with her now.

"Thanks, Reggie," Baz said. "Your opinion means a lot."

"Cheers," Reggie said, the sarcasm lost on him.

"Who are you, anyway?" Baz asked, his attention now back on Rachel.

"Rachel Adams," she said. She held her hand out but he ignored it.

"We're in the middle of filming my show. Why are you asking now?"

"No particular reason. I was in the building so I thought I'd pop in."

"Why ask Marvin?" Baz didn't wait for her to answer and turned to Marvin. "Was she asking anything else?"

"She asked if the parties were safe."

Baz turned back to Rachel, jabbed his finger in her chest and said, "I think you had better clear off."

"Ah, right. I…"

"Just fuck off!"

Rachel turned and walked away.

Kieran and Nat were still there when she closed the room door behind her.

"Are you okay?" Kieran asked. He moved to grab her arm and she shrugged him off.

"Fine," she said and walked past the two of them towards the lift, her eyes starting to fill with tears as she realised what a complete shambles she had made of everything.

Chapter 18

Luke couldn't wait for the week to end.

There was only a limited amount of work he could do without being in the office, but it wasn't just the boredom. His father was driving him up the wall.

"You should have stayed in the police," Hugo said. He was standing at the conservatory window staring at the manicured gardens, something he seemed to spend the majority of his time doing.

"You know why I left, Father," Luke said, not for the first time. "I couldn't go on, not after what happened to Jess."

"But a sourcing company of all things."

"Outsourcing."

"What?"

"Filchers is an outsourcing company. I've told you this."

"Whatever it is, it's not the same."

Luke sighed. "Of course it's not the same. But the work I do is important and I've got a great team."

"Mmm." Hugo turned to face his son. "I should come with you today."

"I'm fine, Father," Luke said. "There's no point in you sitting around waiting for Mother to be seen. You're better off staying here. Plus, it will give me the chance to talk to Mother properly."

"Good luck with that." Hugo's voice broke slightly as he continued. "She's going downhill awfully quickly."

There was nothing Luke could say. His father was right and their only hope was that the consultant would prescribe something to slow the process down.

There was a small cough and Luke turned to see Amy, the young housekeeper, at the door. "The Duchess is ready, your grace," she said.

"Thank you, Amy," Hugo said.

"I'll see you later, Father," Luke said. There was no reply and he turned to follow Amy out of the room.

"She thinks she's going to a ball," Amy whispered once they were out of earshot. "I don't know why. I told her she's seeing a doctor but she doesn't seem to have taken it in."

His mother Daphne, the Duchess of Dorset, was staring at one of the oil paintings when they got to the Front Hall.

"That's Hugo's great-great-grandmother," she said.

"That's right, Mother," Luke said.

She turned and scowled at him. "Where's Hugo? He's taking me to the Osberts."

"No, he's not, Mother. We're going to see your consultant."

She looked past him at Amy and pointed her finger. "You. Come here."

Amy walked hesitantly over. "How can I help, your grace?"

"Fetch Hugo, Emily. He needs to take me to the ball."

"It's all right, Amy," Luke said. "Leave it with me." He turned back to his mother as Amy stepped away again. "I'm taking you to see your doctor, Mother."

"I'm not dressed correctly."

"You look fine."

"I need a ballgown. I'm going to the Osberts."

"Come on," Luke said and put her arm through his, shocked as always by how frail she was. He led her outside and opened the passenger door of the BMW.

"Where's Hugo?" she asked as he leaned over to fasten her seatbelt.

"He's not coming," Luke said. He walked round to the driver's side and climbed in.

They set off for Salisbury and Daphne was quiet for

the first few minutes until they passed a large gated driveway.

"The Osberts lived there," she said, "but they're dead now."

She remained quiet for the remainder of the journey.

When they reached the hospital, Luke parked and went to the passenger side to help her out.

"Thank you, Marcus," she said as she took his hand.

"I'm Luke."

"I know that," she snapped. She looked up at the red brick Victorian building in front of them "Why are we here?"

"We're going to see your doctor."

She nodded and he put her arm through his. They walked to the steps and she stopped at the bottom. "Why are we here?"

"You've got an appointment with your consultant."

She nodded again.

*

Hugo was seated in the old armchair in the library reading when Luke returned.

"Where's Daphne?" he said, looking up from the FT.

"Amy's taken her for a nap," Luke said. "The journey tired her out." He collapsed into the brown leather Chippendale opposite his father.

"What did Mr Hargreaves say?"

"He's prescribed some drugs but there's not a lot he can do." Luke paused. "He asked if we had considered putting her in a home."

"Mmm."

"Have you thought about it, Father?"

"I don't see the need. We can bring carers in here."

Luke decided to let the matter drop. Money certainly

wasn't a problem, and at the moment his mother was relatively easy to cope with. The trouble was that it was going to get harder. He'd done some reading and it was clear that her Alzheimer's could affect her in one of two ways. She might become increasingly stressed and take that stress out on others, becoming loud and possibly even violent. On the other hand, she could go to the other extreme and withdraw completely within herself.

Only time would tell.

"Please excuse me," Luke said. "I have a few calls to make."

"Fine," Hugo said, his nose now back in his newspaper. "I'll see you at dinner."

Luke made himself a coffee and headed upstairs to his bedroom. He had just settled behind his desk when his phone rang.

"Luke Sackville," he said.

"Hi Luke, it's Rachel, Rachel Adams." She sounded on edge, her voice not as lively as it had been when they had met the previous week.

"Hi, Rachel. Is everything okay?"

"I, um…"

"What is it?"

"I completely messed up."

"What do you mean?"

"I managed to see Damon, Ozzy, Reggie and Marvin yesterday. Even Baz."

"That's great."

There was a pause before Rachel continued. "I asked all the wrong questions."

"Don't worry about it. As long as you didn't tell them about Josh there's nothing lost."

"There's worse."

Luke sensed that she was on the edge of tears. "What happened, Rachel?"

"I've been sacked."

"What?"

"John Steadman called me in this morning. He's the Head of Light Entertainment. He told me I'd upset people by spreading rumours."

"About who?"

"He specifically named Baz Hartman. He said Baz is one of their biggest stars and content designers are two a penny." He heard her voice break. "God, it was awful."

"Can he do that? Sack you for supposedly spreading rumours."

"Easily. I'm not a permanent employee. I'm on a rolling contract. He told me I'll be paid until the end of the month and then it won't be renewed."

"I'm so sorry I've put you in this position, Rachel."

"Don't be silly. It's not your fault and it was about time I moved on. I'm upset because it's just happened, but I'll be fine. Talking to you has helped." There was a moment of silence before she continued. "The funny thing is I was going to ask if you…" She paused.

"If I what?"

"Nothing. It's silly. "

"No, go on."

"I wondered, um, I wondered if you might like to meet up sometime."

"Oh."

"Sorry if I'm out of line."

"No, not at all. I'm in Dorset this week but, yes, I'd love that."

Luke smiled to himself. He had taken a liking to Rachel immediately and it would be great to spend more time in her company. In the back of his mind was the question of whether Jess would approve, but he knew she would. *Get out there, Luke,* he could hear her saying. *You're young and you need to make the most of life without me.*

"Perhaps we could go for a drink?" he asked. "How are you fixed next Monday or Tuesday?"

She gave a hollow laugh. "I'm pretty free as it happens."

"Yeah, I guess you are." He echoed her laugh. "Look, why don't I come by yours at seven on Monday? I know a great bar around the back of Broad Street. We could go for a meal afterwards."

"That would be lovely, Luke. I'll see you then."

Chapter 19

It wasn't the first time there had been rumours, but in the past they had been easy to suppress.

He smiled and put his feet up on the coffee table. Senior management at GNE were so fucking easy to manipulate it was laughable. The stupid idiots were ready to do anything to protect their necks and the reputation of their precious organisation. Whenever they heard someone was up to no good they could be relied on to do one of two things. If the someone was a nobody, a minor cog in the GNE machine, they would be elbowed out, perhaps paid some money and made to sign a non-disclosure agreement. If, on the other hand, one of the so-called star talent had been named, then the big honchos would do their utmost to create a fog of silence, even going so far as to put out counter-rumours if necessary. Staff would be ordered to be silent and threatened with dismissal if they stepped out of line.

The trouble with Rachel fucking Adams was that she was so close to the truth.

He wondered how much more she knew. She had never been to any of the parties, that was for certain. Could she be related to one of the guests, perhaps to the kid he'd killed? Yes, that could well be it.

He'd heard that Steadman had terminated her contract but that might make her even more determined. What if she went to the press or even to the BBC or NTV or Sky? They always liked to get one over on GNE and would lap up the story. If they did that the police would get involved and all hell would break loose.

He couldn't afford for that to happen.

She had to be stopped before she opened her big

mouth again.

But how?

He took a glug of his coffee and worked through his options.

He held up the thumb of his left hand. The first was intimidation. He could put the fear of god into her. It would have to be remote using letters, phone calls, emails or social media, or even a combination. Bombard her with death threats and make it clear she needed to back off or else.

His index finger joined his thumb. Second, go for a loved one. Perhaps she was married or had an elderly ailing mother. There was bound to be someone in her life she cared for dearly. If she believed that person was going to be badly hurt or worse then that might be a very effective way of shutting the bitch up.

Up went his middle finger. Option three was blackmail. In his experience, everyone had at least one skeleton in their closet. If he could discover her darkest secret he could threaten to tell the world and make her a disgrace. The trouble was that it meant lengthy research. Secrets were secrets because they were well hidden and unearthing the details could be hard.

Finally, he raised his ring finger to join the others. Last but not least, there was the nuclear option. He loved the expression 'terminate with extreme prejudice'. It didn't make any sense but it had a certain ring to it.

He leaned forward, put his coffee down on the table, and nodded to himself.

It was a no-brainer really.

Options one, two and three took time and he didn't have time. Rachel Adams was stirring it up and he had to stop her double quick.

He clasped his hands together as if in prayer, then pushed them up and spread them out above his head.

"Ker-pow!" he said.

Chapter 20

Rachel was in a good mood.

Scrub that. She was in a fantastic mood.

Not only had she found another contract quickly, this time at a media agency in the City, she also stood to be quids in. Today was her last day at GNE, but they were paying her until the end of the month and she started at Waltham Hobbs on Monday. Moreover, her daily rate at the media agency was going to be fifty quid higher.

Things were definitely looking up.

Her new boss had asked if she could be in London all week, which meant she wouldn't be able to meet up with Luke on Monday as planned, but she didn't think that would be a problem. She'd ring him when she got home and see if they could meet up next weekend instead.

Rachel had a spring in her step as she mounted the stairs to the first floor. Yes, she thought, things had worked out for the best. She had a short day too, so she'd be back in her apartment by mid to late afternoon. It was simply a case of handing her work over to the new guy, talking him through her plans and then she could leave and get the train back to Bath.

She was surprised when she got to her usual spot to see Baz Hartman sitting there tapping out a beat with the fingers of his right hand.

"Hi, Baz," she said. "Are you waiting for me?"

He looked up. "I was told you'd be in about now," he said. "Look, this doesn't come easily to me, but I wanted to say sorry."

He was using the word 'sorry' but it was apparent from his tone that he was anything but.

"For what?" she asked.

"For getting you the push. Don't get me wrong. You were bang out of line with those questions but, well, you didn't deserve what you got."

"Thanks. Don't worry about me though, I've got another job and I start on Monday." As she said this, it dawned on Rachel that Baz wasn't listening.

"I gotta ask you a question," he said.

"Fire away."

"How did you hear there was trouble at my parties?"

She hesitated. "From a friend, um, a male friend."

"Who?"

"I'd rather not say."

"I'd like to know."

She looked at him and he saw the defiance in her stare.

"Right," he said and stood up.

"See you around," she said, but he had already started walking away and didn't respond.

Rachel shook her head. The guy was so up himself it was untrue.

A few minutes later her replacement arrived and she got to work handing her plans and ideas over to him. Even with a break for lunch, they were finished just short of 2:30. She said goodbye to the new guy and headed out of GNE for the last time, thinking that with any luck she'd be home by five. She had a new book to read, but first she would run herself a foamy bath and wash away the stresses of the week.

As she walked past reception she saw that Reggie and Marvin were leaving just ahead of her, filming of 'Hall of Flame' presumably finished for the week. She held back for a moment, hoping that they wouldn't turn around and see her, and was relieved when they walked into the Starbucks on the opposite side of the road.

It was less than a five-minute walk to Regent's Park underground station and the sun was out. Suddenly, the world seemed a brighter place and she was almost whistling as she took the elevator down to platform level. She had had enough of GNE. The office politics were crazy so it was good she was out of there, even if she had been pushed rather than jumped. Waltham Hobbs would be a new start.

As would Luke Sackville.

Rachel looked up absent-mindedly at the screen to see that the next train was due in one minute. Even her timing was working out well.

She stepped towards the platform edge as the sound of the train grew closer. There were a lot of people waiting but she understood the reason why. It was Friday afternoon and they were leaving early to make the most of the weekend.

As was she. A warm bath, a read of her paperback in her onesie. Bliss. And then on Monday a new job and later in the week an evening out with Luke. Life was good.

The noise of the train grew louder as it approached the tunnel at the far end of the platform.

Rachel felt someone brush against her back.

"Sorry," she said automatically as she turned round. "Oh, hi," she added with a smile.

The smile wasn't returned as the man put both hands on her chest and pushed with all his might. She tried to grasp his shirt but he was already moving away, a cold look in his eyes as he realised he had done enough.

Rachel's right foot was the first to find fresh air, and her arms windmilled as she attempted to regain her balance by putting all her weight forwards and onto her left leg. Her efforts were in vain, however, and her last memory as she fell back was of her attacker weaving through the crowds towards the exit.

*

Angus Middleton was in the middle of justifying Arsenal's latest signing when he saw a woman behind Leon put her hands to her mouth, scream and point. He pushed his friend aside and saw that a woman had gone over the edge and lay splayed across the rails on her back. Blood was pooling beneath her head and she looked to be unconscious.

Several people were staring, a few were shouting and some, to his horror, were holding their phones in the air to video what was happening.

Angus jumped down onto the tracks, bent to his knees and slid both arms under the woman's back. He raised himself to a standing position, turned and slid her onto the platform.

It was only at this point that he became aware of a low growl and turned to see that the approaching train was less than twenty yards away and showing no signs of stopping.

He turned back as a line of people held their arms out to him and screamed for him to be quick. Angus grabbed the two nearest wrists and jumped up and forwards as the train raced past. Stumbling to his feet, he saw that one of the hands that had pulled him up belonged to his friend.

"That was close," Leon said. "Pretty fucking stupid too, if you ask me."

"How is she?" Angus said as he tried to catch his breath.

Leon gestured to the unmoving body on the floor beside them. "It doesn't look good, mate," he said, shaking his head. "It doesn't look good."

Chapter 21

"She's still not answering," Helen said. "It's going straight through to voicemail."

"Perhaps she's on the train," Sam said. "Reception could be poor."

"Aye, could be."

Josh looked up from his laptop. "What was that?"

"We're trying to get hold of Rachel," Helen said, "so that we can brief our wee teenage undercover agent."

Josh considered whether he should be pleased or irritated by this. He liked the sound of 'undercover agent' though and decided it trumped being described as 'teenage'. It took him back to his experience of working alongside MI6.

"I thought I might use the name James Broad," he said and went through the motions of adjusting a bow tie on his shirt. "You know, tomorrow. When I'm an undercover agent."

Helen snorted. "Not very subtle, Josh. If anyone asks, are you going to say your name's 'Broad, James Broad'?"

"I might," Josh said, but there was a slight blush on his cheeks.

"Why don't you use your real name?" Sam asked.

Josh drew his head back. "But I'll be undercover," he squealed.

"It does make sense to use a false name," Helen said.

"Thank you, Helen," Josh said.

"What about Rabbie Burns?" Josh considered this for a second while Sam stifled a laugh. "You could wear a kilt," Helen went on, "and carry bagpipes. How's your Scottish accent?"

Sam decided to help him out. "I suggest you keep it

simple. What's your brother's name?"

"Noah. But I'm not using that."

"What's his best friend's name?"

"He hasn't got any friends."

"Seriously, Josh."

Josh shrugged. "I guess his three best friends are Mohammed, Tyler and George."

Helen laughed. "You don't look much like a Mohammed."

"I'm certainly not being called Tyler," Josh said. "He's a right idiot."

"George it is then," Sam said.

Josh considered this for a minute and was about to speak when Helen held her hand up. "Not Clooney," she said.

"What about George Bailey?" Sam said.

"Aye, that would work," Helen said.

"Oh, I like that," Josh said with a smile. I love that film. "My name's George Bailey," he said, trying it on for size. He nodded. "Done."

"I'll try Rachel again," Helen said. A few seconds later she ended the call. "Still no answer."

"Perhaps she's updated Luke," Josh said.

"Aye, could be. I'll call him on the conference phone."

She dialled Luke's mobile and he answered straight away.

"Hi Luke," Helen said. "I'm with Sam and Josh. We've been trying to get hold of Rachel but she's not answering. You haven't spoken to her by any chance have you?"

"Yes, she rang me on Wednesday. Sorry I didn't tell you but to be honest there's nothing to report."

"Hasn't she been able to speak to any of them?" Sam asked.

"She did but it didn't go well. She couldn't find anything out. What was worse was that senior management heard she'd been prying and ended her contract."

"That's awful," Helen said.

"She's in GNE today but only for handover to her replacement."

"Is there any chance she'll find anything more out?"

"I don't think so. She's had a stressful week so I think it's best we leave her out of things."

"I feel kind of guilty," Sam said.

"Me too," Helen added. "We got her into this mess."

"I wouldn't worry about it," Luke said. "She seemed fine when I talked to her. I'm seeing her on Monday evening and I'll pass on your concerns." Helen and Sam exchanged a look as he said this.

"Thanks," Helen said.

"Are you ready for tomorrow, Josh?" Luke went on.

"I think so, guv," Josh said. "I'm going to use a false name for the evening. I'll be George Bailey."

"Good idea. I'll ring Victor Robertson and tell him."

"We're going to run through the crazy wall again before we leave today to make sure I remember all the key names."

"That's great. Give me a ring at the end of tomorrow evening will you, to let me know how you got on."

"It'll probably be late, guv."

"No problem. Helen and Sam, have a great weekend."

They said their goodbyes and Helen ended the call.

"Why were you two looking at each other like that?" Josh asked.

Helen and Sam looked at each other again.

"There," Josh said, pointing at each of them in turn. "Like that." He raised an eyebrow. "Did I miss something?"

"Did you learn nothing on that detecting course, Josh?" Helen asked.

"What, I, uh, wait." He paused as if the answer was on the tip of his tongue then shook his head. "No, missed it."

"Luke said he's seeing Rachel on Monday evening."

"I got that. He said he'll pass on our concerns but…" He smiled as realisation dawned. "Oh, I see. You think he, well, uh, he and Rachel, they're like, uh, going on a date?"

"Aye."

"Wowza."

Helen looked over at Sam who had been silent for the past couple of minutes. "Are you okay, Sam?" she asked.

"Sure," Sam said. "Sorry, I was miles away."

"Right." Helen rubbed her hands together. "Let's work our way through the names on the board. Is that okay, George?"

Josh was turning the pages of his notebook and didn't look up.

Helen poked him hard in the arm and raised her voice. "I said, is that okay, George?"

Josh looked up and his smile returned. "Oh, yeah, that's me. George Bailey. Gotcha."

They all turned as Maj walked into the Ethics Room.

"Hi, Maj," Helen said. "Good timing. We're just about to go through the names to prep our teenage spy for tomorrow's adventure."

"I heard you say George Bailey, Josh," Maj said. "I take it that's your name for the evening?"

"Sure is."

Maj perused the whiteboard. "No update from Rachel yet?"

"She did nae get anywhere," Helen said. "So we're reliant on you."

"Fair enough. I'll start with Baz Hartman, the host."

They spent the next thirty minutes running through the key names.

"If I were you," Maj said when they'd finished, "I'd pair up with someone. I think that'll make it easier to do the rounds."

"Makes sense," Josh said, "though to a large extent, I guess I'll have to play it by ear." He paused and looked around the others, a slight edge to his voice. "Wish me luck, guys."

"Dinnae worry," Helen said. "You'll be fine. There may be some unsavoury stuff going on but all you've got to do is observe and report back. It's not as if you're going to be in any danger."

Chapter 22

Sam opened the door to her apartment, threw her bag onto the sofa and flopped down beside it. It had been a tiring week and the last thing she felt like doing was going out for a meal. Soaking in a hot bath held a lot more appeal.

But on the other hand, a bath would refresh her and it was going to be fun celebrating with her mum. They had booked La Papillon to celebrate her fifty-ninth birthday in style. Modern French dining with a twist apparently.

She was looking forward to hearing what the 'little secret' was that her mum had mentioned when they'd last talked on the phone. Anyone else and she might have thought she had a new man in her life but no, that was never going to happen. It had been over ten years since she had kicked her father out and not once had she shown an interest in men since then.

As for Sam's love life, that was also non-existent, although she wasn't overly disappointed things hadn't worked out with Chris Nevin. He was nice but that was as far as it went. There had been no spark between them and when they met for dinner before she left Supracomm they had agreed to remain friends but no more. She smiled to herself, thinking that 'remain friends' was code for never seeing each other again.

She wanted to be in a relationship but it had to be a man she could talk to, in the way she could talk to Luke. He wasn't her type of course. He was tall, which she liked, and he had a dry sense of humour, which was appealing, but she liked men who were more…

More what?

More available, for a start. Luke was going out with Rachel Adams, and besides he and Sam worked together and a relationship with the boss was always destined for failure. He had a scar on his face too. And he was recently widowed.

So what was her type?

It certainly wasn't Tony and yet she'd fallen for him hook, line and sinker, even given him the key to her flat. She'd fallen into lust, that had been the problem. Tony was good-looking but his conversation, unless he was talking about himself, was non-existent and he had the intellectual depth of a cockroach.

At least Tony had stopped nagging her to meet his girlfriend. What on earth was that about? He'd said she wanted advice on karate classes but he had to have some ulterior motive. She clicked on their last WhatsApp conversation from a couple of weeks earlier.

Tony: *Hi Sammy. Jazelle is still keen to meet you.*
     Sam: *Why?*
Tony: *She wants the Dan advice.*
     Sam: *Tell her to google it*
Tony: *I'd like you to meet her.*
     Sam: *No*

Was 'Jazelle' even a name? It conjured up an image of a lap dancer which made her smile. That would be Tony through and through.

But was he really stupid enough to think 'the Dan advice' made any sort of sense? Possibly.

No, probably.

God, she was pleased she'd finished with him.

Perhaps being single for a while would do her good. She was only thirty-two, for goodness sake. There was plenty of time to settle down. She should be like Hannah who hadn't had a relationship for over a year and was revelling in her single status.

Her phone rang and she saw it was her friend.

"Hi," she said. "I was just thinking about you."

"Something positive I hope."

"Hannah, do you like being single?"

"Definitely. I'm not going to do it forever, mind you. When the right man comes along and all that. But yes, for the time being, I'm enjoying the freedom."

"Mmm."

"There's a big difference between your situation and mine though," Hannah went on.

"What's that?"

"I haven't got the hots for my boss."

Sam almost dropped the phone in shock. "Don't be silly, Hannah," she spluttered. "That's nonsense."

Hannah laughed. "If you say so."

"Whatever gave you that idea?"

"You're always talking about him, the great decisions he's made, how well he stands up to people."

"We work together, that's all. And he's a great boss but that's as far as it goes. He's not my type."

"Mmm."

"Anyway," Sam said, keen to change the subject. "Why did you ring?"

"I wanted to check you're still on for tomorrow."

"Sure. I'll see you at the Leisure Centre at four."

"Great."

"I have to go now. I'm going out with Mum to celebrate her birthday."

"Wish her a happy birthday from me."

"Will do."

Sam hung up, pleased the call was over.

Where on earth had Hannah got that idea from? Luke was pleasant and a good manager but the idea that she fancied him was utter tosh. She wasn't attracted to him in the slightest. She liked men who were...

She struggled for a moment trying to think what she looked for in a man. If her recent track record was anything to go by she was attracted to men who were either completely up themselves or had the potential to be international terrorists.

The common link between Tony and Chris was that they were straightforward, she decided after a moment's thought. They said what they wanted and everything was up-front. What you saw was what you got. Luke, on the other hand, was complex and hard to read. In truth, he was almost completely the opposite of the men she went for.

Sam smiled and shook her head. She'd put Hannah right when she saw her the next day. Got the hots for her boss! The very idea.

Chapter 23

Sam spotted her mum as soon as she entered the restaurant.

"'Ave you a booking, Madame?" the waiter said in an over-the-top French accent.

"Chambers," she said absent-mindedly and gestured to the far end of the room. "I can see my mother over there."

The waiter gave a very low bow and gestured for her to make her way over. As she weaved through the other tables Kate looked up and gave her a beaming smile. Sam was immediately struck by how she somehow looked brighter than normal, almost as if there was an aura around her. But how could that be? It had only been three weeks since they last met.

"Hi, Darling," Kate said as she stood up to give her daughter a hug.

Sam raised one eyebrow as she sat down. Was it her mum's hair? No, that hadn't changed. Her clothes looked good on her, but she always dressed well. What was it then?

"I've ordered a bottle of champagne to celebrate," Kate went on. "Ah, here it is now."

The same waiter approached clutching an ice bucket and a bottle. With a flourish, he placed the ice bucket in the centre of their table and held the bottle up so that the label was only a couple of inches from Kate's nose. She pushed it away with her index finger and looked up at him bemused.

"Moet et Chandon, Madame," he said proudly.

"Yes, I can see that," Kate said. "It's what I ordered."

The waiter nodded, clearly pleased to have brought the correct bottle, then pulled a small knife from his waistcoat pocket, unfolded it and delicately sliced through the foil around the stopper, smiling at both of them as he slowly turned the bottle. When he had finished he gently placed the foil on the table, folded the knife away and returned it to his pocket. With a flourish, he flicked back the metal catch holding the stopper in place, placed it next to the foil, paused to smile at Kate again, then lifted the white cloth from the ice bucket to wrap it around the head of the bottle.

Before he could do so there was a loud bang and the cork exploded out, bounced off the ceiling and landed in the soup bowl of a middle-aged man at the next table.

Sam stifled her laughter as the man gave a little scream of horror. He turned to reveal pieces of French onion soup dribbling from his beard.

"Oh shit!" the waiter said, his accent now more Tower Hamlets than Notre Dame. He stepped towards the man and started dabbing his beard with the cloth. "I'm so sorry, ah, monsieur," he said, recovering his French accent halfway through the sentence.

"Get off me," the man said as he pushed him away. He grabbed the cloth and wiped his face before handing it back to the waiter. He turned to his partner. "I'll go to the bathroom and wash this off."

"Good idea," his partner said and Sam could see that she too was trying to conceal a smile.

The waiter shrugged his shoulders and turned back to their table. He picked up Kate's champagne flute and poured a tiny amount into it, then lifted the glass and, as with the bottle earlier, held it two inches from her nose.

"It's fine," she said, pushing it away.

"But Madame must taste…"

"No, it's fine. Just fill our glasses." She paused. "No, on second thoughts, we'll pour our own."

"But…"

Kate smiled up at him and took the bottle from his hand. "Leave it to us." She gestured to the other table. "Why don't you fetch them a fresh bowl of soup."

The waiter nodded and gave another deep bow before shuffling away towards the kitchen.

"That was an entertaining start to the evening," Sam said, a broad smile on her face. "If he's our waiter for the entire meal this should be very entertaining." She paused and lowered her voice. "Did you notice how his accent changed? It went from the Sorbonne to Shoreditch and back."

Kate nodded and they both started laughing.

"So, how are you?" Kate asked when they'd calmed down.

"I'm fine, Mum." Sam looked across at her mother and could see that she was itching to say something. "What's your little secret, then?"

"I've…" Kate paused and the colour rose in her cheeks. "Gosh," she went on, "I didn't think it would be so difficult telling you, but…"

"Out with it, Mum."

"I've got a boyfriend."

Sam stared at her mum.

"You can close your mouth, Darling," Kate said.

"Sorry, but I'm, uh, well, it's a bit of a shock, that's all."

"I know I'm fifty-nine, but…"

"It's not your age, Mum. I thought you'd resigned yourself to being single."

"You remember I told you to try Tinder and Plenty of Fish."

Sam laughed. "I do indeed. You called it Cinder." Realisation dawned. "You met him online?"

Kate nodded.

"You have met him in person though, haven't you?" Sam added hastily, remembering the romance scams the Ethics Team had had to deal with.

"Several times," Kate said.

"What's he like?"

"You can see for yourself. I've invited him tonight."

"What?"

"Ah. Here he is now."

Sam turned to see their mock-French waiter approaching.

She turned back to her mother, eyes wide. "You can't be serious?"

"Not him," Kate said and Sam turned back to see the waiter stand to one side and bow as a tall man in his mid-fifties walked past him and bent to give Kate a kiss on the lips before turning to Sam. He had neat salt-and-pepper hair with a similarly shaded short beard, but his sparkling blue eyes were what drew her attention. There was something about his smile that struck her as disingenuous, but she realised that was nonsense. She was shocked that was all. The thought of her mum having a boyfriend had taken her aback.

"You must be Sam," he said and she thought she detected a trace of an Irish accent. He looked down at her and offered his hand. "You look lovely this evening. I can see you've inherited your Mum's looks."

Sam wasn't sure whether to take that as a compliment or be creeped out but took his hand and said, "Pleased to meet you. Sorry, I don't know your name."

"I haven't had a chance to tell her," Kate said. She turned her eyes to the waiter who was busy laying up an extra table setting. "We were a bit distracted." She looked back at her daughter. "Darling, this is Brendan."

Sam nodded. "Hi, Brendan."

There was a theatrical cough and Sam looked over to see the waiter holding the chair back with one hand, his other hand palm up inviting Brendan to sit down. As he did so the waiter thrust the chair forward into the back of his knees causing Brendan to give a little squeak before falling back into it.

The waiter appeared not to notice. "Champagne?" he asked, his French accent now on full speed ahead.

"It's okay," Sam said hastily. "We'll pour our own."

"Very well, Madame."

"Mademoiselle."

He raised his eyebrows.

"I'm not married," Sam went on.

"Indeed." He hesitated, apparently confused, before saying. "Then I will be back for your order shortly."

"He was our distraction," Kate said once the waiter had gone. She told Brendan what had happened with the bottle.

Sam watched Brendan while her mother was talking. He was certainly attractive, and his accent was delightful. She wanted to find out more about him though, make sure he was good enough. She took a sip of her bubbly and waited for her mother to finish then asked, "So what do you do for a living, Brendan?"

"I'm an executive producer," he said. "Kate told me what you do and I believe we've outsourced some of our back-office services to your company."

Sam almost spat out her champagne. "Not GNE?" she spluttered.

"Would that be a problem?"

"It's just that we're working quite closely with them at the moment."

"That sounds ominous." He winked. "Are you undercover again?"

Sam glared at her mother. "Mum!"

"I wanted to tell Brendan all about you," Kate said defiantly. "I'm proud of what you do."

"Don't blame your mother," Brendan said. "I was prying more than I should but your job sounds fascinating. That business where you were taken to the hills sounded awful."

Sam glared at her mum again.

"Let me put your mind at rest," Brendan went on. "I work for NTV in Bristol and I've never worked for GNE. I know a fair few people there of course, but that's as far as it goes."

"You do?" Sam said, her interest piqued. "So do you hear stories about what goes on there?"

"And some." He chuckled. "The media industry is rife with gossip and there's a load comes out of that place I can tell you."

"Really? Please, tell me more."

Chapter 24

Luke felt like a chauffeur as he waited outside The Randolph for his parents. It was his own fault. His father had wanted to take his mother for afternoon tea, something they had done once a month for the previous decade or more, and Luke had insisted on driving.

He tapped his fingers on the steering wheel and looked down at the clock on the instrument panel. It wasn't even 4 pm so they'd probably be another thirty minutes at least. He wanted to ring Josh to wish him well for the evening but there was no point. Better to leave him to get ready in peace.

He sighed. The week had dragged and dragged and he couldn't wait to get back to Bath. It was hard work living with his mother and father. They were difficult people to deal with, always had been, and his mother's illness brought additional stress.

However, the main reason he wanted to return was his job. He'd been working at Filchers for a few months now and while the office politics, not to mention individuals like Edward Filcher and Glen Baxter, could drive him up the wall, it was his team that made it all worthwhile.

He could hardly believe how lucky he, Luke Sackville, ex-DCI, had been in acquiring four people so hard-working and easy to work with. To be fair they were a bunch of misfits, but they had gelled so well together. They were courageous too, and showed initiative. The learning curve from graduate, contracts consultant, accountant and security guard to investigating serious breaches of ethics had been as steep as they come, but they had all risen to the challenge.

Josh had been the biggest surprise. He was still a big kid

at heart, but he was smart and a quick learner.

Helen's experience and knowledge of the company had proved to be invaluable as had Maj's deep technical skills.

As for Sam, her bravery had been second to none. There was more to her than that though, a lot more. Obviously, there were her accountancy skills, which had been of use on several occasions, but what he really appreciated was the way she lifted the team if anyone was feeling down. She had a radiant smile and when she walked into the room…

His phone rang and he couldn't help smiling when he saw Sam's name on the screen.

"Hi Sam," he said when he'd accepted the call. "I was just thinking, um…" He coughed. "What's up?"

"I've heard more rumours about GNE," she said, her voice flat and lacking its usual warmth. "I thought you ought to know. It may be useful information for Josh before this evening."

"Are you okay?"

"I'm fine." She paused. "Do you want to know or not?"

"Of course. Who did you hear this from?"

"Brendan Doyle. He works at NTV but he knows a lot of people at GNE."

"How do you know him?"

"That doesn't matter."

She was sounding annoyed now and Luke couldn't fathom why.

"Are you sure you're okay, Sam?" he asked.

She ignored his question. "I'm meeting someone so I haven't got long."

"Fire away then."

"Ozzy Vaughan has been the host of 'Rock-n-Roll-n-Rap' for three years. Brendan heard that after the first season, which did incredibly well and surpassed everyone's expectations, there were two complaints about his behaviour."

"Who from?"

"I'm getting to that," she snapped. "They were both from men. One was a member of the crew who accused him of bullying, and the other was a production assistant who said that Vaughan tried to assault him in the bathroom."

Luke wanted to ask what happened but decided to wait. Sam was upset with him for some reason and he couldn't fathom why.

"Both stories were hushed up," Sam went on, "and Brendan heard that the two people involved were given pay-offs and forced to sign non-disclosure agreements."

"That's interesting," Luke said.

"There's more. A few months ago one of Hartman's parties was raided by the police."

"Why?"

Sam's sigh was audible. "Give me a chance," she said.

Luke bit his lip.

There was an uncomfortable silence before Sam continued. "Apparently, the next-door neighbour rang the police because she'd heard someone crying out for help."

Luke waited, not wanting to poke the beast.

"Aren't you curious what happened next?" Sam asked after a few seconds.

"Of course."

"Well, it seems that your lot were completely useless. The police went to the house but didn't get past the front door."

Luke waited for a few seconds to make sure she'd finished, then said. "Is that everything that Brendan heard?"

There was another pause. "I think that's quite a lot of new information."

"Oh, it is, Sam. Well done."

"There's no need to patronise me, Luke."

"I wasn't…" Luke looked up to see his father guiding

his mother towards the car. "Oh shit," he said. "I've got to go, Sam. I'll pass the info on to Josh."

There was no response and he looked down to see she had hung up.

＊

Sam put her palm to her forehead as she put her phone back in her bag. That had been a very uncomfortable phone call and she wasn't sure why. She looked up to see Hannah jogging towards her.

"Sorry I'm a bit late," Hannah said, before adding when she saw the expression on her best friend's face, "Are you okay?"

"Can we give the leisure centre a miss?" Sam asked.

"Yes, sure. Why?"

"I've just had an argument with my boss."

Hannah smiled. "Lover's tiff?"

"For fuck's sake, Hannah!" Sam held her friend's eyes for a second then her top lip started trembling. "Sorry, I…"

Hannah grabbed her hand. "Come on," she said. "Let's find somewhere quiet where we can talk."

She led Sam to a nearby cafe and to a table in the corner at the back. "Sit here," she said. "I'll order a couple of coffees and then you can tell me all about it."

Sam watched her friend walk over to the till and realised there were tears in her eyes. She used her index fingers to brush the wetness away. What on earth was she crying for? She'd had an argument, that was all. Nothing to get upset about.

The call had wound her up but she found herself struggling to remember what Luke had done to annoy her so much. She'd been thrilled to share what she'd found out but he hadn't seemed excited. Was that it? Or was it because he'd patronised her?

Hannah placed their coffees down on the table and then reached out to grab both Sam's hands in hers. "What's wrong?" she asked.

"He belittles me," Sam said. "And he patronises me."

"Does he?"

"Yes."

"And that's it? That was the reason for the argument?"

"I don't know, Hannah." Sam shook her head. "It may have been my fault in part."

"Why? What did you say?"

"I wasn't myself. I was abrupt, rude probably." She thought back to their conversation. "Yes, I was definitely a tad difficult. But I'm not sure why."

"Have you had a visit from Aunt Flo?"

Sam couldn't help but laugh at this. "No, Hannah," she said.

"Then has he said or done something to wind you up?"

"He hasn't said anything, but he's…" She paused. "Yesterday, I found out that he's…" There was a sinking in the pit of Sam's stomach as the truth hit her.

"He's what?" Hannah asked.

Sam's next words were almost whispered. "He's got a date," she said.

Chapter 25

Josh placed a third dollop of max-hold gel onto his hair, massaged it in and stood back to admire himself in the mirror. It was looking good, he thought. Better than good. It was awesome. No way was it going to lose shape, even over a full evening. Hey, the skies could empty on top of him and his hair still wouldn't budge. He patted the top and it bounced before returning to its perfect sculpted shape.

"Gucci," he said under his breath.

"You're not leaving it like that are you, Joshy?" Leanne asked from behind him.

"Eh?" He gave a half-jump, looked at his girlfriend's reflection in the mirror, then returned his gaze to the front and turned his head to one side and then to the other. "I think it's cool. Does it make me look too old?"

She laughed. "No, it makes you look younger if anything."

"What's wrong with it, then?"

"Isn't it a bit, well…" She hesitated for a second. "… old-fashioned?"

"Nah, it's cool. I've had it this way for years."

"Exactly." She paused. "Shouldn't you have a fade either side? You know, have it shaved to a number 1 or 2."

"I know what a fade is, Leanne."

She saw his expression and decided to drop the subject. Hair was his thing and she knew from experience that he didn't take kindly to being challenged on it.

"The outfit's good," she said. "I love the rainbow t-shirt."

"It's multi-coloured, not rainbow."

"And the Vans. Much more this century than those old Adidas trainers you usually wear."

Josh gave a little huff of exasperation. "That's exactly what Maj's daughter Sabrina said."

Leanne smiled. "You look great, Joshy, you really do."

Josh shrugged. "Thanks."

"Are you going to meet some famous people?"

"Possibly," he said. "Obviously, Baz Hartman will be there. It's his party. And other people from his show, plus some from 'Rock-n-Roll-n-Rap'."

"Ozzy Vaughan?"

"Yeah, I think so."

"Wow. Can you get his autograph for me?"

"Hardly. I'm on a secret mission, Leanne. Undercover. Spying."

"Like James Bond."

"Exactimo." He made a finger gun and pointed it at the mirror before saying in his best Sean Connery voice, "The name's Bailey, George Bailey."

"But seriously, Joshy, is there any danger? Should I be worried?"

"Nah," he said. "It should be fun. All I've got to do is mix and mingle and watch. If I see anything untoward I make a mental note and feed back. That's it."

"What time have you got to be there?"

"I was told around 8." He looked at his watch. "Shittedy-shit-shit. It's 8 now. I'd best be off."

He grabbed his car keys and kissed Leanne. "Don't wait up," he said. "I'm guessing it'll be well after midnight before I'm back."

Josh drove to Charlcombe and parked on one of the tree-lined roads off Lansdown Road. This left him only a few hundred yards to walk to Whistler House and he set off with a spring in his step.

Undercover, eh? Wowza. This was proper investigative work. It was going to be brillianto putting his detecting course to work.

His phone rang and he saw Luke's name on the screen.

"Hi, guv," he said. "I'm almost there."

"I hope it goes well, Josh," Luke said. "I'm ringing because Sam found a couple of things out from a friend of a friend which might help you focus."

"Gotcha."

"First, Ozzy Vaughan's had a couple of accusations levelled at him within GNE which have been brushed under the carpet. One of bullying and the other of assault. Second, a neighbour complained to the police that they'd heard someone crying out for help at one of Baz Hartman's parties. The police went around but nothing came of it."

"Right, guv. So you think Baz Hartman and Ozzy Vaughan should be my main focus?"

"My advice is to keep your eyes and ears open, Josh, but pay special attention to them. It doesn't sound like either of them are nice guys but there could be a lot more to it than that."

"Right. Will do. Better go."

As Josh hung up he heard footsteps and turned to see someone a few paces behind. It was a man, he could tell that much, and he was big but his face was in shadow.

"Hey, you," the figure shouted from the darkness.

Josh swallowed. Buggery-buggery, was he about to be mugged?

The voice came again. "Are you going to Baz's party?" He was only a couple of yards away now and his face was visible under the light from the street lamp. He was smiling, wore a beanie and Josh put his age at eighteen tops, probably a year or two younger.

"Yeah," Josh said with a sigh of relief. "You too?"

"Sure am." He held his hand out. "Owen."

Josh shook his hand. "George."

"We might as well, like, walk together," Owen said. "It's the next turning on the right."

"Sure. Makes sense."

They started walking down the hill.

"This is my first time at one of Baz Hartman's parties," Josh said. "Same for you?"

"No, I came a couple of weeks ago." He stood back and looked at Josh. "I'm guessing you're, like, the same age as me. Or are you younger?"

"I'm sixteen."

"Same age then. Most of the guests were old, like thirty or more. We need to fit in by saying we're at Uni."

"Okay." Josh realised this was an opportunity to find good stuff out before the party had even started. "Did you have a good time?"

"It ended early." Owen paused. "And it was weird."

"Weird? How do you mean?"

"It's this road here."

"What do you mean weird?" Josh asked again.

"Fucking weird, that's what I mean. It was, like, cut short after a fight. I'll tell you all about it when we're in." He paused. "Did Eve invite you?"

"No, I was invited by a friend."

"Wait 'til you meet her, man." He whistled. "She's well fit."

"Gucci."

"What did you say?"

"Gucci. You know, cool."

Owen laughed. "My little brother uses that phrase. You wanna look older at this gig, George, not younger."

"Ah, right."

Josh hesitated, trying to decide how best to probe. "When you came before," he said, "did you come alone?"

"Nah, I came with a mate, or at least he was a mate."

"Was?"

"I left before he did and he's been snubbing me ever since. Don't know what I did, but what the fuck? I've got other friends."

"What's his name?"

"Why?"

"Just in case I know him."

"I doubt you would. He and I are from Bristol. I assume you're from Bath?"

Josh tried to hide his disappointment. "Yeah," he said. He'd try again later.

"There it is, George," Owen said, gesturing ahead. Look at those awesome cars."

"Gu..., uh, cool."

"I bet that Lambo's Baz's. Fucking awesome."

"Fucking awesome," Josh agreed.

They walked to the front door and Owen turned, his smile stretching from ear to ear. He offered his fist and Josh looked at it, up at Owen's face, and then back at the fist.

"Well?" Owen prompted, moving his fist slightly in Josh's direction.

"Oh, right." Josh bumped his own fist against Owen's then put it to his mouth and blew on it.

"Cool," Owen said. He turned back to the door and pressed the bell.

It was answered a few seconds later and the woman who opened the door was indeed, as Owen had put it, well fit. She was blonde with perfectly proportioned facial features but it was her figure-hugging mini dress that really showed off her assets.

"Hi, lads," she said, looking at Owen, then Josh and then back to Owen. "Ah," she added. "Owen, isn't it?"

Owen's mouth opened but he didn't say anything and after a few seconds it became clear he wasn't going to close his mouth any time soon either. Josh decided he had better say something.

"I'm George," he said.

"Ah, right." Eve looked down at her clipboard and Josh could see there were a dozen or so names on it. "Got it." She looked up at him and smiled. "George Bailey, friend of Vicky's. Is that right?"

"Definito," Josh said. He put on his best smile and gave

her a double thumbs up. "Owen and I met on the walk here."

"That's terrific. Why don't the two of you go on through to the back? There's a bar set up next to the pool so grab yourselves a drink and make yourselves at home."

"Thanks." Josh started to move past Eve but realised Owen was still standing staring at her. He turned back and grabbed him by the arm. "Come on, Owen. Let's get a drink."

Owen let Josh pull him past Eve into the corridor behind. They had only walked a few yards when a man in a dinner jacket emerged from a door to their left.

"Hi, lads," he said, a beaming smile across his face. "Welcome to Baz's party."

Without waiting for him to say anything else, Owen took his iPhone from his pocket and handed it over.

"Thanks," the man said. "You were here a couple of weeks ago, weren't you."

Owen nodded and gave a half-laugh. "Yeah, I know the drill." He turned to Josh. "They take your phone to stop photos being taken. You get it back at the end though."

"Oh right," Josh said. He fished his own phone out and handed it over.

"What's your name?" the man asked. He was still smiling.

"George," Josh said. "George Bailey."

"As your friend said, I'll give you your phones back when you leave. If you can't find me just ask someone to fetch Kieran."

"Will do."

Kieran stepped back into the doorway so that he was no longer blocking their path and gestured towards the back door. "Have fun, lads," he said and winked, sending a shiver down Josh's spine.

For the first time, he wondered what he was letting himself in for.

Chapter 26

"They're here again," Owen said when they emerged onto the patio at the back of the house.

"Who are?" Josh said.

"Damon Prendergast and Ozzy Vaughan." Owen pointed to a group of five men on the other side of the pool.

Josh looked over at the group and recognised both of them from the photos he'd stuck to the investigation board. Ozzy was the bald man with several bracelets on his wrists and a big gold medallion. He appeared to be dominating the conversation and was gesticulating wildly. Every few seconds he clicked his fingers together. It all seemed contrived to Josh, but three of the group were paying rapt attention.

Damon Prendergast, on the other hand, seemed totally disinterested and was gazing off into the middle distance. He seemed upset to Josh, but whether it was with any of the men he was with he couldn't tell.

"Is Damon the bald one?" he asked.

"Where have you been, George? Don't you watch 'Rock-n-Roll-n-Rap'?"

Josh decided to pretend ignorance. "Rock-n-Roll-n-what?"

Owen shook his head. "I can't believe you don't watch it. You must have heard of 'I'm Wiv Da Hood'."

"No."

"It was Ozzy's big hit."

"Right. So, uh, which one's Ozzy Vaughan?"

"Duh! Which one looks like a rapper to you?"

"Oh. Gotcha. The bald guy. So Damon Prendergast is…"

Owen sighed. "Damon's the tall guy with a beard."

"The one who looks bored?"

"Yeah, that's him. He wrote 'The Boss'."

Josh sighed with relief. This time he knew what Owen was talking about. "Gotcha," he said. "Alan Sugar gives people tasks then chooses one to work for him."

Owen looked at him askance. "Where have you been, George? 'The Boss' is a West End show about Bruce Springsteen."

"Oh, yeah. Sure."

"Anyway," Owen went on. "Damon and Ozzy both present 'Rock-n-Roll-n-Rap'. Fucking cool them being here, isn't it?"

"Fucking cool," Josh agreed.

"I wonder who else we're going to see. Hey, there's the bar. I'll get us some drinks. What do you want?"

"I'll have a coke."

"No drugs here," a nasal voice said behind him.

Josh turned to find a tall and very overweight man grinning down at him. Weirdly, the man also had his eyebrows raised and this brought back memories of 'The Shining' which Leanne had cradled him through a couple of nights earlier.

"Here's Johnny," Josh said before he could stop himself.

"No, it's Reggie," the man said and presented his hand.

"Uh, right," Josh said. He took the offered hand and immediately wished he hadn't. It felt distinctly damp, almost slimy. "I'm George," he said, breaking the handshake at the earliest opportunity.

"I was joshing with you," Reggie said.

"No, it's George," Josh said.

"What?"

"Oh, I see." Josh laughed. "Gu… Cool. Like, uh, josh-*ing* with me. Because coke is cocaine. But also Coca-Cola. So…"

"Right," Reggie said, and Josh noticed for the first time

that he had his left arm around the shoulder of a much smaller and younger man. No, he corrected himself, not a man. Boy, more like. He was around five foot nine and slight of build but it was the bum fluff above his upper lip that was the giveaway. Maybe sixteen, possibly younger.

"This is Callum," Reggie said.

"Hi," Callum said.

"I'm Owen," Owen said. "I'm getting George and me a drink. Do you want anything?"

"I'll come with you," Callum said immediately and squirmed out of Reggie's grip to follow Owen to the bar.

"I'll have a bourbon," Reggie called after them.

"So, uh, are you on the telly?" Josh asked him once the other two had gone.

"Don't you watch Towie?"

"Eh?"

"Essex."

Josh swallowed. "Ethics?"

"No, Essex."

Josh breathed a sigh of relief.

Reggie nodded his head to one side. "Surely you've heard of 'The Only Way Is Essex'."

"Oh, right. Gotcha. Yeah. Heard of that. So are you on it?"

"I was the second-hand car salesman."

I might have guessed, Josh thought but said. "Was?"

"Before I got fucking famous."

"Right. Uh, so, how did you become famous?"

"I told you, I was on Towie."

"Gotcha."

Suddenly it hit Josh who the man was. He was on the middle right of the crazy wall, next to Marvin Winespottle. He flicked his fingers and pointed at Reggie.

"Reggie Dowden," he said. "You and Marvin Winespottle are on 'Hall of Flame'."

The smile and elevated eyebrows returned. "Fucking

got it at last."

A suspect. Right, here we go. Day 3, session 1 had covered using bugs to listen in to conversations, and session 3 had been about interviews. This was a bit of both, so he had to probe, but also listen if the other person was talking to someone else. He couldn't take notes, didn't even have his phone, which meant he had to file everything away in his memory. Not a problem. He could do that.

He realised Reggie was saying something.

"As I said, I'm pretty big," Reggie said.

Odd thing to say. He was of course. Christ, the man was obese. But to say it out loud like that, well it showed a certain amount of self-awareness.

"Not as big as someone like Kim Kardashian," Reggie went on.

"But she's…" Josh paused for a second, the cogs turning. "Oh, you mean you're not as famous as her."

"That's what I said. On my fucking way though."

"Right, yeah. On your fucking way."

"Your bourbon," Owen said as he reappeared and handed Reggie his drink.

Callum gave Josh his drink and stood close by his side rather than returning to stand next to Reggie.

"Nice talking to you, George," Reggie said. "Maybe catch you later, but I promised Callum I'd show him something."

"It's alright, Reggie," Callum started to say.

"Nonsense. You'll fucking love it. It's massive. Really impressive."

Reggie reached over and took Callum's hand then pulled him towards him and patted him on the head. It was an odd thing to do but Callum merely shrugged. "Okay," he said. He turned to Josh and Owen. "See you guys later."

Chapter 27

Sam and Hannah had decided on a girls' night out: a cheap but cheerful meal then a couple of drinks and back to Hannah's.

So far they'd had a great time. They both loved pasta and Ask Italian had been as good as ever. They'd talked about school, they'd had fun at the expense of early paramours, and they'd fallen into fits of laughter recalling the time Mrs Kirby, the geography teacher, had been caught in flagrante with Mr Watson, the Head of English, in the sixth form common room.

And now they were in the Saracen's Head.

Sam looked at her watch. It was just gone ten which meant Josh would be at Baz Hartman's party. She wondered how he was getting on, and whether Luke had been able to pass him the info she'd got from her mother's new boyfriend.

"Here you go," Hannah said, placing Sam's Prosecco in front of her.

The pub was packed but Hannah spotted an elderly couple getting ready to leave and raced to grab their table which was right at the back of the pub.

"You're not going to believe this," Sam said as Hannah took the seat opposite, "but my mum's got a boyfriend."

Hannah's eyebrows went up. "Kate?"

Sam smiled. "I've only got one mum."

"Bloody hell. Good for her. What's he like?"

Sam hesitated for a second. "I can't quite make up my mind. He was friendly enough, and he gave me some info that's useful for what I'm working on at the moment, but there was something about him that felt wrong."

Hannah laughed. "Probably the fact he's dating your

mother."

"Yes, you're probably right."

"Is he attractive?"

It was Sam's turn to laugh. "Hannah, what are you like?"

"Well. Is he?"

"Yes, he is. Tall, solidly built, bright blue eyes, neat beard, big smile."

"How long have they been seeing each other?"

Sam was about to answer when she spotted movement behind a man at the bar. She saw part of a man's face and tilted her head to one side to get a better view.

"What is it?" Hannah said, turning to follow Sam's gaze.

"He's over there," Sam said.

"Who is?"

"Brendan. Mum's boyfriend."

At that moment Brendan spotted Sam looking at him and raised his hand in acknowledgement.

"I see what you mean about him being attractive," Hannah whispered. "Mind you, your Mum's hardly had the ugly stick thrown at her."

"I ought to say hello," Sam said. She stood up from the table. "I'll be back in a moment."

As she approached Brendan she saw that he was with two other men, both younger, perhaps forty or so.

"Hi, Brendan," she said.

"Hi," he said. "Fancy seeing you here." He turned to his two companions. "Grant, Phil, this is Sam. She's a friend of a friend."

Sam nodded hello to the two men and kept the smile plastered on her face, but what on earth did he mean by a 'friend of a friend'? Clearly he was keeping his relationship with her mum a secret. The bastard wasn't married was he?

"I'm glad to have run into you, Sam," Brendan said. "I've got some more info on that stuff I was telling you about."

"Really? What's that?"

Brendan turned so that Grant and Phil couldn't see his face and mouthed 'they're GNE' before saying, "I'll pop over in a minute."

"Great. See you in a tic."

Sam returned to Hannah and bent forward before whispering. "Well, that was odd."

"What was?"

"He introduced me as a 'friend of a friend'. Why on earth would he do that? Do you think he's married?"

"Honestly, Sam," Hannah said, smiling and shaking her head. "Your mum gets a boyfriend and suddenly you're reading things into everything he says. I can think of countless reasons why he might say that."

"Like?"

Hannah held up her right thumb. "One, it could be because it's early days in the relationship." She raised her index finger to join her thumb. "Two, he doesn't want to talk about his girlfriend with people he works with." Next came the middle finger. "Three, Kate's asked him to keep it quiet for the time being…"

"Okay. I get the picture." Sam paused. "Or it could be because he's married."

Hannah laughed.

"See what you think of him," Sam went on. "He's got more info for me and he said he'd pop over with it." She looked up. "Oh, here he is now."

"That was quick," Sam said as Brendan approached their table. "This is Hannah. Hannah, this is Brendan."

"Hi," Hannah said. "Sorry, there's no spare chair."

"It's okay," Brendan said. He turned to Sam. "The info I've got is pretty sensitive. Do you think we could talk outside?"

"Fine with me," Hannah said.

"It won't take long." He turned to Hannah. "I hope you

don't mind, but I don't want to risk anyone listening in."

"Not at all."

Sam followed Brendan to the front of the pub. It was a mild evening and there were several groups of people standing on the pavement outside.

"Too crowded here," Brendan said. "There's an alley up there which should be quiet."

Sam was beginning to wonder just how sensitive this new information was. Brendan was certainly going out of his way to ensure they weren't overheard.

He walked briskly and she had to almost jog to keep up.

"Is this really necessary?" she asked and almost bumped into him as he stopped abruptly.

"Sorry," he said, "but I really can't afford for us to be overheard." He was standing next to a small alley that she had never noticed before. He gestured to it with his thumb. "Let's go down here and talk."

She followed him down the alley which bent to the left after twenty yards or so. Once past the bend, it became very dim, the only light coming from a room some four storeys above them.

"This should do," he said.

Sam turned so that her back was to the wall. "So what's the new information?" she asked.

Brendan smiled, but it was more hesitant than it had been before. He moved so that he was directly in front of her.

"Don't worry, Brendan," she said. "Anything you say I'll keep to myself."

He hesitated for a second before lunging forward and pressing his lips to hers, at the same time putting his hands on her breasts. She used all her force to push against his chest and hold him back.

"What the fuck do you think you're doing?" she screamed.

She tried to manoeuvre away but he shoved her hard

and she stumbled backwards and onto the floor on her back. She tried to call out but he knelt astride her and put his left hand over her mouth.

"You're gorgeous," he hissed.

He moved his right hand to the zip of his jeans and Sam spotted her opportunity. She slid her left arm between his arm and his body and rotated slightly so that she could push her right arm through the gap. Then she clasped her hands together and pulled with all her force.

Brendan screamed as his elbow moved inwards. He raised himself slightly and she used her hips to bump herself to one side, all the while increasing the pressure on his elbow. He was forced to fall away to the right and she released her grip and scrabbled away on her bottom.

He lunged for her foot but she pulled it clear and moved further away from him. He rolled over and got to his feet as she did and started to move towards her, his hands outstretched. Without hesitating she drew her leg back and kicked out with her right foot.

Brendan gasped and put both hands to his groin.

Sam drew her foot back and rotated her leg out from her hip. She continued rotating before straightening her leg and striking the side of his face with her foot.

He went down like a sack of potatoes.

Sam bent forward, hands on her thighs. "You bastard," she said as she gasped for air.

After a few seconds, with Brendan now flat on the floor and whimpering, she reached into her pocket for her phone.

Hannah answered immediately. "I was beginning to wonder where you were," she said.

"I need your help," Sam said between breaths and without lifting her eyes from Brendan. She explained where she was and ended the call.

Brendan pushed himself to a sitting position and put his hand to his face. To Sam's amazement, he was smiling again. "It'll be your word against mine," he said.

Sam heard a noise and turned as Hannah emerged from the darkness.

She looked at Brendan and then back at Sam. "What happened?" she asked. "Did he try it on?"

Brendan spoke quickly before Sam could answer. "Sam brought me to this alley," he said. "She wanted me and then changed her mind. She's a prick-tease."

Hannah ignored him completely. "What did he do?"

"He was going to rape me."

"That's nonsense," Brendan spluttered. "You wanted it as much as I did."

He started to get up but Sam put her foot on his chest and pushed him down again. "Don't even think about getting up," she said.

"I'll call the police," Hannah said.

Sam shook her head. "I'm not sure that will achieve much."

"What then?"

"I'm going to call Luke. He'll know what to do."

Chapter 28

Luke's phone pinged and he looked down to see a WhatsApp from his brother. 'Had to stop for a toilet break but should be back inside 30 mins.'

Thank Christ, he thought. He looked across at his father who was deep in that day's Financial Times. He was still formally dressed despite it being past ten in the evening, shirt pristine and tie tight to his collar.

"Mark, Erica and Marion are well on their way," he said. "They should be back in half an hour or so."

Hugo folded his paper, huffed and laid it on the table beside him. "Ruddy nuisance," he said. "It'll be bad for your mother having an eight-year-old running around the house."

"I think you're wrong, Father," Luke said. "I'm sure Mother will love it."

In reality, he thought this highly unlikely. His mother had never even liked her own offspring and, while her illness made her unpredictable, he was sure the chances of her taking pleasure in someone else's child were minimal.

Hugo seemed to be thinking the same. "It's not as if the little beggar is even one of our own," he said and then huffed again. "Mark was bloody stupid agreeing to take her in."

"He didn't really have a choice."

"Mmm. That's as maybe. Ruddy Erica shouldn't have got pregnant in the first place."

"For goodness sake. She was raped."

"Bah. She should have got rid of it at the time. Had an abortion." He picked his paper up again and stood up. "I'm going to bed."

"No," Luke said, his voice firm. "That's not on."

"It's my house. I can go to bed when I like."

"Whatever you might think, Father, we need to make Marion feel at home. The poor girl has been through a lot. The least you can do is stay here to welcome her when she arrives."

Hugo slapped his newspaper down on the table and sat back on the sofa. "Very well," he said.

"Thank you."

Hugo glared at his son and then reached for his FT again. He opened it and raised it in front of him so that Luke could no longer see the expression on his face.

He smiled to himself, pleased that the old man had listened to him, but even more pleased at the thought that he'd be able to go home in the morning. It meant he'd be back in the office on Monday morning.

And that evening he'd be seeing Rachel. That was going to be interesting. He'd liked her, but their brief meeting had been pretty much business-focused. Why had she asked him out? It was flattering, especially given how attractive she was.

He felt a twinge of guilt, but deep down he knew Jess would approve. More worrying was what the twins might think. It was less than a year since their mother had died. Would Chloe and Ben think it was out of order for him to be out with another woman so soon? He decided he would tell them after Monday if the evening went well and they agreed to go out again. No point in saying anything until then.

He dived back into his book and had read a few chapters when his phone rang. He was expecting the call and accepted it without looking at the screen.

"How's it going, Josh?" he asked. There was silence at the other end. "Hello?"

"Hi, Luke," Sam said.

"Oh, Sam. It's you." Luke remembered the afternoon's call all too clearly. He hoped he wasn't going to get more of the same.

She spoke slowly and shakily. "I, ah, I'm sorry about this afternoon. I was…" She paused. "I was out of order."

She was clearly upset. "What's wrong?" he asked.

He heard her sobbing and then a different voice came on the line.

"Luke, this is Hannah. I'm a friend of Sam's."

He sat upright. "What's happened, Hannah?"

"Sam's… Oh, hang on."

Sam came back on the line. "Sorry, Luke." She was still sobbing but trying to hold it together. "Give me a moment."

He waited.

After a few seconds, she continued, her voice still trembling. "You remember Brendan Doyle from NTV?"

"Of course."

"He… he…"

"What did he do, Sam?"

"He tried to rape me."

"My God." Luke stood up.

"What's happened?" Hugo said, dropping his newspaper to his lap.

Luke waved his hand to shush his father.

"Are you okay?" he asked.

"I'm bruised and…" She tried to laugh but it was a weak attempt. "As you can tell, it's shaken me up a bit."

"Where is he now?"

"He's lying on the floor and I've got my foot on his chest."

"What?"

"Luke, I don't know what to do. Should I call the police?"

"First things first, Sam. Are you safe?"

This time her laugh was genuine. "Don't worry about that. He's not going anywhere until I allow him to."

He heard Hannah's voice in the background. It sounded

like she said 'third dan' which didn't make any sense, unless…

"Were there three of them?"

"Brendan was with two friends."

"Dan and someone else?"

Sam hesitated before she replied. "I see what you're thinking but, no, their names are Grant and Phil. When Hannah said 'dan' she was referring to my karate."

This was the first Luke had heard of Sam's karate but he decided to let it drop for the time being. "Where are they now?"

"Still in the Saracen's Head as far as I know."

"And do you know anything about them?"

"Absolutely nothing other than their names." Sam hesitated for a second. "I'm convinced they didn't know what was going to happen though," she said. "Brendan lured me outside on the pretext of giving me more GNE information, but it was pure chance that the three of them were in the same pub as Hannah and me."

"Right, give me a second to think."

Luke had already decided that calling the police was a waste of time. His twenty years in the force had taught him that the most that would result would be a warning. Brendan hadn't managed to hurt Sam. In fact, it sounded like he might have come off worse in the encounter. And when it came to it, it would be her word against his. Being interviewed would be traumatic for her too.

The question was, what should they do? Brendan couldn't be allowed to get off scot-free. What he'd done to Sam was awful.

Luke realised his hands were in fists. God help the bastard if he ever ran into him. He wanted to be there to support Sam and to deal with the man personally, but he was well over an hour's drive away.

He came to a decision.

"Are you able to restrain him without Hannah's help?"

"No problem."
"Good. This is what I want you to do."

Chapter 29

Sam turned as she heard footsteps.

After a few seconds, Hannah emerged around the corner with Brendan's friends following behind. She had her phone's flashlight on and pointed it first at Sam and then down at Brendan's face. She held it there for a few seconds.

He put his hand over his face and shouted, "Get that away."

Sam still had her right foot pressed firmly down on Brendan's chest but he wasn't making any attempt to get up.

"What on earth's going on?" the taller of the two men said, and she realised it was Grant.

"She attacked me," Brendan said. "She lured me…"

Sam pressed harder with his foot and he spluttered to a stop.

"Your friend tried to rape me," she said matter-of-factly.

"Christ." It was Grant again.

"He's a colleague," Phil said. "We work together but I wouldn't call us friends."

"I thought you both worked for GNE?"

"No, we work for NTV Bristol, same as Brendan."

"Another lie, Brendan?" Sam said, and nudged her foot up his chest towards his chin. He lifted his head away.

"I'd heard a rumour," Grant said. "But I thought it was nonsense."

"It is nonsense. I've…" Sam moved her foot again and Brendan stopped mid-sentence.

"What rumour?" Sam asked.

"That he'd come on heavy with a trainee," Grant said. "He denied it, and she left soon after, so I assumed there was nothing to it."

"Well, now you know otherwise," Sam said. "What would happen if you reported it to someone senior in NTV Bristol?"

It was Phil who answered. "Bugger all, probably."

"Worth trying though," Grant said.

"I'll make your lives hell if you do," Brendan said from the floor.

"Can he do that?" Sam asked. "He's an executive producer so I assume he's senior to you."

"Executive producer?" Grant said with a dry laugh. "That's what he told you, did he?"

"What is he then?"

"He's a producer, plain and simple. Same grade as us. Phil's also a producer and I'm a broadcast journalist." He seemed to come to a decision. "Phil," he said, "I think we should take it to Terence. If we go together we might get somewhere."

"I'm up for that," Phil said.

"Who's Terence?" Sam asked.

"Terence Nix is the Director of News at NTV Bristol," Grant said.

Brendan started to say something but Sam nudged his chin with the toe of her shoe and he stayed silent. She looked at Grant and Phil. "Can we exchange contact details?" she asked. "I'd appreciate it if you could let me know how you get on."

"Of course," Grant said.

"Sure," Phil added. He gestured to Brendan. "What are you going to do with him?"

Sam took her foot off Brendan's chest and stood back. "Get to your feet," she said.

He scrambled to his feet. "You won't get anywhere with this," he hissed.

"Piss off, Brendan," Grant said.

Brendan edged his way past them and round the corner.

"Let's go back onto Broad Street," Sam said, "and we

can swap details there."

They walked to the end of the alley and then exchanged numbers.

"Are you two okay?" Grant asked.

"Sure." Sam turned to Hannah. "I don't think I can face the pub. Can we head back to yours?"

"Of course," Hannah said.

"We'll be in touch," Grant said.

They said their goodbyes and Hannah and Sam headed off down Broad Street.

"I hope we don't run into Brendan," Sam said.

"Not as much as he hopes he doesn't run into you," Hannah said with a laugh. "How did you put him down? He's a big strong guy."

"It was a combination of karate and Jiu-Jitsu. I finally put him down with a high twist kick, but it was Jiu-Jitsu that got me out from under him. We had sessions on it at our dojo a couple of years ago. It's all a matter of using leverage and body position."

"Impressive stuff."

"Bloody useful stuff." Sam hesitated. "Christ, Hannah. If I didn't know martial arts…"

"Best not to go there." Hannah paused for a second. "So, Luke advised you not to go to the police?"

"Yes, which surprised me. I thought he'd be all for getting them involved."

"Do you think you ought to ring him to tell him what Grant and Phil are going to do?"

"Oh no. It's late Saturday evening. He won't want to hear from me again this evening. I'll tell him when I see him in the office on Monday."

Sam's phone rang and she looked down at her screen. "It's Luke," she said.

Hannah elbowed her. "See," she said. "He cares."

Sam clicked to accept the call. "Hi, Luke," she said.

"How did it go?"

"Good. Brendan's colleagues are going to raise it with someone senior at NTV."

"How are you? Do you want me to come to Bath? I could be there in just over an hour."

"There's no need, Luke. I'll be fine, honestly. I'm going to stay with Hannah tonight."

"If you can, stay with her tomorrow as well. I know from experience that this kind of thing can be very traumatic, and it can sometimes hit you hours, days or even weeks afterwards. Be ready for that, okay?"

"I will, Luke."

"And if you get the chance, can you give me a call tomorrow? I'd like to hear how you're getting on."

"Okay. Goodnight, Luke."

"Goodnight, Sam."

Hannah, who had been listening throughout, smiled and nudged her friend again. "I told you he cares," she said.

Chapter 30

Luke put his phone back in his pocket. Poor Sam. It must have been incredibly frightening but it sounded like she had handled herself very well. The mention of 'third dan' hadn't been lost on him either. He made a mental note to ask her about it.

He heard a noise and realised it was the front door shutting. "I think they're here," he said.

Hugo put his paper down, stood up and tightened his tie, even though it was already right up against his collar. "Better greet her I suppose," he said.

"Be nice, Father," Luke said.

"I will, if she's well-behaved."

"She's eight remember."

"Mmm."

Luke led the way to the hall where Erica was standing next to the door with a young girl by her side. It was immediately obvious they were mother and daughter. Marion had inherited her mother's wide eyes and the shape of their faces was similar too. Where they differed was in the shape of their mouths. While Erica's seemed designed never to smile, with both sides turned down as if she would forever be disappointed with her lot, Marion's was the opposite. For someone who had been brought up by drug dealers she seemed on first appearance to be a cheery little girl.

"Hi, Erica," Luke said. "Where's Mark?"

"He's fetching the luggage in," she said.

Luke bent forward. "You must be Marion."

"This is Luke," Erica said.

"You're even taller than Mark," Marion said, her Californian accent immediately apparent.

Luke smiled. "I'm six foot six."

"Wow." She smiled. "That's awesome."

"And this is your grandfather," Erica said.

"Step-grandfather," Hugo corrected.

"You're old," Marion said.

"Well I, um…"

"What should I call you? I've never had a step-grandfather before." She didn't wait for an answer. "I know," she said. "You can be Grandpabbie."

"My name's Hugo," Hugo said. "I'm the Duke of Dorset."

"Yes, I know," Marion said, clearly unimpressed. "Mark told me."

"Do you mean Grandpappy?" Luke asked.

"Jeez, no. That's awful old-fashioned. Grandpabbie is old and he's wise. He's a…"

Luke stepped in before she could finish. "Sounds good to me, Father," he said.

Hugo nodded approvingly. "Very well, Marion. You may call me Grandpabbie."

Mark appeared with two suitcases. "Did I hear that Marion is going to call you Grandpabbie, Father."

"She is, yes." Hugo's chest was out. "Apparently because I'm old and wise."

"And because you look like a…" Marion started to say.

Luke interrupted again. "How was the flight, Marion?" he asked.

She turned to him and smiled. "Awesome," she said. It was clearly her favourite word. "We had chocolate cheesecake. And my seat turned into a bed when I pressed a button."

"Mmm," Hugo said. He gestured to the door to the salon. "Shall we go through…"

"And I watched films. I saw two. One was Frozen, which I've seen of course. The other was Little Mermaid but not the cartoon. It had real actors." She put her hands to her ears. "I wore these headphones that were noise-reducing which was cool. Then I fell asleep because Erica said I had to but I wasn't very tired. I did sleep though. When I woke I had another meal. I didn't like the fruit but they gave me Nutella and crackers instead. It was awesome."

"I gathered," Hugo said.

"You must all be tired," Luke said.

"I certainly am," Hugo said under his breath.

"Yes we are," Mark said. "It was a long journey."

"Can't I stay up and talk to Luke and Grandpabbie, Erica?" Marion pleaded.

"God, no," Hugo said.

"Father," Luke said.

"I'm sorry, Marion," Hugo said, "but your Grandpabbie is old and he needs his sleep."

"Can I talk to Luke then?"

"I'd love that," Luke said. "Erica, why don't you take Marion into the salon and I'll help Mark with the rest of the luggage then we'll join you."

"Awesome," Marion said. "Are we going to get our nails done? Or our hair. I like my hair as it is though. But nails would be good. Can I have sparkles? Or glitter? Oh, can I have both? That would be awesome."

Hugo shook his head. "What is she wittering on about?"

"Salon means a different thing in the US," Luke explained. He turned to Marion. "It's not a beauty salon," he said. "It's what we call the grandest room in an English country house. Another name for it is the drawing room."

"Awesome," she said. "I love drawing. And colouring. Have you got craft things as well like clay or buttons or stickers?"

"I'm going to bed," Hugo said, shaking his head. "Heaven knows what Daphne is going to make of this."

"Good night, Hugo," Erica said. "Come on, Marion.

She took her daughter's hand and led her through to the salon.

"Is there much more?" Luke asked after they'd left.

"Just Erica's cases now," Mark said with a grimace. He gestured to the two suitcases he'd already brought in. "That one's mine and that one's Marion's. Six more to go."

Luke gave a little chuckle. "You don't know who Grand Pabbie is, do you?"

"Never heard of him."

"He's a character from Frozen. Chloe had a poster of him up when she was nine or ten."

"That's nice. And I'm guessing he's old and wise."

"Yes, he is. He's also a troll."

Mark laughed. "Probably best if we don't tell Father that."

"No," Luke agreed, "I think you're right."

They joined Erica and Marion in the salon once they'd brought the luggage in and taken it to their rooms. Erica had found some paper and pencils and Marion was sitting at the desk bent over a drawing.

"Is my luggage in our room, Mark?" Erica asked.

"Yes," he said.

"Good. I'm desperate to get into something more comfortable. Look after Marion, will you?"

Luke and Mark walked over to the desk.

"I'm doing this for Grandpabbie," Marion said without looking up.

Luke looked at the picture and couldn't help smiling. She had drawn a round face with a very large flattened nose and two big round ears. The figure had spiky fronds of hair emerging from the top of his head and from all around his chin.

"It's excellent," he said.

"I know. I'm very good at drawing. I could do with some colour though. His hair should be dirty yellow."

"I think we should try and find you some so that you

can make it perfect. What do you think, Mark?"

Mark shrugged. "Why not?" he said. "In for a penny…"

Luke managed to find an old crayon set in the conservatory and Marion was delighted when he gave it to her.

"Awesome," she said as she extracted the grey and started shading the face.

He looked at his watch. It was getting on for eleven and still no word from Josh. He shouldn't be worried but couldn't help himself. An update would be great but he knew he'd probably have to wait until the party was over and Josh was safely clear before he heard from him and that was likely to be well past midnight.

Chapter 31

"Look, George," Owen said, pointing. "Girls."

Josh followed his gaze and sure enough there were five, no six, girls emerging from the back door of the house. There was a hush as the various groups of men saw them, then conversations resumed but at a louder volume than before.

"Are they gorgeous or what?" Owen said. "Wow. I wasn't expecting that. There weren't any girls two weeks ago but maybe that was because the party finished early."

Josh watched as the girls separated, each of them making a beeline for one of the groups of men. Owen was right. They were, without exception, very attractive. They were young too, maybe late teens or possibly very early twenties.

With a shock he realised that one of them, a girl with long brown hair, was heading straight for them. She was wearing a tight-fitting white halterneck top, her slim waist visible above her faded blue jeans. He could sense without looking that Owen had adopted his gawking pose, the one he had greeted Eve with when they first arrived.

She smiled broadly as she neared them.

"Hi boys," she said, her voice low and sultry. "I'm Blossom."

"George," Josh said, smiling back. He held his hand out but she ignored it and leaned forward to give him a peck on the cheek.

She turned to Owen. He continued gawping until Josh elbowed him in the ribs.

"Hi, um, Blossom," Owen said. She bent forward and pecked him on the cheek. "Thanks," he said. "I'm Owen."

She gave a little giggle. "You don't need to thank me,

Owen."

"Uh, no. But…"

"So what brings you here?" Josh asked. "Is your boyfriend coming later?"

This question seemed to stump her. It was straightforward enough and Josh wondered why she hesitated.

"I'm single," she said after a few seconds. "Baz invited me."

"And the other girls, the ones you arrived with? Are they friends of yours?"

"No, they, uh…" Another telling pause. "We were all asked to the party by Baz and he sent a limo to pick us up."

"Right. I see."

Josh was about to ask something else when Owen came out of his reverie. "So, you're single, Blossom?" The way he asked the question reminded Josh of Luke's dog, Wilkins, when he begged for a biscuit.

"Yes, I am," she said, on more comfortable ground now.

"So, are you a student?" Josh asked.

"We're both students, aren't we George?" Owen said, nudging Josh with his elbow as he spoke. "We're at Bath University. First year."

"I'm an actress," Blossom said. There was a slight edge to her voice and Josh decided he should stop probing for the time being at least, but he sensed there was more to her than met the eye.

"There are a couple of actors here that Owen and I recognise," he said. He pointed to a group of five on the opposite side of the pool, four men and one of the girls who had arrived with Blossom. "That's Roger Cromwell on the left and Matt something-or-other on the left."

"Matt Viner," Owen said. "They're both in Corrie."

"Oh yes," Blossom said. "I didn't know they were gay."

"What do you mean?" Owen asked.

Blossom's cheeks flushed. "Oh, I…" She gave a little chuckle. "I don't know why I said that."

"Why would they be gay?" Owen persisted.

"Oh, I don't know. The way they're standing?"

It was a pathetic reason and she knew it. Josh decided to help her out.

"It doesn't matter, Owen," he said. He turned to Blossom. "Damon Prendergast and Ozzy Vaughan from 'Rock-n-Roll-n-Rap' are over there." He pointed.

"Oh yes," she said. She indicated another group. "And isn't that one of the Blue Peter presenters?"

"I've met him," Owen said, a note of pride in his voice. "He gave me an orange Blue Peter Badge the year before last." He gulped as he realised what he'd said. "Not then. No. It was several years ago. When I was fourteen, so five years ago. Yes, it was five years ago."

"I understand," Blossom said, smiling. "What did you win it for?"

"It was a competition I entered but I can't remember what it was for. It was a long time ago. Five years ago."

"I used to love Blue Peter," she said.

"So how do you know Baz?" Owen asked, desperate to change the subject.

"I just, um, met him." She paused, uncomfortable again. "At the studios, when I was filming."

"What were you in?"

"It was a small part in, um, a drama. Look, guys, it's been nice talking to you but I ought to mingle. Maybe see you later." She gave a little wave and then turned and headed towards another group of three men.

Josh was desperate to ask her more questions. There was more to Blossom than met the eye and he wanted to find out what it was. Asking her anything with Owen there was useless though. He needed to get her on her own somehow.

He decided he'd leave it for now. It was about time he

got talking to more of the 'suspects' on the crazy wall.

The only one he'd met so far was Reggie Dowden and Josh realised he hadn't seen him since he'd gone off with Callum.

"Have you seen Reggie or Callum?" he asked.

"Not for a while," Owen said.

Josh looked around but couldn't see them anywhere. "If you spot them, can you tell me?"

"Sure. Hey, look. Blossom's on her own again. Shall we go over?"

The last thing Josh wanted was another conversation with Blossom while Owen was there. "Why don't you have a word?" he said. "I'm going to see if I can join Ozzy Vaughan's group."

Owen practically salivated when he heard this. "Right," he said, already moving in her direction. "Catch you later."

Josh walked to the end of the pool then around and up to Ozzy's group. Damon still looked disinterested. The other two men gave way and Josh stood between them.

Ozzy saw him and flicked his fingers. "How is it, bro'?" he asked.

"It's, uh, fine," Josh said.

"Sure thang." Ozzy looked him up and down as if he was a hunk of meat in a butcher's then licked his lips and winked. "Just telling these fellas 'bout my new mix. Gonna be streaming next month. Brixton gangster rap, innit?"

"What's your name?" Damon asked without looking up.

"George," Josh said, "George Bailey." He fought successfully to keep his inner Connery at bay as he said this.

He needed to seize this opportunity and moved closer to Damon as Ozzy resumed his monologue.

"You're Damon Prendergast, aren't you?" he asked, leaning forward so that Damon could hear him above the sound of Ozzy holding forth.

"What of it?" Damon was examining the nails of his left hand.

"Are you okay?"

Damon gestured to Ozzy, but still didn't look up. "Don't know how he can fucking block it out," he said.

"Block what out?"

"What happened to Rachel. Fucking awful."

Josh's heart missed a beat. "Rachel? Who's she?"

"Works at GNE. Well, worked there. Got the sack."

Josh breathed a sigh of relief. It was clearly the same Rachel but he already knew she'd lost her job. "That's not so bad, is it?"

Damon glanced at Josh for the first time, and he looked genuinely upset. "I had a run-in with her, said some bad things, but fucking hell, I wouldn't have wished that on anyone."

Josh felt uneasy again. "Wished what on her?"

"She's in a coma. They don't know if she'll pull through but it's looking unlikely."

"How awful! What happened?"

"She fell onto the tracks at Regent's Park underground station and hit her head. Some guy saw her and carried her out just before a train pulled in."

"Was it an accident?"

"Either that or suicide. Someone said they saw her jump so more likely suicide."

"Who said that?"

Damon glared at him. "I don't fucking know. What does it matter anyway?"

"You're right," Josh said hastily. "It doesn't matter. But there's no point beating yourself up about it."

"Yeah, and if I want your advice I'll ask for it. Why don't you fuck off."

Josh could see this was going nowhere. "Right," he said and backed away until he was standing alone slightly outside the group.

Poor Rachel, he thought.

It dawned on him that Luke wouldn't know yet and was

due to be seeing her on Monday evening. He reached for his phone before remembering he'd had to hand it in when they arrived. He'd have to ring Luke when the party ended.

He looked across to Owen who was deep in conversation with Blossom and appeared to be enjoying himself. She saw him and smiled, but it was a smile that said she wouldn't mind him rescuing her. He smiled back but decided she'd have to suffer for the time being.

Now where was Marvin Winespottle?

Chapter 32

Josh cast his eyes around, but there was no sign of Marvin, and he couldn't see Reggie or Callum either.

There were a few people who were the worse for wear, hardly surprising since the drink was free and it was past midnight. But so far he hadn't seen anything to confirm Victor's suspicions. There had been flirting, which aside from Owen with Blossom seemed to be restricted to men flirting with other men, but that was also to be expected.

However, if it was a party for gay men then why were Blossom and the other girls there? And why was someone like Owen, who was as heterosexual as they come, invited?

It certainly warranted further investigation.

He felt a tap on his back and turned to see Callum and another boy of about the same age, if not younger. He was about Josh's height and had wavy brown hair and baby skin. There was no muscle to him and he looked like he'd done most of his growing in the last year or so.

"Oh hi, Callum," Josh said.

"George, this is Dylan," Callum said.

"Hi, George," Dylan said. He looked around nervously after he said it, then added, "Here they come."

Josh looked behind him to see the imposing figure of Reggie approaching accompanied by a tall man with huge glasses who he immediately recognised as Marvin.

"Is anything wrong?" Josh asked quickly while they were still making their way over.

"I don't want to go with them," Callum said.

"Go where?"

Reggie and Marvin arrived before Callum could answer and it was immediately apparent that Marvin was almost paralytically drunk. He was struggling to stand straight and kept falling against Reggie. Josh recalled that Maj had said he was in much the same way at the awards ceremony.

"Come on, Dyl-boy," Marvin slurred.

"I don't want to," Dylan said.

Marvin reached out and grabbed Dylan by the arm. "Won' harm you," he said.

"He doesn't want to go," Josh said and pulled Marvin's hand away.

"What the fuck's it got to do with you?" Reggie asked, pushing his imposing frame between Josh and Dylan.

"If Dylan doesn't want to go he doesn't have to."

Reggie shoved his over-sized belly against Josh making him stagger back a pace. "It's none of your fucking business!" he shouted, his eyes wide.

Josh returned the glare. "Leave him alone," he said.

At that moment someone pulled Reggie back and Josh saw it was Kieran, the man in the dinner jacket who had taken his phone at the beginning of the evening.

"Can we keep it down, guys?" Kieran said, his voice steady. "What's the matter?"

"I don't want to go with him," Dylan whimpered, gesturing to Marvin.

"Why?"

"He's old and I don't fancy him."

"I just wanna talk," Marvin said.

Kieran gave a little laugh. "No, Marvin. I don't think that's true, is it?" He raised his voice slightly. "I think you need to back away and leave these guys alone."

"Callum's with me," Reggie said.

"No, I'm not," Callum said.

"Right," Kieran said, looking at Reggie. "I think both you and Marvin need to leave these lads alone. We don't want any trouble, not after what happened last time."

Reggie sniffed and wagged a finger at Callum. "I'll remember this," he said before grabbing Marvin and leading him away.

"I'd like to go home now," Dylan said.

"Sure," Kieran said. "Come with me and I'll give you your phone back and you can be on your way."

"Cheers, Callum," Dylan said. "And thanks for trying to help, George."

"No problem," Josh said.

He watched as Dylan followed Kieran back to the house.

"I think I'm going to leave as well," Callum said. He looked upset.

"What's wrong?" Josh asked. "Is it what happened with Dylan?"

"No, it's Reggie. He tried to…" He swallowed. "I don't want to talk about it."

"Can I have your number?"

Callum shook his head. "I'm not gay," he said.

"It's not that, Callum. I'm not gay either. But I need to ask you some questions. Would you be happy to meet me tomorrow?"

Callum hesitated for a second. "Okay," he said. He told Josh his number and Josh repeated it back to make sure he'd got it right. He'd have to enter it into his phone as soon as Kieran gave it back.

"Have you got far to go?" he asked.

"Only a mile or so. I live at the bottom of Guinea Lane."

Josh lowered his voice to a whisper. "Which school are you at?"

"Kingswood." Callum paused. "My father's a barrister," he added as if in apology.

"Year 11?" Callum nodded. "You be careful, Callum. I wouldn't come to another of these parties if I were you."

"Don't worry, I won't." Callum shivered. "No way. Bye, George."

Josh waved him off, walked to the edge of the pool and as casually as possible looked over to the other side to see what Damon and Ozzy were up to.

They were now several yards apart from each other. Ozzy was still giving forth, but to three men now, while Damon's mood seemed to have changed considerably. He was with someone and was smiling and talking but his companion was hidden by his large frame.

Josh walked further down the garden, pretended to notice something on the ground and bent down. As he stood up he glanced over again. He could now see that Damon had his arm around the shoulder of a young lad who made Callum and Dylan look like senior citizens. The boy had mascara on and was smiling up at Damon. As he watched, Damon bent to the boy's ear, whispered something and then took his hand and led him to the house. The two of them reached the back door at the same time as Marvin, who still appeared to be blind drunk but let them go first before staggering in after them.

Josh shivered. What he had just seen was further confirmation that Victor Robertson's suspicions were justified.

Chapter 33

Josh decided it was time to track Blossom down. He glanced around and spotted her sitting on the grass at the far end of the garden with her back against a large conifer. Owen, he saw, had joined a couple of other lads and the three of them were sitting with their shoes and socks off, bare feet dangling in the pool.

He wandered over to Blossom and sat down beside her.

"I don't want to be your girlfriend," she said.

Josh started laughing.

"What's so funny?" she asked.

"Sorry," Josh said. "I used the same line on Mandy when I first met her. She's a friend of mine. It just seemed odd having it turned on me."

"So you don't want to ask me out?"

"No thanks. I've got a girlfriend."

"Thank goodness. I mean you're alright-looking, and I guess you're around the same age as me, but you're not my type." She sighed. "Your friend Owen kept asking me if I'd go out with him and he can't be more than sixteen."

Josh only heard one part of this.

"You think I'm about the same age as you?" he said.

"Aren't you? I'm twenty-one."

"Thank goodness. I mean, I'm supposed to look fifteen or sixteen, hence the clothes." He waved his hand in front of his multi-coloured t-shirt. "But I'm twenty-two and I'm pleased you see me for what I am, a fully developed, mature man."

"I wouldn't go that far," she said.

"I'm not telling Leanne about you though. I've made that mistake before." He paused before adding, "Sorry. I didn't mean to say that out loud."

Blossom laughed before saying, "So if you're twenty-two, why are you pretending to be a teenager?"

Josh ignored the question and asked one of his own. "What's your real name?"

"It's Blossom," she said.

"No, it's not."

She turned and looked him in the eyes then sighed. "It's Lily," she said.

Josh considered what he should do. He didn't want to blow his cover but, on the other hand, Lily might be able to help him. He decided to find out more about her.

"So, why are you calling yourself Blossom?" he asked.

"I *am* an actress," Lily said. "That much was true. But I've never met Baz. The other five girls are actresses too."

"How come you're here?"

"Eve, Baz's assistant, arranged it. We're getting £300 each, which is good money for a struggling actor."

"Any idea why?"

"I was told that it was a party for gay men but they needed some women along. I think the exact words were 'to brighten things up'. I didn't ask any questions, but it's pretty clear all these guys, with the exception of Owen that is, would rather we weren't here."

"And you're from Bath?"

"No, I live in Norton St Philip. The bit about the limo was true as well. It came to pick us all up and is taking us back at 2 am."

"That's interesting. I know someone who lives in Norton St Philip. His name's Luke Sackville. Do you know him?"

"No, it doesn't ring a bell." She raised an eyebrow. "You didn't answer my question. Why are you pretending to be fifteen or sixteen?"

"I, uh... Can I borrow your phone? They took mine when I arrived."

"Sure. Why?"

"I need to ring someone." He held his hand out. "Can you keep an eye open for the guy in a dinner jacket? I'll call from behind the tree."

She entered her code into the phone and passed it over. Josh stepped behind the conifer and entered Luke's number. He hesitated, aware that he had to tell him about Rachel, then hit the green button.

Luke answered immediately. "Luke Sackville. Who's this?"

"It's Josh."

"Hi. How's it going?"

Josh swallowed. No sense in beating about the bush. "I've heard some bad news about Rachel."

"Is she at the party?"

"No." Josh hesitated for a second.

"Out with it, Josh."

"She's had an accident and she's in a coma. Apparently, they're fearing the worst." There was silence at the other end. "Are you all right, guv?"

"I'm fine, Josh. Do you know which hospital she's in?"

"I don't. Sorry."

"No problem. I'll find out."

They were both silent for a few seconds.

"Have you found anything useful out?" Luke asked.

Josh told him about running into Owen on the way in, and about Callum and Dylan and how Reggie and Marvin seemed to be intimidating them. He also explained about Lily and the other girls and why he was using her phone.

"I suspect the girls are there in an attempt to counter the rumours," Luke said when he'd finished. "What about Damon Prendergast and Ozzy Vaughan?"

"It was Damon who told me about Rachel," Josh said. "He seemed genuinely upset."

"It could well be an act. In my experience, it's best to start by not trusting people. Make them earn it."

"Gotcha, guv. Later I saw Damon take a young lad by

the hand and take him into the house."

"How old was the boy?"

"He looked no more than fifteen."

"Christ." Luke paused. "What about the host himself?"

"I haven't even seen him, guv. Seems odd really, given it's his party."

"And Ozzy?"

"He's so full of himself, I don't think I'll be able to get anything out of him. It's all 'innit' this and 'sure thang' that. The man doesn't stop." Josh paused. "Do you think I should ask Lily to help?"

"Can you trust her?"

"Yes."

Luke reflected on this for a minute. "Right, here's what I want you to do. First, make sure you've got Owen's and Lily's numbers as well as Callum's."

"Will do, guv."

"Good. Explain to Lily about me and why you're at the party. Ask her if she can try getting Ozzy's attention. She doesn't have to ask him anything in particular, just talk to him and see if anything odd comes up."

"No problemo."

"I suggest you try to get time with Eve. Wherever she is, Baz is probably nearby. Again, no need to probe heavily, just play it by ear."

"Okay. I can do that."

"And ring me after you leave, will you? Don't worry that it's late."

"Sure, guv."

"And well done, Josh. You've made a lot of progress."

Josh returned to the end of the garden, sat back down next to Lily and handed her phone back.

"Good call?" she asked.

"Very good call. The guv told me to tell you everything."

"Are you in the police?"

Josh was taken aback but puffed his chest out. "Is it my bearing?" he asked.

"No, it's the fact you called your boss 'guv'."

"Ah right," he said, now slightly deflated.

"So, why are you here?"

He reinflated. "I'm undercover. My real name is Josh and I'm finding things out, like really spying. You know, uh…" He tried to think of a different word for it but came up blank. "Uh, I'm spying. Like spies do."

"Like James Bond?"

"Exactly." He gave her a double thumbs up.

"Spying on what?"

He gave her the full story from Victor's suspicions through to Maj's visits to the awards ceremony and finishing with his preparations for the evening's party. She snorted with laughter when he described the horrors of his shopping trip with Sam, Helen and Sabrina.

"What now?" she asked when he'd finished.

He explained about her trying to talk to Ozzy.

"I'm fine with that," she said.

"And can you put my details in your phone and give me a ring tomorrow to let me know how you got on?"

"Yes, sure."

He gave her his number.

"And can I give you Callum's number before I forget it?'

She added Callum's details.

"Finally, if I get Owen's number can you put that in too?"

She laughed. "I've already got it. It was the only way to shut him up."

"Great. Can you text me their numbers in the morning?"

She nodded.

"Marvelissimo." He jumped to his feet. "Right, I'm off to track Eve down."

Chapter 34

As he walked past the pool to the house Josh tried to think of a reason he could give for wanting to speak to Eve. Then it hit him. She was Baz's assistant, his 'fixer', so she had details of everyone at the party. He would use that as an excuse.

He walked through the back door and heard the low mumble of voices in a room to the right. In the hope one of them was Eve he gave a peremptory knock and walked in without waiting for a reply.

There were three people inside. Kieran was sitting at a desk bashing away at a laptop, while Eve and a man who was, like Kieran, in a dinner jacket were seated at either end of an ultra-modern, cherry-red sofa.

"Hi," Eve said, looking up. "George, isn't it?"

"Yes, that's right. Sorry to interrupt. I wondered if I could have a word?"

"Sure," she said and smiled. "How can I help?"

Buggery-buggery-boo, he thought. He wanted her on her own. He had planned to ask for Callum's details but that didn't call for her to leave the room. What reason could he give? An internal injury? No, that was stupid. It was too late to feign pain now. What about wanting her number because he fancied her? Christ, no, not that. What if she said yes? He'd have to explain to Leanne and he could imagine her reaction only too well.

"George?" Eve prompted.

Josh shook his head. "Sorry, uh, it's, uh, it's personal. I've got a personal problem. Could I have a word in private?"

Kieran was still bashing away at his keyboard but Josh thought he heard him snort.

"Of course," Eve said. She turned to the man beside her. "I'll be back in a minute, Nat."

Josh went back into the corridor.

Buggery-twofold, he thought. *What am I going to say?*

She followed him out and shut the door behind her. "Let's go into the kitchen," she said and opened a door on the other side of the corridor.

He followed her in and closed the door. She turned to face him.

"What's wrong, George?" she asked.

"I, uh, I'm gay," he said.

She gave a little laugh. "I guessed that," she said. "It's pretty obvious."

"Obvious?" he squealed. "Why?"

She thought about this for a second. "I guess it's the hair that's the giveaway."

"What?" His voice was even higher this time and he automatically put his hand to his head.

"So what's wrong?" she went on. "You said you've got a personal problem."

"Oh, yes, it's because I'm..." He hesitated for a second, then clicked his fingers and pointed at her with his index finger. "It's because I'm gay, that I've, uh, fallen... Yes that's it, I've fallen for, uh, Callum but he's gone and I haven't got his details. I wondered if you had them?"

"I have, but I can't give them out. Tell you what, though. I can message him and say you want to get in touch and if he says yes I'll pass him your details. How's that, George?"

"Gucci."

"Pardon?"

"Thanks."

"No problem." She moved towards the door.

He put his hand on her arm. "Uh, before you go. I wondered if Baz was around? I mean, it's his party and I've not seen him. It'd be nice to say hello."

Eve turned her head to look at a door at the far end of the room before returning her attention to Josh.

"Sorry," she said. "Baz is a little under the weather this evening and I've promised he won't be interrupted. He'd have loved to meet you otherwise but, well, that's the way it is."

"Okay. Shame, but never mind."

"I'd better be getting back. Enjoy the rest of the party."

"Thanks, Eve. I will."

He followed her into the corridor and headed slowly towards the back of the house. As soon as he heard the click of the door shutting he turned around and walked as quietly as he could back up the corridor then pressed down on the kitchen door handle slowly, praying it wouldn't creak. Fortunately, it made no noise and he pushed the door open and walked in, gently closing it behind him.

He walked to the door Eve had glanced at, took a deep breath and then, as he had before, knocked and walked immediately in.

"What the fuck?" Baz asked, raising his head to see who had walked in. He was lying naked on his back on a large round bed. A second man was kneeling on the floor by his feet and appeared to have been sucking his toes.

"Ugh," Josh said.

The man turned and Josh recognised him as having been in a group of three by the pool earlier.

"Do you want to join us?" the man asked then pushed his tongue out and licked his top lip.

"Right, I, uh…" Josh pointed at the door with his thumb. "Thanks for the invitation, but I'll pass if that's okay."

He grabbed the door handle, pulled the door open and practically sprinted back to the garden.

Once there he thought about what might happen if Baz told Eve, or worse still Kieran, that he'd walked in on him. He needed his phone back before that happened. He turned around, decision made, and made straight for the room Eve had returned to, this time opening the door without bothering to knock first.

Kieran looked up when he heard him. "Oh, it's you again," he said. "What now?"

"Sorry to bother you again," Josh said. "I've got a bit of a headache and I've decided to leave. Do you think I could have my phone back?"

Kieran grunted. "What colour is it?"

"It's gold."

Kieran fished a key out of his waistcoat pocket, unlocked the top drawer of the desk and pulled it open. He fumbled around for a few seconds then held a gold phone up. "Is this it?" he said. He turned it over. "It's got turtles on the case."

Josh smiled. "Yes, that's mine." He walked over to Kieran. "They're Teenage Mutant Ninja Turtles."

Kieran grunted again and handed Josh his phone.

"I hope you had a good time, George," Eve said, smiling.

Josh returned her smile. "It was great. Thanks for inviting me."

"Good luck with Callum."

He almost asked what she meant but stopped himself just in time. "Oh, uh, yeah." He winked, lifted his left hand and gave a little wave as he left the room.

Back in the corridor he stood with his back to the door and took a deep breath. Why did he wink? And what was with the wimpy wave? He cast a nervous glance at the door that led to the kitchen and Baz's bedroom before heading for the front door and his escape.

Once outside, Josh walked quickly back to Lansdown Road and started up the hill before pulling his phone out of his pocket and calling Luke. It was gone one in the morning so he was half-expecting it to go to voicemail but it was answered after only one ring.

"Have you left?" Luke asked.

"Yes. I'm walking to the car now."

"How did you get on?"

"I managed to do everything you asked. Lily's going to text me Owen and Callum's numbers in the morning, and I'll ask her then whether she got anywhere with Ozzy Vaughan."

"Well done, Josh. Did you see anything of Baz Hartman?"

"I saw all of him, guv."

"What do you mean?"

"He was, uh, kind of…" He was starting to feel a little nauseous as he remembered what he'd seen in Baz's bedroom. "Can I tell you on Monday, guv? I feel like getting home to Leanne now."

"Of course, Josh. You've done well. There's no urgency so don't try to do too much tomorrow. We'll have a good crack at everything on Monday. Have a good night's sleep."

"Cheers, guv."

Chapter 35

Dylan was trying his hardest not to cry. His head hurt like mad and he was scared but he was almost sixteen, nearly a man. Whimpering and whining were for babies.

He lifted his head, squeezed his eyes to pin-pricks and peered into the darkness trying to see something, anything, that would show where he was. But it was pitch black, as it had been when the bag was pulled from over his head.

How could it be so absolutely lacking in light? He'd dropped off to sleep at one point in the night but not for long and it was mid-June. It had to be seven, eight in the morning, probably later, so there should be light finding its way in somehow.

The door had made a metallic sound when it had been opened so perhaps he was in a prison cell, or maybe an outhouse with a metal door. The floor was hard which suggested it was made of metal too, although he supposed it could be concrete.

He didn't even know how big the room was. His captor had ordered him to keep his eyes closed when he removed the bag and while he tied his wrists together behind the back of the chair. He hadn't dared open his eyes again until he heard the door clanging shut.

Dylan realised he needed a wee. It was only a slight urge but it would get more pressing and then what? He had to think of something else so that he could take his mind off it.

Escape. That's what he needed to concentrate on.

He tried to wriggle his hands but they were tightly bound and all that happened was that the rope cut more into his wrists. The chair appeared to be bolted to the floor so he couldn't rock it forwards or backwards.

If he knew who his jailer was that might help him think of a plan.

What had happened at the party had left him trembling, so much so that when he left he could barely walk and was forced to sit down at the end of the drive to compose himself. However, he hadn't been able to rid himself of the shakes, and after thirty minutes or so decided to call his uncle and ask if he could come to fetch him.

He had pulled out his phone and was about to ring when he heard a swishing noise and was hit on the head. He hadn't come to until his assailant had dragged him out of a vehicle and shoved him into this place.

He had a sense that his captor was big.

Marvin was tall. He had started eyeing Dylan up as soon as he emerged into the back garden. Those glasses of his made his eyes look bigger, and he had watched him all the way from the back door to the bar area. He shivered as he remembered what Marvin had whispered in his ear when he'd first come over. Reggie had followed it up with a smile and a wink which had been almost as vomit-inducing.

But it couldn't have been Marvin because he had been incredibly drunk unless, of course, he had been faking it.

Reggie was more likely. He'd had eyes for Callum but had kept looking at Dylan in a way that really creeped him out.

He sighed as it dawned on him that it could be any of the men at Baz Hartman's party. Possibly even Baz Hartman himself.

'Why?' was the other question, but he didn't want to go down that route.

He wished now that he had told his mum and dad where he was going. They wouldn't have approved, of course, and probably would have stopped him. Boy, how he wished they had.

Zac was a great friend. His mother had rung him, as he suspected she would, to check it was true that he was coming for a sleepover. And Zac had confirmed it.

His uncle was terrific too, as different from his father as two brothers could be. He was eccentric but very open-minded. 'Sounds like a cool party,' he had said when Dylan told him about it. 'Sure you can stay at mine. Let yourself in. I'll probably stay at my girlfriend's the night, but there's a key under the pot by the door.'

He'd got the train from Cardiff to Bath, dropped his backpack at his uncle's then walked to the party. And for the first couple of hours it had been fun.

Until he met Marvin.

Dylan shuffled his bottom on the chair. The need to pee was urgent now.

With a shock, he realised he could hear a key turning. After a few seconds, the door creaked slowly outwards and he was almost blinded as the sun came streaming in.

He squinted at the silhouette in the door. The figure slowly raised one arm in the air and Dylan gasped as he saw the light reflecting off the blade of a long thin knife.

Chapter 36

Hannah placed her paperback down on the coffee table. "Another chapter finished," she said. "I fancy a cuppa. Do you want another coffee?"

"No thanks," Sam said. "I'm all coffee'd out." She had her phone in her hand and was staring at it.

"Do it, Sam. There's no point in putting it off any longer."

"I'm going to ring Luke first."

Hannah grinned. "The man who cares."

"He insisted I ring today to let him know how I am, that's all."

"I'm having a cup of tea," Hannah said. She pointed her thumb at the kitchen door. "I'll put the kettle on and wait for my drink to brew while you call him. I wouldn't want to be a gooseberry."

"Shut up," Sam said, but she couldn't help smiling. Her friend might be like a dog with a bone but she meant well.

Luke picked up on the third ring.

"Hi, Sam," he said. "Did you manage some sleep?"

"A few hours. I'm feeling fine."

"Do you want to come in tomorrow? Because if you want the day off that's okay with me."

"I'll be there, Luke. I've still got that harassment case on the go."

"Maj can handle it."

"No, really. I want to be in. Brendan's a bastard and I dealt with him and that's that. There's no point in sitting at home brooding about what might have happened." She hesitated. "One thing I didn't tell you was that I met Brendan through my mother. They were dating."

"I see." Luke paused for a second. "Are you going to

tell the rest of the team?"

Sam hadn't thought about this. Helen knew about her mum's boyfriend, and Josh and Maj had been in the room when she'd told her, so it made sense to bring them up to date. The trouble was she felt so embarrassed by what had happened. She had let a near stranger lure her into a quiet alley. How stupid was that?

"You shouldn't think you did anything wrong," Luke said.

It was as if he had read her mind.

"I don't. I…"

She hesitated as the enormity of what might have happened hit her with a force so strong she might as well have been punched in the solar plexus.

What if she hadn't known martial arts? Or if he'd been too strong for her and had kept her pinned down? Or if he'd spiked her drink? Or…

"Sam, are you okay?"

She could feel her eyes welling up. "Yes, I'm fine. I…"

"Take a deep breath. Is Hannah there?"

"She's…" she was struggling to get the words out. "She's in the kitchen."

"You need to sit down with her and tell her everything that happened last night."

"I've already…" She took a deep breath and then exhaled. "I told her everything last night."

"Tell her again. In detail. And then tell her a second time, and a third after that. Let her ask questions until she knows every step you took and every word that was said. It will help you rationalise what happened."

Sam took a deep breath. "I will, Luke. Thanks."

"I'll see you tomorrow, Sam."

"Yes, see you tomorrow."

She was shaking as she put the phone back down on the coffee table.

A couple of minutes later Hannah reappeared cradling

a cup of tea and smiling from ear to ear.

"How was…" she started to say and then saw the expression on her friend's face. She put her drink down, sat on the sofa next to Sam and took her hand.

"What happened?" she asked. "You weren't all periodic with him again were you?"

Sam laughed but it was a half-hearted attempt. "No."

"What's wrong then?"

"The events of last night caught up with me while I was talking to him. He suggested I talk it all through with you, that if I do that it might help me come to terms with it."

Hannah nodded. "Sounds sensible to me. After all, what are friends for?" She grabbed her drink and took it back to the armchair. "Right then," she said. "Start with when you first caught sight of the Irish bastard in the Saracen's Head."

*

Sam felt a lot better after talking it through with Hannah, but it didn't make telling her mother any easier.

"Should I go round to see her?" she asked. "I feel I ought to tell her face-to-face, not over the phone."

"I think you're right," Hannah said. "It's going to be a hell of a blow for Kate, especially if she's got real feelings for the guy."

"The other problem is working out exactly how to tell her. I want to tell her quickly and not mess around but I can hardly say 'Hi, Mum, your boyfriend tried to rape me last night,' can I?"

"You're right. But…" Hannah stopped speaking when Sam's phone started ringing.

"It's Mum," Sam said as she looked down at the screen.

Hannah shrugged in a way that suggested 'rather you

than me', and Sam accepted the call.

"Hi, Mum," she said.

"What on earth were you thinking?" her mum said. She was furious but also sounded like she was on the edge of tears.

"What's wrong?"

"Brendan's finished with me." There was silence for a couple of seconds before she continued. "He said our relationship couldn't work, not after what you did."

"What do you mean?"

"I know he's attractive," she went on, and she was talking through tears now, "but how could you do that?"

"Mum, I don't know what you're talking about."

"He told me what happened at the Saracen's Head last night."

It dawned on Sam what he'd done. She looked across at Hannah as she delivered her next words. "Did Brendan tell you I tried to chat him up?"

"You know what you did, Sam."

"Yes, Mum, I do."

Hannah pointed to the phone and mouthed, "Give it to me."

Sam started to shake her head then thought better of it and handed it over.

"Kate, it's Hannah," Hannah said. There was silence at the other end. "Brendan lured Sam to a quiet alley and tried to rape her." Still nothing. "He's told you a cock-and-bull story to stir it up because he's a fucking bastard and you're well rid of him." She paused. "Your daughter needs your support, not your anger."

There was silence for a few more seconds then Kate said, her voice weaker than before, "Can you put Sam back on please?"

Hannah handed the phone back to Sam and she put it to her ear.

"Sorry, Sam," her mum said between sobs.

"Don't worry, Mum," Sam said. "Do you want me to come over?"

"Yes please, darling."

"I'll be there in fifteen minutes."

Chapter 37

Marion was incorrigible and Luke was loving it. She reminded him a little of Chloe at that age, mainly because of her smile and her endearingly cheeky manner. However, when it came to word count and volume Marion was in a league of her own.

"Awesome," Marion said for the umpteenth time as he put hotels down on Whitechapel Road and Old Kent Road.

"They don't earn much," he said.

"It's the names. They're so cute. And the little tokens. I like the cannon, but the top hat is cool too, and the battleship as well. Not the thimble, though. No one wins a game with a thimble. Grandpabbie," she added without skipping a beat, "can I buy Kings Cross from you? I need it because it's where Harry goes."

"Harry who?" Hugo asked.

Marion looked at him as if he'd lost all his brain cells. "Duh. Potter, silly."

"Mmm. I'm not sure." There was a glint in his eye that Luke hadn't seen in a long, long time. "It's a very valuable property."

"Can I? Can I?"

He pretended to be undecided and then held it up. "Okay," he said. "You can have it. No charge."

"Gee, thanks."

Hugo handed it over, his face devoid of emotion, though it was clear to Luke that his father was already growing fond of his step-granddaughter.

Luke threw the dice and moved the boot around to Mayfair.

"That'll cost you 2,000," Mark said.

"Right, I'm out," Luke said. He handed his two paltry

sets and tiny amount of cash to his brother and pushed his chair back. "I have to be getting home anyway."

"Can't you stay, Unc?" Marion pleaded. "You're, like, awesome, and you didn't finish reading me that story about the dragon and the princess. We got as far as the dragon losing his fire, but the prince was stuck in the forest and couldn't get out so the next thing has to be the princess helping him perhaps by cutting her hair, because it's made of gold so she can sell it and pay the ransom."

"Sorry, Marion," he said. "I have to go, but I'll try and come back next weekend."

"That would be good," Mark said.

"Cheers, Dad," Luke said. "Say goodbye to Mother when she wakes will you?" Hugo grunted and nodded his head without looking up.

Luke turned to Mark. "Where's Erica? I ought to say goodbye."

"I wouldn't worry," Mark said then cupped his hand to the side of his mouth and whispered, "She's in a sulk."

"Why is Erica in a sulk?" Marion asked.

"Right," Luke said. "I'll leave you to handle that one, Mark. Bye, Marion."

"Bye, Unc. Why is she in a sulk, Mark?"

As Luke walked to his BMW he reflected on how Marion had seemed to settle in so quickly. What's more, the impact she had already had on his father was incredible. Mark seemed to love having her around too.

Erica was certainly fond of her daughter but she was hard to read, always had been. He wondered why she was sulking. Knowing her, it was probably something trivial.

He turned the engine on and headed for the road that led north towards Bath. Now that he had left the house his thoughts returned to Sam and Rachel.

Sam's experience had been truly awful but she had handled herself very well, both in defending herself against Brendan but also since. Her emotions were running high but he had no doubt that she would come out stronger the other side. He would have liked to see her and reassure her that she had his full support, but she was having a relaxing day with her friend Hannah so Luke decided it was best to leave her in peace. He'd catch her alone in the office tomorrow.

It was hard to believe that Rachel was in a coma and near to death. She had been so lively on the one occasion they'd met, and her personality had come shining through when they'd talked on the phone. He hardly knew her but it was awful to think she could now be so lifeless.

He decided to ring to find out the latest.

The phone rang several times and he was resigned to leaving a voice message when there was a click and a woman said, "Hello. Who's this?"

"Hi, it's Luke Sackville," he said. "Sorry to bother you, but I'm a friend of Rachel's and I've only just heard what happened."

The woman sighed. "Rach is in a coma." She was clearly very upset. "Sorry. I'm Wendy, Rach's mum. She told me about you on Friday. Aren't you in the police?"

"Ex-police."

"Ah yes, I remember now."

"What do the doctors say?"

"She was brought in unconscious on Friday and they found a bleed on her brain…" She paused. "Sorry, it's so hard seeing my daughter like this."

"It's okay. When you're ready."

She continued after a few seconds. "They performed an emergency craniotomy but she's been in a coma ever since. They've told me…" He heard her take a deep breath. "They've told me to prepare for the worst."

"I'm so sorry, Wendy. Is there anything I can do?"

"You can catch the bastard who pushed her."

Luke's heart missed a beat. "I thought it was an accident."

"She was pushed, I'm sure of it."

"What do the police say?"

"They think she tried to kill herself, but that's nonsense. When we spoke on the phone on Friday morning she was in a really good mood. She was excited about the new job and about her date with you. There's no way she'd commit suicide."

"But what makes you think she was pushed?"

"She told me she'd upset some people at GNE and she was worried they'd hold it against her."

"That doesn't mean one of them would try to kill her."

Wendy sighed again. "You sound like the officer I talked to. He thought I was talking rubbish too."

"I don't think you're talking rubbish at all, Wendy. You know your daughter better than anyone." Luke hesitated. "I can't promise anything, but I'll do what I can."

"Thank you, Luke."

"Will you keep me up to date with how Rachel's getting on?"

"Of course. I'll text you my mobile number."

"Stay strong for Rachel, Wendy."

"I will, Luke. Speak soon."

As soon as the call ended Luke rang Pete Gilmore, his ex-colleague from Avon and Somerset Police.

"Hi, Luke," Pete said when he answered. "Sounds like you're travelling."

"Yes, on my way back from Dorset."

"I sense you're not just ringing for a chat."

"Correct. I need a favour. Are you on for breakfast tomorrow?"

"Sure."

"Great. See you at 8?"

"Fine."

"I'll explain everything when we meet. Enjoy the rest of the weekend."

"And you, Luke."

Chapter 38

Josh was pleased with himself. Okay, he'd told Leanne a little white lie, but it was the best thing to do given how she'd reacted in the past to him meeting women. If he'd told her he was seeing Lily as well as Callum she'd go berserko, ask if she was pretty and he'd have to tell the truth. She had been so annoyed when he'd innocently confirmed that Mandy was attractive. He didn't want to go down that rabbit hole again.

He climbed down from the number 4 bus and turned towards St James Parade. Lily had suggested meeting at the Forum Coffee House which suited him just fine. As long as they did luxury hot chocolate that was. And pastries. He fancied a millionaire's shortbread. Leanne had cooked a big fry-up but that was ages ago and he was ravenous.

Millionaire's shortbread could be a bit on the small side though. He wondered if they had any danish. Or maybe a rocky road. And a millionaire's shortbread. Was that being greedy? Yes, but...

Lily was there when he arrived and he was pleased to see she'd nabbed a table with a couple of comfy-looking grey armchairs. She smiled at him as he approached.

"Good morning, Josh. You look different."

"Older and more mature?"

"No. Just different."

"Right." He indicated the counter with his thumb. "Have you ordered?"

"No, I thought I'd wait for you."

"Gucci. I'll go and get them in. What'll you have?"

"Just an orange juice please.'

"Nothing to eat?"

"No. I'm fine."

Josh went to the bar. "A large luxury hot chocolate, please, with extra marshmallows. Oh, and an orange juice."

"Anything to eat?" the man behind the counter asked. "Aside from the marshmallows," he added drily.

Josh eyed up the pastries and cakes. "One rocky road and…" He pointed at one of the cakes. "Is that lemon drizzle?"

"It is indeed."

"Wowza. My favourite. I'll have a slice of that as well."

"Fine. I'll bring them over in a minute."

Josh paid and returned to the table. Lily was much more casually dressed than the previous evening, still with jeans but a blouse that spoke less of party glitz and more of town centre shopping. He guessed it was because she was now being herself rather than acting out the role of 'Blossom'.

"Thanks for texting me Callum and Owen's numbers," he said.

"No problem. Have you rung them?"

"I've rung Callum and I've arranged to see him after we've finished. I'll leave Owen until tomorrow I think. I want to discuss the best approach with the guv first."

"You rate your boss a lot, don't you?"

"Oh yeah. He's great."

"Here are our drinks. Oh, that's nice of you, Josh. How did you guess?"

"Guess what?"

To Josh's horror, she held her hand out, took the lemon drizzle cake from the waiter and placed it on the table next to her orange juice. "It looks lovely. Thanks very much. It's been my favourite for a long time."

"Mine too," Josh said under his breath. *Maybe they'll have some at the cafe where I'm meeting Callum*, he thought.

"I managed to talk to Ozzy Vaughan," she said.

Josh waited until he'd swallowed his first bite of shortbread before answering. "Excellento," he said. "How did it go?"

She gave a little laugh. "His act has been well-honed but that's all it is."

"What do you mean?"

"His accent's completely false. It takes an actor to see an actor and that man is faking it to the hills and back."

"That's interesting. Did he do or say anything that makes you think he might be taking advantage of anyone at the party?"

"Not at first, but the whole time he was talking to me, or rather at me, he didn't look at me once. His eyes were flitting from group to group and it was obvious he was eyeing up the younger guests."

"And then?" Josh prompted.

"After a few minutes, he seemed to forget I was standing next to him, or maybe he didn't care. Anyway, he called out to a young lad who was walking past. His exact words were 'Hey kid. Wanna go inside and boom boom with Ozzy's shagpile?'"

Josh pulled a disgusted face. "Does that mean what I think it means?"

"I looked it up," Lily said, "and yes, it does."

Josh took his notebook out and jotted down exactly what Ozzy had said.

"That's great evidence," he said as he popped the last piece of millionaire's shortbread in his mouth. He pointed at Lily's drizzle cake which was only half gone. "Are you finishing that?"

"Definitely," she said and picked up another forkful. "It's delicious."

"Mmm."

"So," she went on, "what are you going to do next, aside from speaking to Callum?"

"That'll depend on Luke."

"If you want my help with anything let me know."

"Thanks, Lily. I will. I'd better be off now. It'll take me

twenty minutes or so to walk to where I'm meeting Callum."

"Bye, Josh. And thanks again for the cake."

"Uh, yeah. No problemo."

As he walked away from the cafe, Josh reflected on what Lily had said about Ozzy. His attempt to entice the boy into the house definitely moved things forward, and what she had said about him faking his accent was intriguing. He was probably only doing it to project the image necessary for his rapping and hosting persona but could there be another reason? He'd be interested to get Luke's views on it.

Josh reached the location Callum had given him but could see no sign of the 'Cafe by the Furnace'. He walked back, crossed the road, returned to the location he started at, looked up at the large sign and realised the large blue-on-white sign read 'Shop and Cafe' in small letters underneath the headline 'Glass-blowing Studio'.

"Gotcha," he said, aiming a finger gun at the sign.

He walked inside to find a very different atmosphere from the Forum cafe. There were several groups of customers and big brunches were clearly a thing, but he couldn't see any cakes in evidence.

"Nothing sweet to eat?" he asked the girl behind the counter.

"Home-made lemon drizzle is today's speciality," she said with a smile.

"Brillianto."

"You only just missed out," she added and gestured behind him. "He had the last piece."

Josh turned to see Callum sitting in the corner forking a piece of cake into his mouth. He looked up and said, still savouring his mouthful of lemony wonderfulness, "Hi, George. This is yummy."

"So I see."

"Do you want a Kit Kat?" the girl asked.

"I'll give it a miss, thanks," Josh said. "One luxury hot chocolate please."

"A what?"

Josh sighed. "A mocha then? With extra chocolate."

She shook her head. "I can do a cappuccino."

"Fine."

Her smile returned. "I'll bring it over."

Josh went to join Callum who was shovelling the final piece of cake in his mouth. "Hi," he said. "The cake's all gone."

"Shame," Callum said, wiping his mouth with a napkin. "It's always good here."

"Of course, you live near here, don't you?"

"Just up Guinea Lane. I often come here with Ava. She's my girlfriend. Where do you live?"

"Opposite Lansdown Cricket Club in Weston." Josh smiled. "That side of the ground is the Combe Park End so that's what my mum called our house. I like living there but my girlfriend and I are going to rent a flat together soon."

"Wow! No way would my Mum and Dad let me rent a flat with Ava."

Josh paused. "Callum," he said. "I have an admission to make."

"Really. What's that?"

"My name's not George." He kept his voice as non-Bond as he could as he added. "The name's Josh. Josh Ogden. I was undercover last night."

"Cool. Are you doing a project for school?"

Josh sucked his jaw in. "I'm twenty-two," he said.

Callum laughed and then saw the expression on Josh's face. "Seriously?"

"Yes. I work for Filchers."

"I see." Callum leaned forward and whispered his next words. "Are you a private detective?"

Josh hesitated. "Nearly," he said.

"Nearly?"

Josh waved his hand. "It doesn't matter. The fact is we, that's me and my guv, he's an ex-Detective Chief Inspector by the way, we're looking into Baz Hartman's parties on behalf of, uh…" He thought about how to describe Victor Robertson and settled on, "…a client."

"I see." Callum hesitated before continuing. "Actually, I don't. Why are you looking into them?"

"Our client believes they're being used as a front to groom young boys."

"I'm sixteen," Callum said. "It was my birthday last Thursday. I'm above the age of consent."

"That's not the issue, Callum. And besides some of the others were definitely younger than you. How old is Dylan?"

"He's fifteen."

"Exactly." Josh removed his notebook. "Do you mind if I make notes?"

"Sure."

Josh felt around in his pockets. "Buggery-buggeroo," he said.

"Your cappuccino," the waitress said as she placed his drink in front of him.

"I don't suppose you have a pen, have you?" Josh asked.

"Yes," she said. She returned behind the counter and started drying crockery.

Josh called over. "Could I borrow it please?"

She looked up. "Borrow what?"

"The pen."

"Yes, of course." Her smile returned. "Why didn't you say?"

"I, oh…never mind." Josh stood up, walked the counter and took the pen she held up in front of her. "Thanks," he said.

"No problem."

"Right," Josh said when he was seated again. He

opened the notebook, wrote the date and time down and looked across at Callum. "What's your name?"

"Callum."

"I meant full name."

"Callum Indiana Jones."

"Why did your... No, never mind." Josh wrote the name down. "How were you invited to the party?"

"Eve invited me. I love 'Hall of Flame' and applied to be in the audience for filming. I was unlucky but she sent me a questionnaire and after I completed it she emailed back to say I could come to the party and bring a friend."

"What questions were you asked in the questionnaire?"

"Nothing odd. Where I lived, my age, who I most admired on the programme, why I wanted to be in the audience, that kind of thing."

"I see. And did you bring a friend?"

"No. I said I'd like to bring my girlfriend but she said unfortunately they no longer had space for there to be two of us."

"So Eve knew you weren't gay?"

"Yeah."

Josh made another note. "Who did you meet at the party?"

"Not many people, actually. I got landed with Reggie early on. To begin with it was fine, because he's famous from Towie so it was cool chatting to him. But then he started to get a bit creepy. And when he asked me to go see something which was massive and really impressive I thought he meant... " He pointed through the table in the direction of Josh's groin and lowered his voice. "...his tallywhacker."

"His what?"

"You know." Callum lowered his voice still further. "His wee willy winkie."

Josh stared across the table bemused, then clicked his fingers and exclaimed, "Penis!"

A silence descended on the cafe, and Josh turned to see a woman holding her hands over her young daughter's ears and shaking her head at him disparagingly.

"Sorry," Josh mouthed to her.

"It was an award," Callum went on. "Baz Hartman won it for the first series."

"Right." Josh made a note. "So, aside from Reggie, who else did you meet?"

"Marvin, of course, and he's just as creepy."

Josh jotted this down. "Do you know anything else about Dylan?"

"Only his phone number."

"You've got his number. Great? Could I have it?"

"Sure."

Callum read out Dylan's number from his phone and Josh jotted it down.

"I'll be sitting down with Luke tomorrow to agree next steps," Josh said. "He's the ex-DCI I mentioned. I'll probably be back in touch with more questions. Is that okay?"

"Yes, fine."

After they said their goodbyes Josh headed back to the bus station. He'd achieved a lot and he was feeling pretty pleased with himself. What he fancied now was going to see a movie with Leanne. Yes, that would be great. There was a new Avengers film out that he was dead keen to see.

He was on the bus back to Weston when his phone pinged and he looked down to see a text from Callum.

'Hi Josh,' it read. 'Dylan's texted and he's still at his uncle's. He asked me to go over this afternoon before he returns to Cardiff. Do you want me to tell him about you or to ask him any questions?'

Josh considered suggesting he go along as well but he'd already done enough and it was a Sunday. Besides, he was very attracted to the idea of an afternoon spent in the cinema with Leanne on one side and a jumbo-sized bucket of popcorn on the other.

'Please tell Dylan I'll be in touch,' he wrote. 'I'll contact him tomorrow.'

Chapter 39

He was taking a risk but it would be worthwhile and besides the opportunity was too good to miss.

Two of them! What a stroke of luck that the second fucker was walking right into his grasp.

He considered how to make the most of it and decided he would play them off against each other. He'd really enjoyed threatening the little Welsh bastard with the scimitar. The look on his snivelling little face had been unbelievably satisfying.

But if he had two!

One could watch while he toyed with the other one, then he'd reverse their positions. And he'd take a long time over it, savour every moment.

They deserved it after all.

But first things first.

He pulled down the extendable steps and clambered up into the attic, brushing away a few cobwebs before putting his head above the opening and turning on the light on his phone. He shone it into the far corner and, sure enough, the battered old brown suitcase was there, exactly as he remembered it. He hadn't opened it for four or five years but he had known the contents would come in useful at some point.

He rubbed his hands together then crawled into the space and over the beams, clicked the latch open and pulled up the top of the case.

The canister was on the left. He picked it up and turned it over in his hand. It was full and he'd forgotten how heavy it was.

He was about to close the lid when he noticed another item which he'd completely forgotten about. He laughed to himself as he remembered putting it there. At the time he'd wondered why he was keeping it but he was glad he had. It was going to make things so much more memorable.

He shuffled to one side where there was a cardboard box, with 'Halloween' written on the side in black marker pen and reached inside to pull something out. It was cheap plastic but still in one piece and would be ideal.

He took the three items and crawled back to the ladder and then backwards down the steps to the landing. He went into his bedroom and laid them next to each other on the bed.

They were perfect.

The little bastard was going to be scared shitless.

How delightful!

With a shock, he remembered Rachel Adams.

Fuck!

The bitch was on the verge of death but there was the chance, slight as it might be, that she might recover. If she did she would name him as the person who had pushed her onto the tracks and he couldn't afford that.

He was going to London in a couple of days so he'd have to make time to go to St Mary's Hospital and finish what he'd started.

Who was it who had said 'a life without risks is not worth living'? Some fancy philosopher he supposed but it was true nonetheless.

He rubbed his hands together.

Dealing with Rachel fucking Adams was going to be fun too.

Chapter 40

The street was rough, much rougher than Callum had expected. At least a quarter of the century-old terraced houses were boarded up, and as he passed number 12 he saw it had a big red-on-white sign over the front door saying 'Do Not Enter - Danger of Collapse'. Dylan had said his uncle was cool so maybe he was squatting, but even so this was a harsh neighbourhood to be living in.

Had he got it wrong? Perhaps it wasn't Lord Avenue. He clicked on Dylan's message to check. *'My uncle's home is 32 Lord Avenue,'* it read. *'We may be in the garden and will leave the front door open.'*

When he reached number 32 he looked at the facade and felt the need to check the text again to be absolutely certain. He did so, looked back at the house and shook his head. The front door wasn't so much left open as hanging off, and all three windows that faced the road were broken and backed by sheets of board.

He shrugged.

Ah well, he was here now. Presumably, the rooms at the back were habitable even if the ones at the front weren't.

The gate was also hanging off its hinges. Callum pushed it out of the way and then stepped hesitantly to the front door. There was a four or five-inch gap between the door and the jamb and he bent his head to it and called out.

"Hi, Dylan. It's Callum. Are you there?"

There was no answer.

He pulled at the door, half-expecting it to collapse, and it swung slowly open with a creak, only held on by the middle of the three hinges, the other two having long since rusted away. After some movement, it stopped and wouldn't budge any further, but there was enough room for him to slide in through the gap.

The house was in no better condition on the inside. There was wallpaper peeling from the walls and even exposed brickwork in several places. To the left were stairs but they didn't look as if they would take a mouse's weight let alone his.

"Dylan," he called again. "Are you there?"

Still no answer.

Callum decided he might as well try the back garden now he'd made it this far. If they weren't there he'd message Dylan and ask what was going on.

He stepped down the corridor towards a door at the far end that he guessed led to a kitchen and onwards to the garden. He passed an open door on his right and then stopped dead in his tracks.

He could have sworn he'd heard something, a soft padding sound.

He hoped it wasn't a rat. He hated rats.

Callum stepped back, looked through the open doorway and his eyes widened in horror. A red skeletal face was staring back at him.

Before he could scream a hand came up from the black-clad body beneath the skull, pointed a nozzle and squeezed.

There was a low hissing sound and moisture hit him across his nose and cheeks. Callum gasped and put his hands to his face, trying to wipe away the liquid that was burning into his eyes and up his nostrils.

Beyond his own screams, he heard a long low chuckle.

The cackling of the devil.

Chapter 41

Luke and Detective Inspector Pete Gilmore were at their usual table in the corner of The Good Bear Cafe.

Over breakfast, a full English for Pete and steak, eggs and chips for Luke, they talked about their weekends. Pete described his strained journey to Leeds for a large family christening, while Luke told his friend about the dramatic, but far from unpleasant, arrival of his step-niece Marion from California. He chose not to mention what had happened to Sam on the Saturday evening.

"So, what's the favour?" Pete asked as he put a serviette to his lips to remove the lingering brown sauce.

Luke explained about the Ethics Team's investigations into possible impropriety by GNE employees, and how Rachel Adams had asked questions for him at GNE's Head Office and put noses out of joint.

"The thing is," he concluded, "Rachel fell onto an underground line on Friday evening. She's in a coma and the doctors haven't given her much chance of coming out of it. Her mother is convinced she was pushed but the Met have told her they're convinced it was attempted suicide."

"What's your view?" Pete asked.

"I spoke to Rachel on Friday morning and she was in a very good mood. She could have slipped or tripped, but I find it hard to believe she would try to kill herself." He paused. "The truth is, Pete, I'd arranged to go for a meal with her this evening."

"Christ! I'm sorry, Luke. So she and you were seeing each other?"

Luke gave a dry laugh. "This would have been our first date."

"I'm guessing you want me to find out where the investigation is at?"

"If you could."

"I'll see what I can find out, but you know what they can be like. Us lot in Somerset are country bumpkins as far as the Met is concerned. I'll do my best though."

"Thanks. I owe you one." He gestured to Pete's empty cup. "Another?"

"Yes please."

Luke turned to the woman at the counter. "Could we have another double espresso and a flat white please?"

"Be with you in a minute," she said.

"I could do with your advice on something," Pete said when Luke turned back to face him.

"Fire away."

"I'm working with West Midlands Police on a murder investigation and they're driving me up the wall."

"What's the case?"

"Last Wednesday morning a woman walking her dog by Chew Valley Lake spotted a bloated hand in amongst the reeds. Turned out to be a young boy but the body was in a right state." Pete shook his head as the memory came back to him. "It wasn't just that he was bloated. Most of him was gone, Luke. I mean, chewed away. Reckon it must have been the pike. Put me off fishing there I can tell you. Ah, thanks."

The waitress put their coffees in front of them and returned to the counter.

"Anyway," Pete went on, "Sally Croft completed the post-mortem and said he'd had his throat slit and had been dead for at least a week, probably more like two weeks. His teeth were about the only part of him left intact so we did a search of dental records but he didn't match with any mispers in our patch."

Luke took a sip of his coffee. "I'm guessing he matched a missing boy in the West Midlands," he said.

Pete nodded. "A fifteen-year-old from Solihull. Ethan Jarvis. Been missing a couple of weeks."

"What's the problem?"

"It's the DI assigned to it in Birmingham that's the problem. Her name's Jill North and she's, excuse my French…" He lowered his voice to a whisper. "…a fucking liability."

"I take it the investigation's on Holmes?"

Pete nodded. "Yes, but she's not updating it as she should."

Luke had seen this happen before. The Home Office Large Major Enquiry System was used by all UK police forces to share information or conduct a joint investigation, but its usefulness depended on the quality of the information entered.

"Who's the Senior Investigating Officer?"

Pete gave a little snort. "Applejack would you believe?"

"You're joking? I thought he was on traffic."

"The Chief assigned him."

Luke shook his head. Detective Chief Inspector Jack Bramley, nickname Applejack, was one of the laziest officers he'd ever come across.

"What do I do, Luke?" Pete asked. "I don't want to go over Applejack's head, but…" He held his hands out, palms up.

Luke gave it a few moments thought. "Have you found anything out about where or when the body was put in the lake?" he asked.

"We've got some tyre tracks we're following up on, and there are a couple of people who've come forward saying they saw two men acting suspiciously."

"I suggest you invite the Birmingham DI down. Tell her you'd value her opinion on what you've found and it would be useful if she saw the lake."

Pete considered this. "Mmm," he said. "That might work. Thanks, Luke. I'll give it a go."

*

Luke was early to Filcher's Monday morning meeting for once.

"Hi, Gloria," he said to Filcher's secretary.

She looked up and smiled. "Good morning, Luke."

He indicated his boss's office with his thumb. "How's his mood?"

"Very good for a Monday. Not sure what he was up to at the weekend but he's full of the joys of spring." She paused and pursed her lips. "Well, as full of the joys of spring as he ever gets."

Luke chuckled. "Am I okay to go in?

"Certainly. You're the first."

He went in to find Filcher standing up and polishing the glass of a photo frame with a white handkerchief.

"Ah, Luke. Sit down, sit down." He almost smiled but not quite.

"Giving Boris a shine?" Luke asked as he took a seat at the conference table.

"I was with him," Filcher said as he returned the frame to pride of place on his mahogany desk and admired it. "On Saturday," he added before returning the handkerchief to the pocket of his waistcoat and turning the photo so that it was facing outwards. It showed a younger Filcher with the then-Member of Parliament.

"That must have been nice," Luke lied. "Where did you see him?"

"At Windsor."

"Castle?"

Filcher was still looking at the photo. "Racecourse," he said absent-mindedly. "Had a catch-up. Good to see him. We go back, you know."

"To Eton. Yes, you've told me."

"He's doing well."

"Despite the challenge in the courts?"

Filcher waved his hand dismissively. "Fiddle-faddle. Good sort, Boris. Decent." He bent down, peered at the image in the frame and nodded. "He's one of us."

"One of you?"

"Yes." Filcher stroked his Old Etonian tie. "We go back, you know," he said again.

"So did you and Boris go to the races together?"

"Not quite. Bumped into him. Literally, as it happens. Hah!"

"And then you had a long chat?"

"Short chat," Filcher corrected. "But enough. Good to see him. Blighter didn't recognise me at first. Must have been drinking. Hah."

Luke was relieved to hear the door open behind him.

"Hi James, Fred," Luke said as the Heads of HR and Marketing walked in.

"Morning, Luke," Fred Tanner said.

"Glen can't make it, Mr Filcher," James said as he and Fred sat opposite Luke at the conference table.

Filcher tore his eyes away from the photo and tutted. "Not good enough." He clicked a button on his desk phone.

"Yes, Mr Filcher," Gloria said.

"Find out why Glen's not here, Gloria." He hung up and harrumphed. "These meetings are important," he said. "Have to keep my eye on the ball, before it, ah…"

"Goes in the net," Fred offered.

"Exactly." Filcher jerked his head up and down a few times, bringing an image to Luke's mind of a nodding dog on a car's rear parcel shelf. "My role," he went on, "is to steady the ship."

"Before it goes off the rails," Fred said, trying but failing to keep the grin from his face.

Filcher nodded again and reached for a stack of papers on his desk. He kept one sheet for himself and handed the rest out. Luke looked down at the agenda in disbelief.

"As you see," Filcher said, "We have fourteen items to discuss today."

His phone buzzed and he clicked the button.

"Glen's had an accident," Gloria said. "Fell over in the corridor on the first floor."

"I need to go," James and Luke said in unison.

"HR matter," James added.

"Ethical considerations," Luke said.

Filcher sighed. "Very well. Be quick. Fred and I will start without you."

Fred looked across at Luke and mouthed, "You lucky bastard."

Chapter 42

Glen was lying on his back when Luke and James reached him. He was grimacing in pain and had both hands cupped over his groin.

"What happened?" Luke asked.

"Fucking… C… C… T… V," Glen said in between gasps. He nodded his head to the security camera on the floor beside him and then up at the ceiling.

Luke looked up and saw that the mount was hanging on by one screw, the exposed cable beside it.

"You're lucky you didn't electrocute yourself," he said.

"Don't… feel… lucky."

Luke looked up to see Helen and Sam emerge from the Ethics Room a few yards down the corridor.

"Hi," Sam said as they approached. She held up a small red bag. "First aid kit."

Helen looked down at Glen. "Have you cut yourself?" she asked.

Glen shrugged "Don't… know." He nodded his head to his hands. "Hit… ghouls."

Helen raised one eyebrow. "Ghouls?"

"Family…"

"Family?"

Glen gave an audible sigh. "Family… ghouls."

"He means jewels," Luke said.

Helen shook her head. "Right, take your hands away, Glen, and let's have a wee look."

His hands pressed down even harder and he gave a squeal of pain. "Fuck!"

Luke looked at Sam and saw that she was fighting back laughter.

"I don't think this needs four of us," James said.

"Are you returning to Filcher's meeting?" Luke asked.

"I'd better log this accident first. How long do you think the meeting will take?"

"Anything up to two hours."

James smiled. "The system's very slow. I think logging this may take as long as a hundred and twenty minutes."

"Stop being a baby," Helen said after James had left. "Unzip yourself. I used to be a nurse so I've seen it all before."

Glen looked at her, gave a grudging nod and then looked pointedly at Luke and Sam.

"We'll leave you to it," Luke said, picking up the hint and grateful for the opportunity to get away.

"Dinnae worry," Helen said. She pointed at Glen's groin. "I'm pretty certain there won't be much to see in there."

Luke followed Sam back into the Ethics Room and was pleased to see that they were alone.

"Maj and Josh are interviewing someone on the third floor," Sam said.

He gestured for her to sit down at the office table and took the chair opposite. "How are you feeling?" he asked.

"Fine," she said, but her attempt at a smile was weak and strained. "I've told Helen by the way."

"How did your mum take it?"

"She was fine, though not at first."

"Why not?"

She gave a thin dry laugh. "Brendan rang her before I got the chance to and told her I'd tried it on with him."

Luke shook his head. "He can't be allowed to get away with this, Sam. You said that his two colleagues were going to raise it with someone senior?"

"Yes, Grant and Phil said they would take it to someone called Terence Nix. Apparently, he's Director of News at NTV Bristol."

"Today?"

"Yes, hopefully."

"Please tell me when they get back to you. If they haven't called by lunchtime I suggest you chase them. And if you want my help with anything let me know. I'll do anything I can to make sure he pays."

"I will, Luke. Thanks." She looked up as Helen walked in. "How did it go?"

"There was nothing to see," Helen said. She grinned. "Aside from his wee fella that is."

"So he's fine?" Luke asked.

"Bruised like buggery, and walking like a cowboy who thinks he's still on his horse, but aye, other than that he's dandy."

"And you used to be a nurse?"

"Who, me? Nah, always been a lawyer."

"Hi, guv," Josh said as he and Maj walked in. "We just passed Glen Baxter in the corridor. He looked in pain."

"He's lost his horse," Helen said.

"Pardon?"

"We'll explain later," Luke said. "I want to add what we learned at the weekend to the investigation board and agree on our next steps. But first, Josh learned some sad news at the party. Josh…"

"I heard it from Damon Prendergast," Josh said. He told me that Rachel Adams had an accident on Friday. She's in a coma."

Sam put both hands to her mouth.

"What happened?" Helen asked.

"She fell onto the line at Regents Park underground," Luke said. "She's in St Mary's Hospital in London and the doctors fear she might not recover."

"Christ, that's awful," Sam said. "Are you going to visit her in hospital?"

"I might do."

There was a moment's pause, then Luke said, "Shall we start?"

They all agreed and Helen walked over to the board, marker pen and Post-its at the ready.

"Josh," Luke said. "Can you start by summarising how the evening went, please? Once you've done that you can run through each of the people you met at the party and if relevant we'll add them to the board."

"Sure, guv," Josh said. He summarised the evening beginning with meeting Owen outside and concluding with his encounter with Baz Hartman.

"And this man was sucking his toes?" Helen asked.

A shiver ran through Josh as he remembered the scene in the bedroom. He nodded. "He asked if I wanted to join in."

"And then you got your phone back?" Luke asked, bringing them back on track.

"That's right, guv. From a man called Kieran. He and another guy, Nat, were in dinner jackets and dickie-bows and seem to be Baz's bodyguards."

"Right, that's an excellent summary, Josh. Now can you run us through the new names?"

"Sure." Josh opened his notebook. "First, the three young lads I met. I saw others but these were the only ones I spent any time with." He waited for Helen to stick three Post-its on the board.

"Owen Lambert's the boy I met outside. He's 16, lives in Bristol, and this was his second time at one of Baz's parties. The first was a couple of weeks ago but it ended early. He told me that the friend he went with has been snubbing him ever since and he doesn't know why."

"Did he tell you his friend's name?" Luke asked.

Josh shook his head. "No, but I've got his contact details so I thought I'd ring him today." He waited until Helen had updated Owen's post-it before continuing. "The other two boys were Callum White, who lives in Bath, and Dylan who's from Cardiff. I don't know Dylan's surname but I met Callum yesterday and he texted me afterwards to say he was meeting Dylan and would check it was okay to contact him. I've got both their phone numbers."

Helen added the names to the board.

"How many other teenagers were at the party?" Sam asked.

Josh thought about this for a second. "There were probably twelve altogether. Eve ticked me off on a list when I arrived so she'll know all their names. One of the youngest-looking ones went off with Damon Prendergast at one point and that really creeped me out."

"How old do you think the boy with Damon was?" Luke asked.

"My guess would be fourteen, guv."

Helen added this information to the Damon Prendergast Post-it.

"Okay," Luke said, looking at the board. "So there were a dozen or so younger lads at the party who we believe were invited by Eve. One of them went off with Damon Prendergast and three others we have contact details for. Can you tell the team about Lily, Josh?"

"Six women arrived together part-way through the evening," Josh said, "and I got chatting to one of them, a woman called Blossom. Only she wasn't."

"She wasnae a woman?" Helen asked.

"Oh yes, she's a woman, but her real name's Lily not Blossom. She's an actress and it seems that she and the five other women were invited to stop the parties being all-male. 'To add some glamour' was what Lily was told."

"What about the others, Josh?" Luke asked, gesturing to three other Post-its. "You've talked about Baz, who it seems likes the company of older men, and Damon, who's definitely now higher on our suspect list. But what about Ozzy Vaughan, Reggie Dowden and Marvin Winespottle?

"Ozzy's a complex character," Josh said. "He's full of himself and affects a gangster rap accent which Lily is convinced he's faking."

"But you didn't see him doing anything untoward?"

"I didn't, but Lily did. She heard him ask one of the young boys if he wanted to have sex with him."

Helen added this information to the board.

"Reggie and Marvin," Josh went on, "were definitely chasing Callum and Dylan."

"It reinforces what Marvin, drunk as he was, told me at the awards ceremony," Maj said.

Luke leaned forward and stared at the board, drumming his fingers on the table as he considered the options. After a couple of minutes, he made his mind up. "I think we've got enough with what Josh and Maj have uncovered," he said. "I'm going to talk to Victor and make an appointment to see someone senior at GNE. In the meantime, let's try and get even more evidence."

He turned to Josh. "Can you get back in touch with Callum and Dylan and see if they can provide anything else useful?"

"Will do, guv."

He addressed his next comment to Sam. "Sam," he said, would you mind ringing Owen? From what Josh has told me I think he might be more receptive if a woman questions him."

Sam nodded. "No problem."

"Great. Once I've rung Victor I'm going to see if I can speak to Eve and persuade her to share her party invitation list with me. Maj, are you okay to join me? You met her at the awards ceremony and it seems like you got on."

"Sure," Maj said.

"Helen, can you do some more digging on everyone we've got up on the board?"

Helen nodded. "Nae problem. I'll start with Damon, Ozzy, Reggie and Marvin as they're the ones you'll most likely be taking to GNE senior management."

"Great. Thanks."

Chapter 43

Callum cowered back in his chair as the man who had tear-gassed him leaned forward, his eyes blazing. The skeleton mask was long gone, but Callum thought of him as Red Skull now. He was big, he was strong and he was the personification of evil.

"Who the fuck is Josh?" Red Skull demanded, spittle hitting Callum on the bridge of his nose as he spat the words out.

"He's... he's a friend."

"From where?"

"S... school. He's in my... my class."

Red Skull turned Callum's phone around. "See here," he said and jabbed at the message on the screen. "He's asking about Dylan. How the fuck does he know about that waste of space?" He gestured to the boy in the corner of the container. "You only met on Saturday night."

"I told him... I told Josh. On Sunday. We m... met for a coffee."

Red Skull grunted. "And he's in your class?"

"Yes."

"Do you think I'm stupid?"

"No."

"Then what fucking day is it?"

"M... Monday." It dawned on Callum what that meant. "He thinks I'm at school. He's on a trip," he blurted out. "A school trip."

"Where?"

Callum thought back to the last outing he'd been on. "Stratford-on-Avon," he said. "To learn about Shakespeare."

"Mmm." Red Skull took a step back. "And why does

your friend Josh want Dylan's contact details?"

Callum swallowed. "I told him about the party. How good it was. And I guess he... he wants to see if Dylan enjoyed it as well."

"Fucking lies!"

"No. It's the truth..."

A hideous smile wrapped itself across Red Skull's face and he tapped his nose with his index finger.

"I've got an idea," he said. "When do they return from Stratford?"

Callum gulped. What answer should he give? And what if Josh texted him again? He might give something away about who he really was.

"Are you fucking listening to me?"

"S... Sorry. It's today. They return today. Late this evening."

"Late?"

"Yes."

"It'll have to be tomorrow then," Red Skull said under his breath. He bashed away on the phone for a few seconds.

"What are you doing?" Callum asked.

"I'm not doing anything," he said, still grinning. "*You're* sending Josh a message." He hit the button. "There. Gone."

"What did you say?"

"I dangled some bait. Now let's see if the little fucker bites."

S J Richards

Chapter 44

As expected, given it was a school day, Owen's phone had gone straight to voicemail. Rather than leave a message, Sam decided to text him.

'Hi,' she wrote. *'I'm George's friend and wondered if we could talk. Samantha.'*

Her phone beeped less than a minute later.

'Hi Samantha. I'll ring at lunchtime. Owen x.'

The kiss was an interesting touch, Sam thought, but not unexpected given what Josh had said about him.

She laid the phone to one side and debated whether to ring Grant or Phil. No, she decided, better to give them until after lunch. If she hadn't heard by 2 pm she'd ring one of them.

She googled Terence Nix, the man at NTV they were due to be contacting, and was pleased to find a LinkedIn entry for him. He had been Director of News for nearly two years, having previously been an anchorman and before that a journalist at Sky.

She went back to the search and looked through photos of several Terence Nixes before choosing a slightly overweight man in his mid to late fifties who somehow looked right. She clicked on the photo and was pleased to see she'd chosen correctly. An article from the Bristol Herald Courier showed him beaming and passing an oversized cheque to a middle-aged blonde woman.

Local Man Raises £1500
for Cancer Research

Terence Nix, father of two and a senior manager at NTV in Bristol, has raised over £1500 through a sponsored skydive. 'My mother died from cancer,' he said. 'I wanted to do what I could to help this worthy cause.' Alison Newton from Cancer Research accepted the cheque and commented, 'Terence has done a wonderful job. We're so grateful.'

Sam scanned through the rest of the article which revealed that Nix was frightened of heights and that he was happily married to Stephanie and had three grown-up children. It wasn't very illuminating but it did present a picture of a decent man.

Hopefully, that meant he would be receptive to what Grant and Phil had to tell him about Brendan.

Her phone rang and she looked down to see Owen had initiated a FaceTime video. Ah well, she thought as she accepted the call, in for a penny in for a pound.

The face that appeared on the screen was unmistakably teenage. It wasn't that his face was overrun with acne, indeed he didn't appear to have any spots at all, but there was a smidgin of brown wispiness on his upper lip and in the middle of his chin that suggested hair was trying to grow but did not yet need paring back.

"Hi," Owen said, looking a little confused. "Is Samantha there?"

"I'm Samantha," Sam said, smiling. "But you can call me Sam."

"But you're… I mean, like…"

"Old," she suggested.

"No, ah, yes. Well, not old, but…" He looked to one side and called "I'll be there in a minute" to someone she couldn't see, then turned back and said, "Sorry, I have to go. I'm between lessons."

"Please ring me as soon as you get the chance, Owen. It's vital I talk to you about Baz Hartman's parties." He looked unsure so she added, "George isn't George. He and I are private investigators and his real name's Josh."

"He's not fifteen?"

"No. He's twenty-two."

"Cool. Yeah, I'll call when lessons end."

The call ended and she wondered if seeing her had frightened the poor lad. Saying 'George isn't George' probably hadn't helped either.

"That was an odd wee call," Helen said from the other side of the office. "Did I hear you say you're old? What does that make me?"

"Young at heart," Sam said.

"Aye. I'll settle for that."

Sam's phone rang.

"You'd best get that," Helen said. "Might be another toyboy." She turned back to her laptop.

The screen said 'number withheld'. Sam clicked to accept the call.

"Hi," she said.

"Sam?"

She recognised Grant's voice immediately. "Hi, Grant."

"Not good news, I'm afraid," he said.

"Is Terence Nix away?"

"No, he's here today. Phil and I have just come out of his office."

Sam sighed as she realised what was coming. "What did he say?"

"That in his view Brendan is a decent and hard-working employee who would never take advantage of a woman."

"What?" Sam shook her head in exasperation.

"He also said that Brendan is an honest man and he would always accept his word over someone he'd never met."

"You told him what he tried to do to me?"

"Of course, but he said we weren't there, and why should anyone believe a story from a woman who had had a few too many glasses of wine."

"I wasn't drunk!"

"I know."

It dawned on Sam what must have happened. "Brendan had already got to him, hadn't he?"

"I think so, yes." Grant paused. "Terence also told Phil and I to be careful."

"Careful of what?"

"Of what we say. He reminded us that we're both on twelve-month contracts which are coming up for renewal."

"You mean he threatened you?"

"Not in so many words."

Sam took a deep breath. "Well, thanks for trying," she said.

"Sorry we couldn't be more help."

"It's okay. You did your best."

Sam ended the call and felt a hand on her shoulder.

"I got the gist," Helen said. "You need to tell Luke."

"Yes, you're probably right. Any idea where he is?"

"With Filcher, I think."

Sam's phone rang and again she saw 'number withheld' on the screen.

"Grant again," she said to Helen who mouthed 'fingers crossed' and returned to her desk.

Maybe something positive had happened after all. She accepted the call.

"Hi, Grant," she said.

"Who's Grant?" Tony said. "Is he the new love of your life?"

"What now, Tony?" Sam said, her voice flat.

"Jazelle's here, Sammy."

"Bully for you."

"We work together."

"At the lap dancing club?"

"In the garage," he said, the sarcasm lost on him. "Jazelle's our receptionist."

"I'm at work, Tony."

She heard him talking to someone and a woman's voice

came on the line.

"Hi, Sammy. I'm Jazelle."

Her voice was gravelly and husky. It was Marilyn Monroe with added nicotine and estuary. Tony doubtless found it sexy, but all it did for Sam was remind her of the danger of smoking near the docks.

"How can I help you, Jazelle?" Sam asked.

"Tone said you know origami."

"Paper-folding?"

Sam heard Tony's voice again. Jazelle replied to him and then came back on the line.

"Silly me," she said and giggled. "Karate. I meant karate."

This conversation was the last thing Sam needed at the moment.

"I have to go," she said.

"Minge," Jazelle said abruptly.

Sam raised an eyebrow. "Pardon?"

There was another mumbled conversation.

"Minge a twa," Jazelle said. "The karate was a rose."

"You mean a ruse."

"Yeah, that. It was Tone's idea, but I'm up for it if you are."

"Up for what?"

"Minge a twa," she repeated.

"Oh. You mean…" Sam put her hand to her forehead. "Please can you put Tony back on?"

"Yeah, sure."

"Hi, Sammy," Tony said. "What do you think?"

"I think I need to get back to work."

"We were good together, babe. We…"

She hung up. What on earth had she ever seen in the man?

Chapter 45

"Your friend needs to hire a private detective," Luke said, looking up at his boss. Despite being almost a foot shorter than his Head of Ethics, Filcher's chair was designed so that he was raised above anyone sitting opposite.

"I paid for that detecting course," Filcher said. "About time it was put to use."

"I assure you that it is being put to use."

"Pah. What's the fellow working on then?"

"He's been doing some excellent work for GNE."

Filcher raised an eyebrow. "Really? GNE, eh? Important prospect."

"Exactly, Mr Filcher."

"Yes, need to keep Joe on it."

"Josh," Luke corrected.

"But what about Bertie?"

"I know some excellent people he could speak to."

"Mmm."

Filcher's desk phone buzzed and he pressed the button. "Yes," he snapped.

"Sam Chambers is here," Gloria said. "She's waiting to see Luke."

Luke stood up and walked to the door.

"We haven't finished," Filcher said.

Luke sighed. "I'll ring him, but I can't promise anything."

"Right. Good." He bent back to his desk phone. "Gloria, give Bertie Fotheringay's contact details to Luke, will you?"

"Certainly, Mr Filcher."

"Hi Sam," Luke said when he saw her by Gloria's desk. "Is everything okay?"

"Sure. I could do with a word though."

"You can use Glen's office," Gloria said. "He's out at a meeting."

"Thanks, Gloria."

"I'll email Mr Fotheringay's details to you."

Luke led Sam to Glen's office and opened the door for her to enter. It was even more of a mess than when he had last been inside, with papers strewn across the desk and onto the floor. There were rubber dumbbells laid across the arms of two chairs. He picked them up, put them on the floor and gestured for Sam to sit down.

"I take it Brendan's colleagues have rung," he said.

"Yes. Grant rang a few minutes ago. He and Phil got nowhere with the senior guy at NTV. What's more, he issued loosely veiled threats about what might happen if they said anything more about it."

Luke shook his head. "How do you feel?"

"Resigned, I suppose, even though I thought they'd get somewhere. This morning I googled the man they were seeing and he seems like such a nice guy. He did a sponsored parachute jump to raise money for Cancer Research."

"What's his name?"

"Terence Nix."

"Right. Leave it with me."

"What are you going to do?"

"I'm going to have a word with Mr Nix. And don't worry about Grant and Phil, I'll leave them out of it."

"You don't have to."

"I know."

Sam hesitated for a second. "What happened to Rachel is horrible," she said. "Are you going to visit her in hospital?"

"I haven't decided," Luke said. "I hardly knew her, but we were supposed to be going out this evening."

"I'm sure her family would appreciate it if you did."

Luke thought back to his conversation with Wendy, Rachel's mum. "Yes," he said. "You're probably right. I could go in after I see Victor, and hopefully someone senior, at GNE."

His phone rang.

"Ah, that's Victor now. Do you mind?"

"Not at all. I'll get back to the Ethics Room."

Luke gave Sam a wave as she left the room and accepted the call.

"Hi, Victor," he said. "Thanks for ringing back."

"No problem, dear. What can I do you for?"

"You were right about the parties."

"Oh my. I was so hoping I was wrong. What have you found out?"

"Quite a lot. I'm thinking of coming to London tomorrow. Could we meet late morning?"

"Of course."

"How difficult is it to line up a meeting with a GNE senior executive?"

Victor gave a little laugh. "I can generally find a way."

"In that case, could you arrange for me to see someone early afternoon?"

"I'll see what I can do."

"Thanks. I suggest we meet at a cafe, say at 11:30, rather than at GNE."

"I know the very place. I'll text you details."

"Thanks, Victor. See you tomorrow."

As soon as the call ended Luke raced back downstairs and was pleased to see all of his team were back in the Ethics Room.

"I have to leave now," he said, "and may or may not be back later today. Tomorrow, I'm going to GNE in London. If any of you get any further with your various lines of enquiry let me know."

"I've found out Eve's home address," Maj said. "Her name's Montgomery and she lives in Midford."

"Great. See if you can find out when she's likely to be at home. I'd like us to try and speak to her today if possible." He glanced at Sam before continuing. "I'm heading to Bristol first so I'll meet you there."

"Okay, Luke."

Luke climbed behind the wheel of his company Beemer and sat quietly for a few seconds. He was seething, but he knew that anger would hinder rather than help. He had to take a measured approach if he was going to get anywhere.

He started the car and headed out of the car park, keeping well within the speed limit. As he drove, his mind whirred as he considered how best to deal with Terence Nix.

Sam had said an internet search had revealed an apparently pleasant man. Perhaps he could play on that.

Yes, that might work.

It took just over an hour to get to NTV's Bristol office which was just outside the city centre, a sparkling new four-storey building in a small business park with glass to the walls and a large 'NTV' sign above the entrance. Luke parked in a visitor's spot and walked into reception.

"Good afternoon," the young lady behind the visitor's desk said as he approached. "What's the name?"

"Luke Sackville."

She scanned a list in front of her, then turned over six or seven visitor's badges that were laid out next to it.

"I'm sorry, Mr Sackville, I don't seem to have a record of your visit. Who are you seeing?"

"Terence Nix."

"And he's expecting you, is he?"

"Yes."

"Okay. I'll ring his secretary."

She rang a number. "Rosie," she said when it was answered. "I've got a Mr Luke Sackville here. He says Terence is expecting him."

There was a mumbling at the other end, then the

receptionist said to Luke. "Who do you work for, Mr Sackville?"

"Cancer Research," he said.

She passed this on. There was a further pause and then she said, "Rosie will come down in a minute. I'm ever so sorry about the mix-up. I'll print you a visitor's pass while you're waiting."

"Thanks."

A few minutes later he was sporting a badge on a lanyard and being escorted upstairs by a slim young woman with short curly black hair.

"I'm so sorry you weren't on the list," she said as they reached the first floor.

"Don't worry," Luke said. "I didn't know myself that I was coming until earlier today."

She led him to an office which had all-glass walls. Inside he saw a middle-aged man dressed casually in a navy sweatshirt and jeans. He looked up and smiled as he saw Luke approach.

Rosie opened the door for Luke to enter. "Would you like a coffee, Mr Sackville?"

"I'd love one," he said. "Strong and black if possible."

"Terence?"

"Yes please, Rosie," Terence said.

She left and Terence rose from behind his desk, shook Luke's hand and gestured for him to sit at one of two orange armchairs. They were angled so that both faced the exterior window, though the view was nothing to write home about, showing only other almost identical buildings further on in the business park.

"I'll stand if you don't mind," Luke said. "I've been in the car for over an hour." He walked to the window.

"Fine," Terence said as he sat on one of the armchairs. "How can I help you, uh, Luke, is it?"

"That's right. It's Luke." Luke said, ignoring the other half of the question. He pointed at the buildings outside the window. "Are those NTV's offices as well?"

"No. The nearest one is Microsoft and the far one is Bannermans."

"Really?" Luke turned around. "Is that the business outsourcing company?"

"I think so, yes."

"I had dealings with them a few months ago."

"Are they corporate donors then?"

"To Cancer Research?" Luke shrugged. "I really wouldn't know. Possibly."

"But I thought…"

"There were ethical problems between my company and theirs," Luke went on, talking over him. "It was a very nasty business."

"I was told you worked for Cancer Research."

Luke took a business card from his pocket and gave it to Terence. "That's me," he said. "As you can see, I'm Head of Ethics. Do you believe in ethics, Terence?"

"Yes, of course. But why…"

"So what's more important to you? Ethics, morality and principles or supporting your staff through thick and thin, regardless of what they've done?"

"Well, I…"

The door opened and Rosie walked in bearing a tray with two cups on it.

"Your coffee," she said.

"Thanks, Rosie," Luke said, smiling. "Terence and I are discussing ethics. Would you like to join us?"

Rosie looked at Luke and then at her boss, confusion written across her face.

Luke decided to take a punt on something.

"Do you know Brendan Doyle, Rosie?"

She tried to keep a straight face but for a fraction of a second her upper lip formed into an expression of disgust. It vanished as soon as it appeared but it was enough.

"I, ah, yes. He's a producer."

"And he's got a certain reputation, is that right?"

"You don't have to answer," Terence said.

Luke could see internal forces vying with each other as Rosie debated whether to support her boss or do what was right. After a few seconds, her back stiffened as she came to a decision.

"Everyone knows about him," she said. "All the women know to stay out of his way."

"Rosie!" Terence said.

"Thanks, Rosie," Luke said. "And don't worry. You won't get into any trouble, I promise you."

Rosie edged out of the room and Luke walked towards Terence until he was towering over him.

"On Saturday night," he said through clenched teeth, "Brendan Doyle tried to rape one of my friends."

"I don't, I mean I…"

"I believe you were told about it and refused to believe it. Can I ask why?"

"He's a good employee. Been here for years. What Rosie just said, I didn't know that."

"So this is the first time there's ever been a complaint about him?" Terence hesitated and Luke sighed. "How many other complaints have there been?"

Terence slumped back in his chair. "Two," he said, his voice not much more than a whisper.

"Attempted rape?"

"No. Of course not."

"What were they?"

"There was an alleged incident at the Christmas party. A woman accused him of exposing himself in the ladies' loo, but…"

"You put it down to drunkenness?"

Terence bowed his head. "Yes."

"What was the other *alleged* incident?"

"He supposedly sent a photo of his, uh, erect penis to someone. But she deleted the image so we didn't have proof."

"And after all, he's good at his job?"

Terence had the decency not to say anything.

"My job is unusual," Luke said. "There aren't many companies who have a Head of Ethics, but my god you could do with one here."

"We have a human resources department," Terence said. "They're responsible for, well, for that kind of thing."

"You can't palm it off," Luke said. "You're a senior executive and you have to take responsibility. When was the first complaint about Brendan?"

Terence shrugged. "Probably a year ago. Maybe eighteen months."

"Christ!" Luke sat down in the second armchair and glared across at the other man. "How easy is it to fire him?"

"That's not…"

Luke held his hand up. "Is it easy?"

"Well, yes. It's simple. I could terminate his contract instantly, but…"

"What about a reference?"

"He would get a standard reference, saying he's a good producer, his timekeeping's excellent, that kind of thing."

"And you think that's okay?"

Terence slumped into his chair. "I guess not."

"You guess not? We're talking about a sexual predator for goodness sake. Do you really believe that these three accusations are false? That three separate women have conjured them up out of thin air?"

Terence had the decency to look ashamed. "I didn't put two and two together," he said.

"I think you did, Terence. Your trouble is that you didn't want to rock the boat, did you? Easier to ignore the accusations." He paused to allow this to sink in. "If I had my way he'd be in prison."

Terence started to speak but Luke held his hand up again. "Actually, that's given me an idea," he said. "Is

Brendan in today?"

"Yes. I saw him earlier."

"Good. I want you to ask Rosie to set up a meeting between you and him for first thing tomorrow. Make it clear it's a work meeting."

"Okay."

Terence didn't make any move so Luke opened the door and put his head out. "Rosie," he said, "could you come in for a moment please?"

She came inside, still looking nervous.

"Don't worry," he said once she was in the office and the door was closed again. "You're not in any trouble. Isn't that right, Terence?"

Terence nodded. "Absolutely. In fact, I need to apologise, Rosie. I've been woefully remiss. I should have done something about Brendan Doyle a while ago."

"Please can you set up a meeting," Luke said. "It's for Brendan and Terence in this office at 8 am tomorrow." He turned to Terence. "What's the reason for the meeting, Terence?"

Terence considered this for a moment before saying to Rosie, "Please tell him it's about a second series of 'Raconteur'."

"Will do, Terence," Rosie said. "Do you want to order coffee for two?"

It was Luke who answered. "For five, please. There'll be six of us, but Brendan won't feel like any."

Rosie's nervousness had disappeared and she was almost smiling when she left the room.

Luke took out his mobile and tapped on one of his recent numbers. It was answered after two rings. "I could do with a favour," he said and explained what he wanted.

"He sounds repulsive," DI Pete Gilmore said when he finished.

"Will you help?"

"Definitely. Anything to teach the bastard a lesson."

Chapter 46

"Brillianto!" Josh said.

Helen rotated her chair. "Made a breakthrough?" she asked.

Josh swivelled around and held his phone in the air. "Callum's texted. Dylan's still in Bath and he's up for meeting."

"It's a school day. Shouldn't he be back in Cardiff?"

"I hadn't thought of that." He passed his phone over and Helen read the message.

'Dylan wants to meet. He's still at his uncle's in Bath.'

She looked up. "Short and to the point," she said.

Josh typed on the screen and held it up. "What do you think?"

'Great news but I thought he'd be back in Cardiff.'

"Looks good," she said, and Josh hit send. He turned back around and his phone pinged a couple of minutes later.

'Dylan has a tummy upset. Hoping to be better tomorrow and go home on Wednesday. Wants to know if you can see him tomorrow evening?'

He typed a reply.

'How's 6pm? What's the address?'

The response was almost instantaneous this time.

'6pm Tuesday is good. I'll find out the address and text it to you. Come alone - Dylan's nervous.'

"It's all fixed, Helen," Josh said. "I'm seeing him at 6 tomorrow."

"Do you want me to come with you?"

"No, I think I should go alone." He pointed to his phone. "Dylan's edgy about anyone else going. Probably because of what he's going to tell me about Reggie and

Marvin."

Helen nodded. "I guess that's understandable," she said. "The poor wee kid had a rough time on Saturday and then a bug. It's no wonder he's on edge."

Sam heard the last part of this as she walked into the Ethics Room. "Are you seeing Dylan?" she asked.

Josh smiled and gave a thumbs-up. "All set up for tomorrow evening," he said. "Any luck with Owen?"

Sam looked at her watch. "It's half three now, so with any luck he'll be out of school and will call soon."

No sooner had she said this than her phone rang and she looked down to see it was another FaceTime video call. "This is him," she said. "I'll take it in the corridor."

She stepped outside and accepted the call.

"Hi, Owen," she said.

His face appeared on the screen, much the same as before but with the addition of a black beanie which made him look even younger. There were trees behind him and he looked like he was sitting on a park bench.

"Hi, Sam," he said.

"Sorry if I confused you earlier when I said George wasn't George."

He gave an edgy laugh. "You did, yeah."

"As I said, he and I work together. We're investigating Baz Hartman's parties. It's been alleged that they're being used to seduce young boys."

"Cool." He paused. "I mean that you're investigating," he added quickly, "not about the young boys. So are you, like, the police?"

"Not quite. Though our boss used to be a Detective Chief Inspector."

"Cool," Owen said again. "I'm not surprised."

"Not surprised at what?"

"What you said about the way the parties are being used. There was some weird stuff going on. In the end, I was pleased to leave."

"What do you mean by weird stuff?"

"There were some right old men, like thirty or maybe more, and they had their arms around the shoulders of guys, like, way younger."

"Your age?"

"One kid looked thirteen or fourteen."

"These 'right old men' as you called them. Do you know their names?"

"Damon Prendergast was one. Also Marvin Wine-something-or-other."

"Winespottle?" Sam suggested.

"Yeah, that's right."

"What about Baz Hartman or Reggie Dowden or Ozzy Vaughan?"

"I saw Reggie and Ozzy but not with boys. I didn't see Baz Hartman all evening."

"Do you know any of the boy's names?"

"Sorry, no." Owen paused. "You know I've been to two of his parties, right?"

"Yes. Josh said."

"The first one was, like, cut short. There was a fight, so I didn't really see much. That's why I was pleased when Eve invited me to the party on Saturday."

"Did you see any evidence of grooming at the first party?"

Owen shook his head. "No, I didn't see any of that. The oddest thing was Alfie's reaction afterwards."

"Alfie?" she prompted.

"Yeah. Alfie's, like, a close mate. Or he was."

"Was?"

"He's been ghosting me ever since. I don't know what happened but it must have been, like, something I said or did at the party. We go to the same school but he won't look at me let alone talk to me. He's even changed his phone number."

"Do you know where he lives?"

"Yeah. Do you want me to text it to you?"

"Yes, please. And if I have any other questions, is it alright if I get back in touch?"

"Sure. And if you find out why Alfie's snubbing me…"

"Don't worry, if I do I'll let you know."

Sam ended the call and went back into the office.

"How did it go?" Josh asked.

Sam held her phone up. "Very well and with luck…" There was a ping and she looked down to see Owen's text.

"What's that?" Helen asked.

"It's the name and address of the boy who went to the party with Owen a couple of weeks ago."

Sam removed the Post-it on the investigation board with 'Owen's friend' on it and replaced it with a blank one on which she wrote 'Alfie Inskip'.

"What's your plan?" Josh asked.

"He lives in Kingswood," Sam said, "and I think I might head for his house now." She looked around. "Where's Maj?"

"He's gone off to meet Luke," Helen said. "They're also planning on a wee bit of doorstepping."

Chapter 47

Luke pulled up next to Maj's Volkswagen in the car park of the Hope and Anchor, walked in and ordered himself a sparkling water.

The pub was more modern inside than he had expected, given the building looked to be 17th Century, but it retained a homely feel through the use of rough-hewn pine tables and chairs. There were a couple of middle-aged men at the bar, one doing a crossword and the other staring into his pint. Aside from them, the only other person in the pub was Maj who had found a table in the corner and was leafing backwards and forwards through his notepad.

"Revising?" Luke said when he took his drink over.

Maj looked up. "Sorry, Luke," he said and closed his notepad. He put it down on the table as Luke sat down and shook his head. "I still find it hard to believe Eve Montgomery's involved in all this. I know you say not to trust people, but she seemed so genuine when I met her at the awards ceremony."

"How did you find her address?"

"Instagram. She posted a photo of her and her parents in the garden of this pub, and another of her with a couple of girlfriends outside the house. I used Google Streetview to find it."

"Good work, Maj." He took a sip of his drink before continuing. "The Old Manor sounds like a grand property for a woman in her twenties so I suspect it's her parents' house. Still, it's worth a try. It's on my way home too, so that's a bonus." He paused. "Remind me how Eve described her job."

"She said she's Baz Hartman's PA and organises his diary and events."

"Did she say what he's like to work for?"

"Demanding, but that some of his friends are worse."

"Mmm. From what Josh says, it appears she's the person who invites these teenagers along. She also personally greets them when they arrive so she must know how young they are. It's hard to believe she doesn't also know how they're treated by some of the older guests."

"Josh also said that he didn't see her outside the house all evening, so maybe she doesn't see what's going on." Maj shook his head and smiled sardonically. "But on the other hand, it could be I'm too trusting."

"Come on," Luke said, draining his drink. "Let's walk around the corner and see if we can find out."

A manicured lawn lay in front of The Old Manor, a three-storied stone building with leaded windows to all floors. A pillared portico led to a pale green entrance door, while to the right there was an attached orangery, also in green. On the left, a bright yellow Lamborghini was parked in front of a stone garage.

"Somebody's got money," Maj whispered as they walked to the front door.

Luke pressed the bell and there was a resounding 'bing bong' from inside, then a man shouted, "Just a minute."

"I know that voice," Maj said.

A minute passed before the door was pulled open. Luke had been expecting someone in their fifties or older but the man who answered was in his early to mid-thirties. He was about six feet tall and would probably have been handsome were it not for the broad scowl across his face.

He looked at the notebook in Maj's hand and then up at Luke. "Are you selling religion?" he snapped.

"No, we're here to see Eve," Luke said. "Is she in?"

The man turned his attention to Maj and raised an eyebrow. "Do I know you?"

"We met at the awards ceremony," Maj said. "I'm Maj." He held out his hand.

The hand was ignored. "Yeah, well you can still fuck off."

A female voice called from somewhere deeper in the house. "Who is it, Basil?"

"No one, Mum," he called back, his voice much softer. "I'm dealing with it." He edged out, pulled the door closed behind him and then eyeballed Luke. "So, what the fuck do you two want with my sister?"

"My name's Luke Sackville," Luke said. "My colleague and I want to ask Eve a couple of questions."

"What about?"

"I assume you're Baz Hartman?" Luke went on, ignoring the question.

"Of course I'm Baz Hartman." He shook his head. "Are you living in a fucking vacuum?"

"We're acting on behalf of someone at GNE who believes your parties are being used for illicit purposes."

"That'll be Rachel fucking Adams." The words were hissed.

"It isn't Rachel Adams, Mr Hartman."

"Who then?"

"I'm sorry. I can't tell you that."

"Gay-bashing, that's what it is." Baz paused. "So are you two police?"

"No."

"In that case, you can definitely fuck off." He stepped back inside and slammed the door closed.

"That was a shock," Maj said as they walked back to the road. "I'd never have guessed they were brother and sister."

"It might explain a couple of things," Luke said. "There's no more to be gained here. Let's head back to the pub and agree what we do next.

As they turned off Old Midford Road, Maj put his hand on Luke's arm.

"That's Eve," he said, pointing to a woman standing on the other side waiting to cross. She was much as Luke had expected from Maj's and Josh's descriptions, slim and classically beautiful.

Eve saw Maj looking, crossed over and gave him a peck on the cheek.

"Hi, Maj," she said, smiling. "Fancy seeing you here."

"Hi, Eve," Maj said. He gestured to Luke. "This is Luke."

"Nice to meet you, Luke. So what brings you two to Midford?"

"We came to see you," Maj said.

Her smile faltered as she considered this. "You came to see me? I don't understand."

"If you wouldn't mind sparing us a few minutes, we can explain," Luke said. "Perhaps you could join us in the pub?"

She gave a little laugh and the smile returned full force. "I'm intrigued so, yes, okay."

Luke led them back to the Hope and Anchor. "Wine?" he asked when they reached the bar.

"Just an orange juice," Eve replied. "I'm working."

Luke bought the drinks. Once they were seated he said. "We owe you an explanation."

"You certainly do." She looked at Maj and then back at Luke. "How you knew you'd find me in Midford for a start."

"Instagram," Maj said.

She shook her head, but she was still smiling. "You have been busy." She paused. "Are you from the newspapers? After some kind of scoop on Baz?"

"No," Luke said. "We're both employed by a company called Filchers."

She looked at Maj. "Is that where you work as a software programmer?"

It was Luke who answered. "Maj works for me," he said, "and he's not a software programmer. He was working undercover when he went to the awards ceremony."

"What? So is Filchers a detective agency?"

"GNE is one of our clients," Luke said, keeping his answer deliberately vague. "They've asked us to investigate Baz's parties."

Eve's smile disappeared for the first time and she looked genuinely confused. "Investigate them? Why?"

Luke decided he needed to be blunt if he was going to gauge how deeply she was involved.

"Male guests are using the parties to groom underage boys," he said.

"No." She shook her head vigorously. "That's not true."

He looked directly into her eyes. "And you, Eve, are the person who procures children for them."

"This is nonsense. I don't…"

Luke didn't let her finish. "You entice them with a promise of meeting the stars," he said, "but instead they are laid out like cattle for your brother's guests to inspect and select."

"It's not like that," she said weakly.

Her eyes started to become moist and Luke decided he had gone far enough. "Then please explain," he said, his voice softer now.

She took a deep breath and looked at Maj. "Is this all true?" she asked.

"I'm afraid it is," Maj said. "We have incontrovertible evidence."

"Someone else who works for me went to Saturday's party," Luke added. "He saw it for himself."

"It's not Baz," she said, but it was more of a question than a statement.

Luke elected not to react and waited for her to continue. After a minute or so, the words came tumbling out.

"A few months ago I suggested to Baz that we invite fans," she said. "He thought it was a good idea but we agreed they should be men because the parties are all-male.

Not that they had to be gay or anything, just so that they would fit in." She looked at Luke as if for approval.

"I understand," he said.

"They were mixed ages at first, but then people started telling me to focus on younger fans. They said it was because they were more enthusiastic. I never dreamt that…" A tear fell from her left eye. "God, I've been so stupid."

"Who told you to focus on younger fans?" Luke asked.

She hesitated.

"You need to tell me," he went on. "For your sake as much as anything."

She nodded. "It was Damon Prendergast and Ozzy Vaughan."

"What about Reggie Dowden and Marvin Winespottle?" Maj asked.

Eve looked at him and shook her head. "No, though to be honest Baz hasn't got any time for them, so he'd probably tell me to ignore them if they did ask for anything."

"But he was happy with you being led by Damon and Ozzy?" Luke asked.

"It wasn't like that!" She put her head in her hands for a few seconds and then looked up, her eyes now full of tears. "I was trying to help," she spluttered. "That's all. I was only trying to help."

"Right now," Luke said. "It's important that you give us as much assistance as you can."

She nodded. "Anything."

"Have you got a list of the fans you've invited?"

"Yes. I've got their names and email addresses."

Luke gave her his email address and she entered it into her phone. "Please send them to me as soon as you're back," he said.

"I will."

"And Eve," he added as they got up to leave. "Don't tell

your brother you've talked to us. I don't want him saying anything to Damon or Ozzy." He paused. "One last question before you go. Why did you pay for six actresses to attend Saturday's party?"

"Kieran and Nat suggested it. They're Baz's minders. The four of us were talking about the parties being a bit dull and Kieran said women would help brighten things up. Baz resisted at first but not for long." She half-smiled.

"What is it?" Luke prompted.

"I was totally in favour of the idea because I thought it would give Kieran someone else to focus his leering eyes on. He's hit on me so many times I've lost count and to be honest he gives me the creeps."

"So the only reason was to add glamour?"

She nodded. "Yes, that was it."

Chapter 48

Sam was stationary waiting for the lights to change to green when her phone rang for the umpteenth time.

She looked down and, as expected, it was Tony's name on the screen. As it had been ten minutes earlier, and ten minutes before that. Again she was tempted to answer and give him an earful, but he was so stupid he'd see any kind of reaction as a positive. No, she had to ignore him.

She pressed the red button.

Two minutes later the phone rang again.

Sam sighed, glanced down and found herself smiling when she saw Luke's name on the screen.

It was good to have someone sane and balanced to talk to, that was all. Nothing else.

"Hi, Luke," she said, fighting to keep her tone measured.

"Hi, Sam. Helen said you managed to get Owen's friend's address and you're going to try to speak to him."

"Yes, that's right. I'm on my way now. How did you and Maj get on?"

"Pretty well. Eve's sending us a list of the boys she invited."

"That's great."

"We learned something surprising as well. It turns out she's Baz Hartman's sister."

"That is a surprise."

"Anyway, I just thought I'd ring to wish you luck." He paused. "How are you feeling?"

She knew he would ask, but god did it feel good that he cared. "I'm fine, Luke," she said, and for some reason, the words caught in her throat.

"That's good. I'm on the case with Terence Nix. One

more thing to do first thing tomorrow. I'll let you know how I get on."

"Thanks."

"I'll see you on Wednesday."

Sam felt a twinge of disappointment as she remembered he was going to London.

"Oh yes," she said. "You're going to GNE aren't you? Are you seeing Rachel?"

"Yes. I think I owe her that much."

Sam hung up and decided that she would try 'Hinge' when she got home. She hadn't got on with online dating apps in the past but Hannah had said 'Hinge' was great if you were after a serious relationship, and that was definitely what she needed.

There was a beep and the SatNav's posh female voice patronisingly informed her that she had arrived at her destination. She parked up and sat for a couple of moments trying to decide how to play it.

Owen believed that Alfie had been upset by something that had happened at Baz Hartman's party. It must have been pretty serious for him to break off with a close friend and go so far as to change his phone number.

The challenge was how to get him to tell all to a complete stranger.

Sam wished she'd asked Luke for his advice when she'd talked to him a few minutes earlier. He was always good in this kind of situation. She wasn't going to ring him back though. It would send the wrong message. She didn't want him to think that she liked talking to him. She did, obviously, but as a boss.

One of Alfie's parents was likely to open the door so she'd have to say who she was and why she was there. She couldn't out-and-out lie, but she couldn't tell the full truth either. If Alfie had distanced himself from Owen because of what happened, it was highly likely his parents weren't even aware he'd been to the party.

She had to find a middle ground and be economical with the truth in a way that enabled her to be alone with Alfie.

Then it hit her. She could use Owen.

She got out of the car and walked down the short drive of number 18 to the front door. It was a tidy Edwardian semi-detached house which spoke of sufficient money but no more. Sam rang the bell and stood back.

The woman who answered had a black apron decorated with a cartoon sunflower, below which were the words 'I'm sunshine mixed with a little hurricane'.

"Hi," she said, wiping floury hands on the apron then holding them up and smiling. "Can't shake hands, sorry. I'm making a birthday cake."

"Hi," Sam said. "Is Alfie here?"

"He's upstairs." She turned and bellowed in a voice that would have sunk a battleship, "Alfie! Visitor!"

"I'll leave you to it," she said and headed back down the hall, presumably en route back to the kitchen.

There were footsteps on the stairs and Sam looked up, expecting to see a sixteen-year-old boy. Instead, it was a woman of nineteen or twenty who descended towards her.

"Hello," the girl said as she reached the bottom of the stairs. "Is he in trouble again?"

Sam smiled. "No. Why would you think that?"

"Aren't you from his school?"

"No. Owen asked me to come."

There were more steps on the stairs, and this time it was indeed a teenage boy who drew into view. It was immediately obvious that they were brother and sister. Their hair was black, but the real likeness was in their eyes which were deep-set and vivid blue.

"Who are you?" Alfie asked when he saw Sam.

It was his sister who answered. "She's a friend of Owen's," she said. "I thought you'd fallen out with him."

"I'm not exactly a friend," Sam said. "But Owen needs

your help."

"What do you want?" Alfie asked.

"Can I come in so that we can talk?" Sam walked in as she spoke, not wanting to give Alfie the chance to say 'no'.

"We can go in the sitting room," Alfie said and pointed to the first door off the hall.

"I'll leave you to it," his sister said and bounced back up the stairs.

Sam went into the sitting room, which was single-mindedly a television room and nothing else, the brown leather three-piece suite directed firmly at a way-oversized television above a weedy electric fire. The only other ornaments were a couple of family photos and a gaudy and flower-free 'Lanzarote' vase.

"Is it okay if I sit down?" Sam asked.

"Sure," Alfie said.

She sat on one of the chairs and he sat opposite, perched on the edge as if ready for a quick getaway.

"What's wrong with Owen?" he asked.

"I have to be honest," Sam said. She smiled but it wasn't returned. "Owen's fine. I'm here to ask you a few questions about Baz Hartman's party."

Alfie stood up and turned to look at the door as if frightened someone could hear what she was saying.

"They don't know I went," he hissed.

Sam held her hands up. "Don't worry, Alfie. I won't tell them. I need a couple of answers, that's all, and then I'll leave you be."

"No," he said, a desperate look on his face. "You don't understand. I can't say anything."

"Please, Alfie. It won't take a moment."

"You have to go."

There was an imploring tone in his voice and she could see he was frightened.

"What's wrong, Alfie? What are you scared of?"

"Please. Just go."

"Can I at least give you my card?"

She held her hand out and he practically tore the card from her grasp. He stuffed it in his pocket, opened the sitting room door and headed down the hall.

"Give me a ring when you're ready to talk," Sam said as he guided her outside.

Alfie didn't reply and the front door closed behind her with a resounding thud.

Chapter 49

Luke reversed up the drive of the farmhouse and turned the engine off. He undid the seat belt and sat still for a moment, unable to shake off thoughts of what had happened to Rachel. It was an unbelievable tragedy to beset a woman in the prime of her life. He'd talked to her on Friday morning and she'd been really happy, looking forward to them meeting up, no idea that within hours she would suffer life-changing, and possibly life-ending, injuries.

The same thing had happened to Jess. In her case, it was a hit-and-run driver that took her life away. You couldn't anticipate these things, all you could do was live for the present. At least he and Jess had had over twenty happy years together and had seen their children grow into wonderful adults.

He sighed and climbed out of the car. What he needed was a brisk walk to clear his head. After that, he'd ring the twins. Speaking to Chloe and Ben always cheered him up.

He put his key in the door and it wouldn't turn. He checked he had the right one and then tried again.

Still no joy.

He stood back, pressed down on the handle and the door swung open.

Something was wrong.

He stiffened and listened carefully. There wasn't even the hint of a noise, which in itself was odd. He stepped through the front door and sure enough, the dog crate was empty, the slatted iron flap wide open.

"Wilkins," he shouted. "Where are you, boy?"

There was no mewling in response, nor any rush of paws on wooden flooring.

Luke's heart sank.

He reached above the settle and took hold of an umbrella. It wasn't a baseball bat but heaven help anyone if he had to use it on them.

He walked from the hall through to the lounge. Still not a sound.

It was as he entered the kitchen that he heard a faint whimpering. He glanced up at the door and stepped slowly towards it.

He was still a few paces away when it flew open and a muddy Wilkins leapt forwards and up at him, flicking mud from his ears and tail onto his shirt and trousers. Behind him, a man of nearly Luke's height stood grinning in the doorway.

"Sorry, Dad," Ben said. "He's been in the river."

"Christ, you frightened me," Luke said. The cocker stepped back and sat on his haunches, tilting his head to one side. "Got any treats?"

"Of course." Ben produced a bone-shaped biscuit from his pocket and held it out. One second later it was gone.

"Right," Luke said. "In your bed to dry out, boy."

Wilkins immediately darted into the crate, rotated twice and flopped down. Luke shut the door.

"How come you're here?" he asked. "Exams aren't done already, are they?"

Ben wiped his hands together. "Yup. All done. Back to torment you for the summer."

"That's brilliant. Heard from Chloe?"

"I don't think hers finish until Friday."

"We ought to go out on Saturday to celebrate." Luke paused. "Talking of going out, do you fancy another walk? I could do with some fresh air."

"Let me guess," Ben said with a smile. "Towards Faulkland?"

Luke returned his son's smile. "Got it in one. Give me a few minutes to get changed and we'll head off. The wet one," he indicated Wilkins with a nod of his head, "can dry off on the way."

Fifteen minutes later they were heading off across the fields towards Tucker's Grave.

"I was going to ring you tonight," Luke said as they set off. "Do you remember Bertie Fotheringay?"

Ben thought for a moment before he answered. "Was he one of Granddad's golfing buddies?"

"That's right. Do you remember anything about him?"

"I remember he was younger than Granddad, but then that's not saying much. Was he in banking?"

"Close. He works in insurance in some capacity for Lloyds of London." Luke paused. "You're holding back on me, Ben. There's something about Bertie Fotheringay that I'm sure you remember. How old were you when he brought his wife and daughter to Granddad's 70th birthday party? Thirteen? Fourteen?"

Ben gave an embarrassed laugh.

"Your eyes were on stalks," Luke went on, "and it's no wonder. I remember your granddad's face when they turned up and he caught sight of Fotheringay's twenty-odd-year-old daughter wearing a string vest and no bra." Luke chuckled. "He was apoplectic with rage. It was just as well Grandma didn't see her before your mum whisked her upstairs and persuaded her to change into one of her blouses."

Ben shook his head. "Why are you asking, Dad?"

"Do you remember his wife's name?"

"Now you're asking." He thought for a second. "Didn't it begin with 'F', which made it odd with the surname?"

"I can't remember at all."

"Was it Fenella? Or Florence?" Ben shook his head in exasperation. "No. It was shorter I'm sure. Was it Fay?" He paused, then flicked his fingers. "Got it. Her name was Fiona. Yes, that was it. Fiona Fotheringay."

They reached the door of the pub and both men ducked and walked in. A middle-aged barmaid with a

Mallets Cider apron was filling pint glasses from one of the barrels on the left, while three men sat at the pine table in the alcove to the right. Two were solidly built, in their forties with ruddy, textured faces that spoke of people who laboured in the countryside. The man opposite them, on the other hand, had a pale face and was thin, in his late sixties, with wisps of white hair combed across the top of his head in true Bobby Charlton fashion.

It was the older man who spoke.

"Yer fine to join us, Luke," he said. "That yer lad?"

"Thanks, Stan. Yes, this is my son, Ben."

Luke slid in next to Stan and Ben sat opposite while the spaniel curled up under the table. The other two men introduced themselves and then resumed their conversation with Stan.

A minute or so later the barmaid called over. "What'll it be, my luvvers?"

"Two Mother Tuckers please, Doris," Luke said.

"Why did you want to know Fotheringay's wife's name, Dad?" Ben asked, picking up their conversation from earlier.

"Filcher, my boss, is a friend of his and asked me if I'd do some investigating for him. I suspected it was your Granddad's old buddy, but now I know the wife's name is Fiona it has to be him."

"Does he think she's having an affair?"

"No, it's not that that's worrying him. He thinks she's trying to poison him."

"Yer drinks," Doris said, placing their ciders in front of them.

"Thanks," Luke said.

"Poison him!" Ben said as he took a glug of his cider. "Wow. What makes him think that?"

"She's taken to cooking him dishes with mushrooms in and one of them gave him really bad indigestion."

Stan nudged Luke in the ribs. "I 'eard that," he said.

"Ain't no Destroyin' Angel."

"She is if it's true," Luke said.

Stan shook his head. "Yer missin' the point, me kidder. She be givin' yer man a mild sort if he only be ill. Destroyin' Angel looks like yer normal mushroom, but yer liver's gone after a small bite and yer dead in days. 'Spect she be usin' Yellow Stainers. Gives yer a belly ache but ain't no killer."

"Or Fool's Funnel," one of the men opposite Stan said.

The man next to him nodded sagely. "Fool's Funnel. Cou' be."

Stan considered this "Nah," he said. "Dey be rare. Yellow Stainers fer def'nite. I'z allus seein' girt great clumps of 'em." He turned back to Luke. "Tell yer mate to rub the top. If it goes yellow it's a stainer fer sure."

"And if it doesn't?" Luke asked. "What if it's pure white like a supermarket button mushroom?"

Stan laughed. "Then he needs to look in the bin, see if he can find the packet. Destroyin' Angels are pure white as well see. Once they're in a pot no tellin' they'll kill yer 'til you're rolling round the floor an' screamin' fer your ma."

"Thanks, Stan, that's useful information."

"Any time, me ole mucker." Stan said. "Any time." He returned his attention to his two friends.

"Are you going to help him, Dad?" Ben asked.

"I might do, Ben. It's certainly intriguing. He lives in Lacock too, so not far."

"Do it, Dad."

"I'll think about it. Anyway, enough about me. How's the course?"

"It's good thanks." Ben stopped and took another sip of his drink. "I've made good friends with a girl on the course. Would it be okay if she came down to stay for a few days?"

"Of course. What's her name?"

"Pippa."

"And she's just a friend?"

Ben's cheeks went slightly red. "Yes, Dad. She's just a friend."

Chapter 50

"Dylan!" Callum shouted.

There was no response.

He peered into the corner of the container. It was very dark but he could just about make out Dylan tied to a chair in the same way he was, arms tight behind his back. His head was down over his chest, and his eyes appeared to be closed. Callum tried to see if he was breathing, but he was at least ten yards away and there wasn't enough light to tell.

He was getting more and more worried. Dylan hadn't moved or made a sound for several hours.

Callum felt his lower lip trembling. He tried to stop it but it seemed to have a will of its own.

Why, oh why, did he have to go to that party?

He'd said he was going to his friend's for the night but his Mum and Dad expected him back on Sunday. They would have reported him missing when he didn't come home. The police must have been looking for him for at least 24 hours, possibly more.

So where were they?

There was a sound and he realised it was a key turning. After a few seconds, the container door opened. He was immediately forced to close his eyes as light tore into the confined space.

Red Skull marched forward, put his hand under Callum's chin and raised his head.

"Open your eyes," he demanded.

Callum squinted, letting in enough light to see Red Skull grinning down at him.

"I've got him," he said triumphantly and lifted Callum's phone in the air so that he could see the screen.

'6pm Tuesday is good. I'll find out the address and text it to you.

Come alone - Dylan's nervous.'

Red Skull cackled. "He's coming, see. Your friend Josh is joining us. Won't that be fun?"

"I'm worried about Dylan," Callum said.

Red Skull let go of his chin and poked him in the chest with his index finger. "It's you you should be worried about, you little runt."

"He hasn't moved or spoken for hours."

Red Skull grunted, looked over in Dylan's direction and shouted. "Hey, Dylan-baby. What's up?"

There was no answer.

Callum watched as his captor walked over and lifted Dylan's head up from his chest. After a few seconds, he let go and it flopped back down.

"Fuck," he said. "Fuck, fuck, fuck."

He inspected the wound on the back of Dylan's head, shook his head and turned to face Callum. "Must have hit him harder than I meant to," he said and grinned. "Well, I suppose it means there's space for your friend Josh."

"What do you mean? Is he…" Callum swallowed. "Is Dylan dead?"

Red Skull took a knife from his pocket, moved behind Dylan and cut through the ropes binding his wrists. He replaced the knife, bent forward and hoisted him onto his shoulder in a fireman's lift and walked to the door.

"You haven't answered me," Callum screamed. "Is he okay?"

Red Skull stepped outside, put his back to the door and shoved it closed. Callum heard the thump of something heavy hitting the floor then the key turning in the lock.

After that, the only sound was of Callum crying.

Chapter 51

"I've arranged for two uniforms to meet us there," Pete said as he climbed into the BMW. They had agreed to meet in the car park of Keynsham Police Station and drive to NTV together.

Luke started the car and headed towards the Bath Road roundabout. "Do they know what's what?" he asked.

"Not yet. I thought it best if you brief them before we go in."

"Fair enough." He indicated right and turned onto the A4 towards Bristol. "How are you getting on with your Chew Valley Lake enquiry?"

Pete gave a humourless chuckle. "Applejack's showing a complete lack of interest."

"Nothing new there."

"However, the Birmingham DI is coming down today."

"Jill North was it?"

"Well remembered. That was a good call, Luke. She bit my hand off when I said I'd appreciate her looking at where the body was found."

"What about the investigation itself? Any suspects?"

"The body was in such a state that we've got very little to go on. At the moment we're assuming he was killed in the Midlands but there's no clue as to why his body was dumped in Somerset."

"Has he got any friends or relations down here?"

"None. I can only think his killer's either from around here, or else made a long journey to make it more difficult to tie it back to him."

It was 7:45 when they pulled into the visitors' spaces at NTV Bristol. Already in the spot next to them was a police Volvo.

"Hopefully, the blue and yellow checks will give him an added scare," Luke said, as he and Pete climbed out and walked to the police car.

Pete bent down to the driver's window. "Good morning," he said, holding his badge up. "I'm DI Pete Gilmore and this is ex-DCI Luke Sackville. If you pop in the back seat of Luke's car he'll explain what we're up to."

Five minutes later Luke led the other three into NTV's reception area where Rosie was waiting for them.

"Hi, Rosie," he said. "Is everything ready?"

She smiled. "Yes, Brendan's in with him now. Please follow me."

The four of them followed her to Terence Nix's office where he was making a good show of listening intently to the man opposite.

Rosie opened the door. "The police are here," she said.

Brendan stood up and looked at the officers and then back at Nix. "Shall I leave?" he asked.

Terence didn't answer.

"Are you Brendan Doyle?" Pete asked.

Brendan turned around, drew his head back in surprise, and then looked back at Terence. "What's going on?" he asked.

"Please answer the question," Pete said.

"Yes, I'm Brendan Doyle. What's this about?"

"I'm Detective Inspector Pete Gilmore from Avon and Somerset Police. This is PC Lucy Trotting and this is PC Adam Birkenshaw."

Brendan looked at each of the officers in turn. "I don't understand," he said.

"My name is Luke Sackville," Luke said. "I believe you know Samantha Chambers who works for me."

"This has to be a joke," Brendan spluttered. "That woman…"

Luke didn't let him finish. He walked up to him and looked down menacingly. "I am deadly serious, Mr Doyle," he said, his voice firm.

Brendan shook his head and gave a small laugh. "This is rubbish."

Luke stepped back. "Please continue, DI Gilmore," he said.

Pete took out his notebook. "Last Saturday the 17th of June you attempted to rape Miss Chambers," he said.

Doyle was still shaking his head.

"And it's not your first offence," Pete went on, looking down to be sure he got the details right. "On the 12th of December last year, you exposed yourself to a woman in the ladies toilet on the second floor of this building."

"That's baloney. I…"

"Please be quiet, Mr Doyle. I haven't finished." Pete waited until he was certain Brendan wasn't going to speak again before continuing. "In October last year, you sent several photos of your erect penis to another NTV employee."

"I only sent one." As soon as Brendan said it he realised what he'd done. "She asked me to," he added hastily. "We were in a relationship."

"Have you ever been on the sex offenders' register, Mr Doyle," Pete asked.

"No, of course not."

"Mmm." Pete tapped on his notebook. "I'm surprised, given all of this. And our investigation has only just started."

"Investigation. What do you mean?"

"We're still building up our evidence, but you can be certain we'll be back in touch. For the moment, you're free to go."

"I can echo that," Terence said.

Brendan turned to him. "What do you mean?"

Terence smiled, but there was a genuine edge to it. "You're free to go, Brendan. Your contract is terminated with immediate effect."

"You can't do that."

"I most certainly can. And before you ask," Terence added, "I will also be writing a reference and sending it to my peers in NTV, GNE, the BBC, Sky and so on. Don't worry, there'll be nothing in it that's unfair. Just the unvarnished truth, that's all."

"PC Trotting, PC Birkenshaw," Pete said. "Please can you escort Mr Doyle from the building?"

"Certainly, sir," PC Trotting said.

"This way please," PC Birkenshaw said, opening the door and gesturing for Brendan to leave the room.

"Thanks, Pete," Luke said, once Brendan was out of earshot. He turned to Terence. "Were you telling the truth about the reference?"

"Absolutely," Terence said.

"Just be careful not to say anything that might be construed as libel. Nothing's been proven, remember. If you'd like, I could draft a form of words for you."

"Thanks, Luke. That would be very helpful." He stood up. "I'll ask Rosie to bring the coffee and biscuits in."

The two PCs had returned and helped themselves to a coffee each when Pete's phone rang. "It's Applejack," he mouthed to Luke. "I'd better take it."

He stepped outside, returning after a couple of minutes.

"Sorry," he said. "There's been a development. Can we leave now, Luke? I'll explain in the car."

"Sure." Luke turned to the two PCs. "Thanks for helping."

It was PC Trotting who answered. "No problem, sir," she said. "Anything we can do to put a man like that in his place."

"They've found another body," Pete said, once he and Luke were back in the car.

"Linked to the first one?" Luke asked.

Pete nodded. "Looks to be another teenage boy so it

could be. Two women were wild swimming in Vobster about thirty minutes ago and got the fright of their lives when they bumped into him."

"Any idea how he died?"

"Applejack told me that there was a gash on the back of his head and it looks like he hadn't been in the water for long. Have to see what the post mortem reveals."

"Sounds ominously like the same killer, Pete. And whoever it is, they're very bold."

Chapter 52

Luke got off the carriage and turned towards Platform 1, apologising as he weaved his way through the other passengers who were all heading for the exit.

Once there, he waited while people clambered into the northbound train. It was as the platform cleared and it started to pull away that he saw the sign.

He had anticipated that it would be there, but it still gave him a jolt as he read the stark words, written in black on a yellow background:

SERIOUS INCIDENT

There was a serious incident on this platform on Friday 16th June at 2:40 pm.

If you saw anything please ring the police on 0800 555 1111

Luke sighed as he made his way to the exit. If Rachel had indeed been pushed, as her mother suspected, he was going to find the bastard who'd done it and make him pay.

Once at the Istanbul Cafe, Luke bought himself a Turkish coffee and bagged a table. He took a sip of his drink, which was piping hot and deliciously strong, and considered how best to deal with the senior executive Victor had lined up.

There was incontrovertible evidence that four GNE staff were up to no good. Two of them, Damon Prendergast and Ozzy Vaughan, fronted a popular TV programme which made them highly visible role models. Any sensible person would want them out.

S J Richards

However, if the culture at GNE was anything like that at NTV, and he suspected it probably was, then there would be strong resistance to taking action, especially given the offenders were 'stars'. Terence Nix was a well-meaning man, who provided his personal time to help charities, and yet he had taken no action against Brendan Doyle, who was a relative nonentity, even as the evidence mounted.

His success in turning Terence's opinion around had come from appealing to his better nature. It hadn't been easy, but perhaps that was the best line to take.

Luke looked up as he heard Victor's voice at the counter.

"Extra syrup please, dear," he said. "Or am I already sweet enough?"

The young man behind the counter stared at him blankly.

"I'm only teasing," Victor went on. "How much do I owe you for this saccharined delight?"

Pleased to be back on level ground, the server took his money and passed him his drink.

"Iced coffee latte," Victor said, as he slid in opposite Luke and placed his drink on the table. "Absolutely scrumptious." He smiled before adding, "A little like me."

He was wearing another ridiculously outlandish outfit, a black and white poncho in a paisley design over skintight black satin trousers. At least it wasn't blindingly bright, Luke thought.

"Sorry, this is so dismal," Victor said, almost as though he'd read his mind. "I didn't feel like colour this morning. Not after what happened to poor Rachel."

"I'm going to see her this afternoon," Luke said. "Though she's still in a coma as far as I'm aware."

"Awful thing to happen to that darling girl," Victor said, shaking his head.

"Anyway, thanks for setting this up," Luke said. "Who am I seeing?"

"John Steadman, Head of Light Entertainment. He's expecting you at 12:30." Victor paused. "He's the man who gave Rachel the push."

For a split-second Luke's thoughts went back to the underground platform, before he realised what Victor meant.

"That doesn't bode well," he said. "What's he like?"

Victor took a sip of his latte while he considered this. "Very old school," he said. "Pleasant enough, but never comfortable in my company. Finds me a bit much, I fear."

"Have you told him what the meeting's about?"

"I told him you were an old friend who could take a couple of his stars in a completely new direction." Victor smiled wickedly. "I didn't tell him that the new direction might be towards Wandsworth Prison."

"Any suggestions on how to play him?"

"I wouldn't say there's any point in appealing to his principles. To be honest, I'm not sure his moral compass has ever been activated. Think of John like a stick of Blackpool rock: cut him anywhere and he'll have 'GNE' written all over. You need to convince him he needs to take action for the benefit of the company."

Luke nodded. "That's great advice." He paused. "You're sure you're happy with this, Victor? You set the meeting up so he's going to know you're the whistleblower."

"Absolutely, my dear. Don't worry about me. As Gloria Gaynor said so memorably, I will survive."

Luke outlined the evidence the team had compiled.

"I'm pleased Baz isn't implicated," Victor said when he'd finished, "but those other four…" He shook his head. "Assuming you convince John to take action, will you take all this to the police?"

"Yes," Luke said without hesitation. "I have a contact in the Met who I'll pass this on to. To be honest, I'm not sure we've got enough to stand up in court, but at the very least the police can issue them with warnings about their behaviour."

Twenty minutes later, a young man with an expansive Afro shook Luke's hand.

"I am Fernando, John's personal assistant," he said, his diction clear but laced with a Spanish accent. "Please follow me."

They emerged from the lift on the 10th floor and Luke followed Fernando to the end of the corridor, where the PA gave a peremptory knock before opening the door for Luke to enter.

The corner office was large but minimalist, the only furniture being a desk and chair of light wood and two matching linen armchairs. Luke's attention was drawn to the windows which faced directly onto Regents Park.

"What a magnificent view," he said.

"Yes, isn't it," John Steadman said. He stood up and placed his reading glasses over the 'v' of his dark blue shirt, the top two buttons of which were undone, before walking over to Luke.

"Nice to meet you," he said as they shook hands. He gestured to the armchairs. "Please take a seat."

"Thanks for agreeing to see me at such short notice," Luke said.

"No problem." He glanced at his watch in a very obvious manner. "Unfortunately, I have a commissioning board meeting at one, so we'll have to keep it brief. Now, how can I help?"

"Actually, it's more a case of how I can help GNE." Luke clasped his hands together before continuing. "There is a news story about to break which will cause your organisation serious reputational damage unless you take immediate action."

Steadman raised a questioning eyebrow. "I don't understand," he said. "I thought you had an idea for a new series. Are you from the press?"

"No. I'm Head of Ethics for Filchers, a major private

company which is proud to have GNE as a client. Prior to joining Filchers, I was a Detective Chief Inspector in Avon and Somerset Police."

"I see. So what's this story about?"

"Tell me, John. How much was GNE affected by Operation Yewtree?"

"Not much, fortunately. It was mainly the BBC. Most of the convictions were people who worked for them like Saville himself, Rolf Harris and Stuart Hall." He paused as it dawned on him what Luke was implying. "You're not saying this story is along those lines?"

Luke nodded. "Sad to say, it is. A number of people in the media industry are set to be accused of grooming children for sex, among them four GNE employees."

"Who?"

"Damon Prendergast, Ozzy Vaughan, Reggie Dowden and Marvin Winespottle. These people are role models and for them to behave in this way is reprehensible and something GNE should not tolerate."

Luke spent the next few minutes sharing the team's findings and Steadman shook his head in exasperation when he'd finished.

"It sounds cut and dried," he said. "Damon and Ozzy are very high profile too." He sighed. "When is the story going to break?"

"In the next few days."

"Christ!"

Luke could almost see the cogs turning as the other man weighed up his options. After a few seconds, he got to his feet, opened the door and called to his PA.

"Fernando," he said, "send my apologies to the commissioning board and tell Jarvis and Frank to come up here asap. Oh, and Moira Handsworth too."

He returned to his seat.

"Jarvis and Frank are executive producers for 'Hall of Flame' and 'Rock-n-Roll-n-Rap'," he explained. "Moira is

Head of Communications."

"What do you plan to do?"

"Terminate their contracts, of course," John said emphatically. "We also need to issue a press release and use social media to communicate that GNE has uncovered what those four are up to and no longer wants them in our employ." He was thinking on his feet, Luke saw, keen to minimise any damage to his organisation. "And I want to make it clear that we're passing our findings to the police."

"I'll ask my team to email a full dossier of our evidence over."

"Thanks, Luke. This afternoon?"

"Definitely."

John gave him his email address and shook his hand much more vigorously than he had the first time. "Thanks for bringing this to my attention, Luke."

"No problem." Luke handed over his business card. "If you need anything else, please get in touch."

Chapter 53

Luke rang Helen as soon as he'd left GNE and asked her to email the full Baz Hartman dossier to John Steadman.

He was pleased with what he had achieved in his meetings with Terence Nix and now John Steadman. In both cases, he had brought sexual predators to some sort of justice. It wasn't as much as they deserved, but it was something.

But now, he was getting to the part of the day he had been dreading the most. He marched off towards St Mary's Hospital, trying not to think too much about the state he would find Rachel in.

Fifteen minutes later, the receptionist directed him to the Adults' Intensive Care Unit on the 9th floor. He walked out of the lift to find a deserted nurses station facing him, turned left down the corridor and spotted a woman with greying hair sitting on one of a bank of three plastic chairs. She was bent forward, her head in her hands.

"Are you Wendy?" he asked as he approached.

She looked up, her eyes rimmed with red. "Yes."

"I'm Luke. How's Rachel?"

"Not much change." She shook her head and glanced at the door facing her. "They say the next 48 hours are crucial."

"Can I go in and see her?"

"A doctor's with her at the moment. He said he wouldn't be long."

Luke sat down next to Wendy.

"It's very good of you to come," she said.

"It's the least I can do."

"Have you managed to look into what happened?"

Luke was about to answer when the door to Rachel's

room opened. A man in blue scrubs and a face mask emerged, glanced briefly at Luke and Wendy, then turned and ran down the corridor.

"What's happened?" Wendy called out to him, worry etched into every syllable.

Luke pushed the door of Rachel's room open. She was lying on her back on the bed, eyes closed and a tube inserted in her nose, a second in her neck.

But it was the lack of noise that drew his attention.

He stepped back outside, looked down the corridor and saw a nurse emerging from the lift.

"Quick," he shouted. "In here."

The nurse recognised the urgency in his voice and ran to the ward. She stepped past him and immediately went into action, turning machines on and checking all the tubes were connected correctly.

"Did you see the man who did this?" Luke asked.

"He went through the fire door," she said without looking up.

Luke ran down the corridor, opened the door and sped down the stairs, taking three or four steps at a time. He was about halfway down when he heard the clang of a door closing.

At the bottom, he pulled open the door and emerged into the main hospital entrance area. An elderly man was lying on the floor, a woman bent over him in the process of helping him up.

"What happened?" Luke asked.

"That doctor…" the man wheezed, raising a hand and pointing towards the exit. "He barged into me."

Luke looked up and saw the man in scrubs through the window as he emerged onto the street. He looked briefly back at Luke and he caught a glimpse of heavily hooded eyes above the mask before he turned back and ran across the road, putting his hand on the bonnet of a car as it braked suddenly to avoid hitting him.

Luke ran to the exit and through the revolving door. He saw the man running left then turning right at which point he disappeared around the corner. He ran after him, holding his hand up to stop the traffic as he crossed the road.

The road he had gone down was marked as private and appeared to be part of the St Mary's campus. Luke ran past the barrier and saw that the road bent slightly to the left but not enough to prevent him having a clear view of where it emerged onto Praed Street.

There was no sign of the man, which meant he had to have entered the buildings to the right or left. Luke tried the first door on the right but it was locked.

He was about to cross to the door opposite when he noticed a ramp twenty or so yards further on which led under the building to what he presumed was parking. Sure enough, when he reached the entrance there was a sign which read 'Staff Parking - Permits Only'.

Luke slowed and walked into the parking area. There were flickering overhead fluorescents which gave sufficient light to see that there were twelve spaces on either side, all of them occupied. He stood still, listening for any sound, but there was complete silence.

"I know you're there," he shouted. "Come out where I can see you."

There was no response, then he heard a soft shuffling sound from behind a Range Rover on his left. He edged to the front of the car, lay flat on the floor and peered underneath.

A pair of green eyes stared back at him from the rear of the car, and there was a loud 'Meow" as the frightened tabby scrambled away.

As it did so, Luke heard movement behind him and rolled over just in time as something metallic clanged into the concrete floor. There was a shout of "Fuck" from his assailant who turned and aimed a kick at Luke's head. Luke moved aside in time for it to be only a glancing blow, and grabbed the man's foot in the follow-through.

With a snarl, the man tried to wrestle his foot free, then swung again and Luke was forced to let go as the weapon hit him across the side of his head. He fell back, momentarily stunned, and his attacker saw his opportunity. He swung again, catching Luke with a full blow to the other side of his head this time.

Luke fell back again and there was another clang as the weapon fell to the floor. He was vaguely aware of a snort of satisfaction from his attacker and of the sound of running footsteps.

Slowly, he climbed to his feet and put his hand to his head which was now telling him how hard it had been hit. He glanced down to see that the object he had twice been hit with was a metal bedpan, and that next to it was a small piece of paper. He picked both up, put the paper in his pocket and staggered up the ramp.

There was no sign of the man in scrubs.

Luke took a deep breath and steadied himself. He felt both sides of his head and looked at his hands. There was no blood. He was going to have bumps and bruising, and undoubtedly headaches, but he didn't think any real and lasting damage had been done.

His main concern was Rachel.

He returned to the intensive care unit to find there were now three women in blue scrubs around Rachel with Wendy standing to one side watching them anxiously.

One of the women turned as he walked in.

"Everything's back as it should be," she said, looking at Wendy. "Fortunately, her ventilator was only disconnected for a few seconds."

She noticed Luke. "Who are you?" She asked, then pointed at the bedpan. "And why are you holding that?"

"I chased the man who did it," he said, still panting. He hit me with this." He handed the bedpan over.

"I think we ought to get you checked over," she said, gesturing to his head. "I'm Dr Patel, by the way."

"No, honestly. I'm fine." He paused. "You need to ring the police and tell them what's happened. I don't think there's any danger of that man coming back today, but they need to post someone outside Rachel's door as soon as they can. If you run into any problems, please give me a call."

He handed the doctor his business card and then turned to Wendy.

"Are you going to be okay?" he asked.

Wendy nodded. "My sister's coming over later."

"That's good."

She hesitated. "Do you think that was the man who pushed her onto the tracks?"

"It must have been." Luke put his hand on her shoulder. "And don't worry, Wendy. I'll catch him if it's the last thing I do."

"Would you mind staying with me until my sister arrives? She shouldn't be more than an hour or so."

"Of course."

It was only when Luke was sitting on the train to Bath that he remembered the piece of paper he had picked up. He took it out of his pocket, unfolded it and read what was written on it.

A-582858

C-070615

D-672311

The writing was neat and clear, but he couldn't fathom what the letters and numbers meant. Phone numbers were a possibility, assuming the 'A', 'C' and 'D' stood for cities such as Aylesbury, Cambridge or Dover. Alternatively, it could be the combination numbers for three safes or lock-up boxes.

After a while, he gave up and decided he would tap the collective minds of the team when he was in the office in the morning. Right now, his head was sore and he needed to rest. He clicked his phone to silent, leaned against the headrest and was asleep within a minute.

Chapter 54

Alfie hadn't called. No surprise there, but Sam decided she wasn't going to wait any longer. There hadn't been any update from Luke, but even if he'd had success with the GNE executive he was meeting, she was convinced Alfie knew something that could be vital to bringing these men to justice.

She rang the bell and this time it was Alfie's sister who answered.

"Oh, you again," she said. "What's he done this time?"

"Nothing," Sam said. "I'm not from his school," she added in advance of the anticipated question. "I'm a relative of Owen's and he needs his help with something."

"He's not in."

"Do you know where he is?"

Instead of answering, she turned around and bellowed, in an excellent imitation of her mother's very far from dulcet tones, "Mum, where's Alfie gone?"

The answer came back just as loud. "He's gone to Joel's."

She turned back to Sam and repeated this, "He's gone to Joel's."

"Yes, I gathered," Sam said. "Where's that?"

She turned again and screamed, "Where does Joel live?"

The reply was immediate, and just as ear-shattering as before. "45 Sycamore Street."

She turned back to Sam. "45 Sycamore Street," she said, again unnecessarily.

"Thanks," Sam said, turning to leave.

"What's wrong with Owen?" the girl called, but Sam was already halfway down the drive and elected not to answer.

She entered the address into her maps app and was pleased to see it was only two streets away so decided to leave the car and walk.

The house was an identikit copy of Alfie's, even down to the bright red front door. However, the woman who answered the door couldn't have been more opposite to Alfie's mother. She was petite, blonde and spoke very quietly.

"Hello," she said, smiling. "How can I help."

"Is Alfie here?" Sam asked, returning the smile.

"Yes. He and Joel are working on a project together. Come on in."

She led Sam to a conservatory at the back where the two boys were sitting next to each other on a small sofa, a book open on Joel's lap.

"I'll leave you to it," she said as she left the room.

The boys looked up when they saw her, and Alfie's eyes widened.

"Alfie," she said. "Can I have a word?"

He swallowed, turned to Joel and said. "It's about Owen. He's ill or something."

"He was at school today," Joel said. "I saw him."

"Owen's not actually ill," Sam said, coming to Alfie's rescue. "But he's got a problem at home and needs Alfie's help." She paused. "Alfie, can we go in the garden and talk?"

He nodded, stood up and opened the door to the back garden.

"We won't be long," Sam said as she followed him out.

The garden was neat, mainly lawn with a paved path towards a summerhouse at the back. There was a wooden bench outside.

"Let's sit over there," Sam said, gesturing to the bench.

He followed wordlessly and sat down beside her, but didn't say anything, just stared forwards at the back of the house.

She could tell he was tense.

"What happened at the party, Alfie?" she asked, after waiting a couple of minutes in the hope he might calm down.

There was no answer.

"My colleagues and I," she went on, "have evidence which proves children are being abused at Baz Hartman's parties. Is that what you witnessed?"

"It was worse," he said, his voice so quiet she almost didn't hear him.

"What was worse?" she said. "Did something happen to you?"

He looked at her, shook his head, then returned to staring into the middle distance.

"What happened, Alfie?"

"He threatened my mum and dad, and Milly too."

"Who did?"

"The man with my phone."

"Was this when he gave it back?"

"He didn't give it back. He told me…" He wiped a tear from his eye before continuing. "He told me he needed it for their contact details. That if I told anyone, he'd come after my family."

"Told anyone what?"

He turned to look at her again. "I can't tell you," he said. "I can't tell anyone."

She waited, judging that he would have to come to it in his own time.

He continued to wipe tears from his eyes and after a few minutes started to speak, again so quietly she could hardly make the words out.

"It was a boy, I think," he said. "About my age, maybe younger. He was naked, and…" He sighed again and took a deep breath before continuing. "There was blood all over him, and all over the carpet."

"Was he dead?" Sam asked.

He nodded. "He looked dead to me."

"What was the man's name, Alfie?"

"I don't know. There were two of them who were kind of bouncers. They wore dinner jackets and they were both big, but the one who refused to give my phone back and threatened me was slightly taller.

Sam thought back to the investigation board. These sounded like Kieran and Nat, and she seemed to recall Josh saying that Kieran was the taller of the two.

"You won't tell anyone, will you?" Alfie went on in a plaintive voice.

"Thank you for telling me this," Sam said, ignoring his question. "And don't worry, we'll bring the man who did this to justice."

Sam rang Luke as she walked back to her car but it went straight to voicemail. She left a message asking him to ring her urgently and looked at her watch.

It was just coming up to five-thirty.

Chapter 55

"So where are you off to after dinner?" Leanne asked.

Josh held his hand up until he'd finished his mouthful of chicken kiev, then said, "I'm meeting Dylan. He's one of the boys I met at the party on Saturday." He paused and licked his lips. "This is marvelissimo."

"I heated it myself."

"Yeah, uh…" He was stumped for the right reply. "It's very well heated. It's, uh…"

"Hot?"

"Yes, it's hot."

"I put the chips in the oven too."

"Right. Uh, good. Well done."

"Is it safe?"

"Definito," Josh said. He pointed at his plate. "They're hot, but not too hot."

She raised one eyebrow. "No, Joshy. I meant meeting Dylan. Is it safe?"

"Of course it is. He's only fifteen."

"Yes, well, I don't like you going off on these undercover thingamabobs."

"Operations," Josh said, his head held up.

"Whatever. You could have been in big trouble on Saturday if they sussed you were older than you said you were." She looked him up and down. "Mind you, you're not exactly mature."

"Eh!"

"Stringy almost."

He was about to say something when he noticed the grin spreading across her face.

"Mmm," he said as he put another mouthful of chicken in his mouth.

She slid her hand to his jeans pocket.

"Not now, Leanne," he said, his eyes on the kitchen door. "Mum might come in."

"This isn't foreplay, stupid. I've put my rape alarm in your pocket, just in case."

He moved his hand to his pocket but she stilled him with a glance. "Either you take it, or…"

"Or what, smartypants."

"I'll withdraw privileges."

"You mean you won't…"

"That's right." She nodded. "I won't heat food up for you for a week."

He fired double finger guns at her. "Okay, I'll take it. You sure know how to threaten a guy." He swallowed his last chip and stood up. "Right, I'd better be off."

"What time do you think you'll be back?"

"Probably about seven." He chuckled. "Give it until 7:30 and then send in the cavalry."

Once he was in his car, Josh checked Callum's text to make sure he'd remembered the address correctly. Yes, he'd been right. It was 32 Lord Avenue, which if he remembered rightly was in Walcot. He entered it into his maps app and clicked on the button. Twelve minutes, it said, directing him towards the north edge of Victoria Park.

He had thought long and hard about how to play it with Dylan, and had decided he needed to be straight with him. That's exactly what Luke would do, he knew. He'd be honest about the investigation and encourage him to open up about everything he'd seen at the party.

He'd have to be patient as well. Dylan was a nervy type and the information may well have to be coaxed out of him. However, it was a nice bright evening and Josh enjoyed this kind of work.

Lord Avenue was a turning off the London Road. He pulled up outside number 32 and found it hard to believe it could be Dylan's uncle's house. It was one of several on the street that had their windows boarded up, and the idea that anyone lived in it seemed almost laughable. He rechecked the text. Yes, definitely number 32.

He stepped through the front gate and across the tiny weed-strewn front yard to the door which was open a few inches.

"Hello," he shouted. "Dylan, are you there?"

There was no response.

"Hello," he called again, slightly louder this time.

Still nothing.

He shrugged his shoulders and turned back to the car. He had just opened the driver's door when his phone pinged and he looked down to see another message from Callum.

'Dylan's in the garden. Straight through the house to the back.'

He was confused at first, then realised that Callum must be with Dylan. He should have expected it, and it would make the interview easier.

He returned to the house and tried to pull the door open. It was held on by only one hinge and resisted, but he managed to make enough room to squeeze through.

Once inside, he was struck by the smell of damp, and also by how dark it was. The front door was open a few inches and yet light seemed to struggle to infiltrate the place. It was eerie and more than a little scary. He put his hand into his pocket, feeling for the alarm Leanne had put there.

He stepped towards the end of the corridor. To the right was a partly open door. Beyond it was complete darkness, not surprising given that all the windows were boarded up. He had a sudden need to see what was in the room, just in case. His muscles tightened as he pushed the door open.

As he did so, there was a deafening banshee scream. Then there was another screech, and he fell backwards onto the floor, at which point the second noise, which was from his own mouth, ceased.

The banshee scream continued, however, and Josh realised with a shock that it was coming from his jeans pocket. He jerked the rape alarm out, pressed on it, then harder, until the noise stopped and the bleak silence returned.

"Buggery-buggery," he said, panting from the fear that had enveloped him. "Thank goodness no one was here to see that."

"I'm here," came a deep voice behind him.

Chapter 56

Josh turned to see a vision from hell.

The man in front of him was clad completely in black, his face a red grinning skeleton behind a glass visor. He raised a hand, in it a matt black canister.

"Take this, fuckwat!" he screamed.

Without thinking, Josh threw a punch at the canister. The man's arm fell to one side, and Josh gave a squeal as his knuckles felt the impact. There was a hiss as the aerosol went off, spray covering the wall beside him, and his eyes and nose started to tingle as some of the gas particles bounced onto his face.

He had to act quickly. The man was big, much bigger than he was, and any moment now he would pull his arm back and direct the canister back onto his target.

Josh did the only thing he could think of.

He dropped to his knees and put all his strength into bouncing back up to drive his head into the man's groin. There was a satisfying yelp of pain and surprise as he fell backwards against the wall and the canister fell to the ground.

Eyes still on the grinning skeleton mask, Josh crawled backwards on his knees and felt along the floor for the canister, first with his left hand and then with both hands. *Where the pissy-piss is it?*

As he searched, his attacker started to recover.

"Bastard!" he said, as he raised himself to his full height. He started to slowly move forwards.

Josh stared up at him, his hands frantically jerking backwards and forwards across the bare pine floorboards. Then his left hand brushed something, so lightly he almost didn't feel it. Quickly he moved his hand back, gripped the canister tightly and swung it forwards and up.

For the second time, a solid object smashed into his attacker's groin. He staggered back against the wall again, breathing heavily, and Josh saw his opportunity. He leapt to his feet and pushed past the man, who was now wheezing and bent double, in too much pain to stop him.

Josh ran down the corridor and put all his weight into the door. Rather than creak open, as he had expected, it fell off its single hinge and he fell over with it.

He was on his hands and knees and turned to see sunlight now streaming into the corridor. The man who had attacked him was again beginning to recover, but Josh wasn't going to hang around to watch. He darted to the road, climbed into his car, turned the engine on and accelerated down the road, his only words a soft "Thank you, Horatio," as he tried to breathe again.

Once he was several streets away, Josh stopped the car, put the handbrake on and took his hands off the steering wheel. His hands started shaking so he put them back.

After a few seconds, he let go again, grabbed his phone and called Luke. To his surprise, it went straight to voicemail so he left a message and hung up.

"Come on Josh," he said to himself. "You know what you have to do."

He turned the Clio around and headed back, slowing as he passed a carpet fitter's van, the response to his peering at the driver being a raised middle finger and a mouthed 'Wanker'.

He parked up outside 79 Lord Avenue, a good seventy or eighty yards short of number 32 and on the opposite side of the road. There was a chance the man had already left but he would give it ten minutes. If nothing happened, he would try Luke again.

A few minutes later he was rewarded as a man emerged from number 32 and turned away from Josh. He was wearing a hoody and his face wasn't visible. On his back was a rucksack.

At the end of Lord Avenue, the man took a left into Earlsway. Josh put the Clio into gear and was at the turning in time to see him climb into a large silver pickup truck. He snapped off a quick photo on his phone and decided that following his attacker was definitely the wrong thing to do.

On the other hand...

He waggled his head from side to side. Surely, it would be safe enough. He'd stay a decent distance behind and keep trying Luke.

Yes, he'd follow.

He put the Clio into gear and it slid right out again.

He tried a second time. No luck.

Buggery-buggery, he thought as he bashed his head against the steering wheel.

Ah well, it was probably for the best.

Chapter 57

Luke woke with a start and looked out of the window to see the train was pulling into Bath Spa. He grabbed his bag and darted to the end of the carriage.

Once out he tried to shake himself awake, then remembered he'd turned his mobile to silent. He clicked the button off red and saw that he had an email from Eve Montgomery, Baz Hartman's sister. The subject was 'Party Lists' and the first attachment was '170623-party.xls'. He clicked on it and read through the names, half smiling as he saw 'George Bailey' fifth on the list of twelve.

He clicked on the second attachment '030623-party.xls'. There were eleven names on this list, but it was the ninth that drew his attention.

"Oh, bugger," he said.

He closed the email and saw that he'd also had two missed calls and dialled his voicemail. The first message was from Sam.

"Luke," she said. "Please call me as soon as you get this. I've spoken to Alfie, Owen's friend. You need to hear what he said."

He clicked for the next message.

"Guv, ring me." It was Josh and his voice was shaky.

He decided Josh's call sounded more urgent and rang him

"Hi, guv," Josh said when he answered. He was panting and out of breath.

"What's wrong, Josh?" Luke said, trying to hide the sense of dread from his voice. "You sounded like you were in trouble."

"My car's broken down. I'm walking home."

Luke couldn't believe his ears. "That's it?" he said.

"No. A skeleton in riot gear attacked me."

"You're not making sense."

"Are you in Bath, guv?"

"Yes, I'm at the station."

"Can you pick me up and I'll explain. I'm on Julian Road."

Luke rang Sam as soon as he'd left the car park.

"Thanks for ringing," she said when she picked up. "Owen's friend Alfie told me he saw a body at Baz Hartman's party on the 3rd of June."

"I think I know his name," Luke said. "It's Ethan Jarvis."

"Who?"

"Where are you, Sam?"

"I'm on my way home. Just passing the Globe."

"Can you come into the office?"

"Sure."

"Great, I'll see you there."

He hung up and called Pete Gilmore, who answered on the first ring.

"Hi, Luke," Pete said. "Just running through things with Jill North. Is everything okay?"

"Your second body," Luke said. "Have you identified him yet?"

"No, we're still working on it."

"I'm fairly confident it's either Callum White or Dylan Williams."

"What? How do you know?"

"Can you come to our office, Pete? I'll explain everything and I need you to see our investigation board."

"I'll be there in fifteen minutes."

A couple of hundred yards down Julian Road, Luke saw Josh standing outside a shop.

"We're heading for the office," Luke said, once Josh had climbed into the passenger seat and they were on their way. "This is another time when I wish I could bluelight my way somewhere."

"Why are we going to the office, guv?"

"You first. What's this about a skeleton in riot gear?"

Josh ran through what had happened on Lord Avenue.

"You had a lucky escape," Luke said when he'd finished. "I'm pretty sure the man who attacked you has killed at least two boys, one of them Callum or Dylan."

"It must have been him that texted me," Josh said.

Luke remembered the piece of paper he'd found by Rachel's hospital bed and it suddenly made sense. He reached into his trouser pocket, pulled it out and passed it over.

"Look at this," he said.

Josh unfolded it and read what was written.

A-582858

C-070615

D-672311

"Where did you get this, guv?" he asked.

"I went to see Rachel Adams this afternoon," Luke said. "A man dressed as a doctor disconnected her ventilator in an attempt to kill her. He managed to get away, but dropped that. I couldn't make any sense of it at the time, but I think I know what it is now. How old did you say Callum is?"

"He told me he was sixteen last Thursday." Josh looked down at the piece of paper again and tapped the middle number. "Which would mean he was born on the 15th of June 2007."

"Exactly. I bet those are PIN codes and the middle one's Callum's. It's the same man." He put his foot on the pedal and accelerated to well over the speed limit. "Sod the blues and twos," he said. "Heaven help any officer who tries to pull me over."

Chapter 58

Luke screeched to a halt in Filchers' almost deserted car park and Sam parked next to him a second or so later. The three of them walked into the building and he marched ahead of the others to the security guard manning reception.

"Two police officers will be here shortly," he said, after showing his Filchers ID. "Detective Inspectors Gilmore and North. Please escort them up to the Ethics Room as soon as they get here."

"I'll get the kettle on, guv," Josh said, once they were upstairs. "I could do with a caffeine hit to calm my nerves."

"What happened?" Sam asked, as Josh left for the staff kitchen.

"We've got a double murderer on our hands," Luke said. "He attacked Josh who was lucky to get away."

"Christ!"

There was a knock on the door.

"Your guests," the security guard said.

"Thanks," Luke said.

Pete Gilmore walked in followed by a woman who didn't look to be much more than thirty. She had bright copper hair that fell in curls over her shoulders, an attractive look that lay in contrast to her face which held an air of 'why the hell am I here?'

"This is Jill North," Pete said.

Jill nodded to Luke and Sam then noticed the whiteboard.

"Are you carrying out some kind of parallel investigation?" she asked, her accent definitely Black Country.

"I'm Luke and this is Sam," Luke said, ignoring her

question. "And this is Josh," he added as Josh walked in bearing a tray of coffees.

"I saw you walking past," Josh said, "So I made you both white coffees. I hope that's okay."

"Thanks," Pete said, taking one of the mugs.

"No time," Jill snapped. She turned to Luke. "Why are we here?"

"Let me explain," Luke said. "I am pretty certain the man you're looking for is on our investigation board. He killed Ethan Jarvis and then took Callum White and Dylan Williams."

"Who are Callum White and Dylan Williams?"

"Please sit down, Jill."

"This had better be worth our while," she said, shaking her head as she took the chair between Sam and Pete.

"As Pete knows," Luke began, "my team has been investigating alleged grooming and sexual abuse at Baz Hartman's parties."

Jill started to protest but Luke held his hand up to stop her.

"We didn't involve the police," Luke continued, in anticipation of what she had been about to say, "because there were only rumours. Baz Hartman works for GNE, a client of Filchers, and it was a GNE employee who asked us to look into whether there was any truth behind the stories he'd heard."

He pointed to Baz's name and photo on the board. "We haven't found anything to suggest Baz himself has done anything untoward." He saw Josh pull a face of disgust as he said this, but chose to ignore it.

"However," he went on, "we've done some digging and undercover work and it's become clear that these four…" He pointed to the right of the board at the images of Damon Prendergast, Ozzy Vaughan, Reggie Dowden and Marvin Winespottle, "…are using the parties to seduce, and in at least one case rape, young boys who are invited by Eve

Montgomery." He pointed to the Post-it next to Baz's with Eve's name on it. "She's Baz Hartman's Personal Assistant, and also his sister."

Jill sat forward, her interest now piqued. "And you think Ethan Jarvis was one of the guests?" she asked.

"I know it," Luke said. "Eve emailed me the lists of invitees and he went to the party on the 3rd of June."

"Who's Ethan Jarvis?" Sam asked.

"He's a lad of fifteen from the Midlands whose body was found at Chew Valley Lake last week," Pete said.

Sam stood up, walked to the board and stuck two blank Post-its up next to the existing Post-its for Owen, Callum and Dylan on the left-hand side. She wrote 'Alfie' on one and 'Ethan Jarvis' on another before looking questioningly at Luke.

"Alfie Inskip, Owen Lambert, Callum White and Dylan Williams," Luke said and she added their surnames.

"Alfie and Owen went to the party on the 3rd," Sam said, "and Alfie told me this afternoon that he'd seen a body there. It must have been Ethan's."

"I think the second body is either Callum's or Dylan's," Luke said. "Josh, can you explain who they are?"

"I met Callum and Dylan at the party on Saturday," Josh said, looking at Pete and Jill. "I was pretending I was only sixteen." He waited for a moment but there was no 'how could you pass for sixteen when you're so mature' so he continued. "Callum texted me yesterday saying Dylan wanted to meet me at 6 pm this evening. When I turned up a man in a skull mask tried to spray me with tear gas and I was lucky to get away."

"Any idea who he was?" Luke asked.

Josh considered this. "He was big but well-built so definitely not Reggie," he said, "and probably too tall to be Ozzie. It could have been Damon or Marvin though."

"Who are those two?" Pete asked, pointing to two Post-its with 'Kieran' and 'Nat' written on them. They were next to Baz's in the centre of the board.

"They work for Baz," Josh said. "Kind of bouncers come odd-job men."

"Why do you ask, Pete?" Luke said.

"I'm not sure. There's something about the name Kieran that rings a bell."

"He took my phone," Josh said.

"He was probably the one who took Alfie's phone then," Sam said. "Although in his case he didn't give it back at the end of the party."

Josh and Luke looked at each other and Josh pulled the piece of paper out of his pocket. "Are you thinking what I'm thinking, guv?" he asked, holding the handwritten note out.

"What's that?" Jill asked, pointing at the piece of paper.

"It's a note I found written by the killer," Luke said. He saw her questioning look. "I'll explain how I got it later. The important thing is it's got three pin codes on it." He handed it to her and pointed at the middle line.

A-582858

C-070615

D-672311

"We know that one's Callum's because it's his date of birth. Which means the other two are almost certainly Alfie's and Dylan's."

"So you think this man Kieran is our killer?" she asked.

"It seems likely."

Pete stood up, pointed at the board and exclaimed. "Kieran Leonard!" He turned to Luke. "Do you remember that trouble at the Pride March in Bristol? I think it was 2018."

"Was that the one where someone was batoned by one of our officers?"

Pete nodded. "A bunch of thugs from the far right

turned up and started throwing stones at the marchers. The riot police went in and Leonard fractured the skull of one of the Pride organisers. He said it was an accident but they found neo-nazi pamphlets in a container he was renting where the Harbutt's plasticine factory used to be. He was suspended and later sacked."

"The guy who attacked me had a riot helmet on," Josh said.

"That has to be our man," Luke said.

Jill stood up. "We'd better get back to the office, Pete," she said. "We need to find out where he lives and put out an APB."

"Do you want our help?" Josh asked.

"It's a police matter now," she said. "Thanks for your assistance. You've done well."

Josh started to respond but Luke held his hand up to stop him.

"If you need anything, Pete," he said, "let me know."

"Will do," Pete said. He turned back as he left the room and mouthed. "I'll ring you later."

"Golly, she was patronising," Josh said when she'd left.

Luke gave a thin smile. "Don't worry," he said. "I'll ring Pete later for an update and to tell him what happened to me at St Mary's Hospital. He needs to tie in with the Met's investigation into who disconnected Rachel's ventilator."

"There's a chance Callum or Dylan is still alive though, guv. Isn't there anything we can do?"

"We can bring the board up to date, but not much more. Let's do that and then I'll drop you home. You can call a garage in the morning to sort your car out."

Chapter 59

Kieran drove down the alley to the line of five containers at the back, pulled up outside the burgundy one at the end and turned the engine off.

He sat still for a few seconds and then banged his left hand against the steering wheel. He had been careless, allowing the little fucker to get away. He'd get him back though, and when he got him…

A malevolent grin spread across his face. These faggots had it coming to them and this one would soon learn not to mess with him.

George fucking Bailey!

He gave a deep chuckle as he remembered the film. It wasn't going to be any kind of wonderful life once he'd finished with this particular George Bailey. No rescue by angels for him.

But why the fuck was he also calling himself 'Josh'?

He leaned forward, removed a key and a bottle of water from the glovebox and climbed out of the Isuzu. He was about to unlock the door when he heard a scuffling noise and put his ear to the container wall. Had the little bastard managed to loosen his bonds? If he had he'd teach him a lesson he wouldn't soon forget.

He readied himself in case the kid was hiding ready to pounce and put the key in the lock. He started to turn it and the noise came again, nearer this time. He looked down to see a large grey rat scurry out from beneath a discarded bag of rubbish. It ran around the corner and disappeared.

Smiling to himself, he unlocked the door and tugged it open.

Callum looked across at him from the chair, his eyes squinting against the light, and Kieran walked over, unscrewed the top of the bottle and tipped it up over the boy's mouth. Callum drank noisily, glugging it down and almost retching, so desperate was he for water. After a few seconds he had had enough, but Kieran kept the bottle there, water now sliding off the sides of the boy's chin and onto his t-shirt.

Kieran threw the empty bottle to the side of the container and took a step back.

"Are you hungry?" he asked, looking down at the boy and half-smiling.

Callum nodded.

"I've got sandwiches in the car. Smoked ham and cheese. You're not a fucking vegan are you?"

Callum shook his head.

"What's up? Cat got your tongue?"

"W… w… what have you done with Dylan?"

Kieran marched forward and grabbed the boy's jaw in one massive hand.

"He's past fucking tense," he spat. "Don't you worry about him. He's where your type belong." He let go of Callum's jaw and stepped back again.

"W… what do you mean?"

"Your sort deserve what they get. Dylan. That tarted up one, Ethan. George or Josh or whatever the fuck his name is." He jabbed a finger in Callum's chest. "You."

"Why?"

"You fucking know why. You're perverts, going to those parties and offering your bodies. You make me sick."

"I d… didn't. I w… wasn't. I'm a fan. I l… l… like the show."

"Do you want the sandwich?"

Callum nodded again.

"I need some fucking answers first."

Callum swallowed. "W… what do you want to know?"

"Where does Josh live?"

Callum stared up at him but didn't say anything.

Kieran sneered. "Where does he fucking live?" He repeated, emphasising each word this time.

"I d… don't know."

"Well, here's the truth," Kieran said in a much softer voice, before leaning down so that their noses were almost touching and bellowing, "You're fucking lying!"

Callum shrank back. "I'm not," he said.

Kieran stood back again and considered his options. He could threaten the kid's parents. That might work. Or he could hurt the kid, which might be more satisfying. The important thing was to get results, and get them quickly, before George fucking Bailey went to the police.

Of course, he might already have gone to them. He'd be scared, that was much was for certain, but he was only fifteen or sixteen so his first instinct would be to go home and tell him mummy and daddy.

Yes, the more he thought about it, the more certain he was that he'd be at home.

He needed the fucking address.

"Do you love your mummy?" he asked.

Callum didn't say anything but stared at him, his lower lip trembling.

"I know where she works," Kieran went on. "It's all in your fucking phone. I might pay her a visit tomorrow, or better still, I could follow her out of your house." He grinned. "Your address is on your phone too. She only works a few hundred yards away so she must walk to work. Is that right, Callum? Does she walk to work?"

Tears started running down Callum's cheeks but still he said nothing.

"There was a photo of you and her as well. She's fucking gorgeous. I might…"

"Weston," Callum blurted out.

"What?"

"Weston. Josh lives in Weston."

"Now we're getting somewhere."

Kieran waited.

"Combe Park End," Callum said after a few seconds, so quietly Kieran couldn't quite catch it.

"What did you say?" he asked.

"It's Josh's house. It's called Combe Park End. He told me it's opposite the cricket club."

"You'd better be telling the fucking truth." Kieran walked to the door before turning back. "Mind you," he added with a smirk. "I might pay your mum a visit anyway."

"No!" Callum screamed.

Kieran locked the door, climbed into the 4x4 and reached into the glovebox for a second time. He pulled out a packet of sandwiches, ripped it open and placed it on the passenger seat before turning the engine on and heading back to the main road.

He was ravenous and smoked ham and cheese were his favourite, but he'd have to eat them on the way. He needed to get to Weston pretty fucking quickly.

Chapter 60

"I'm not a little kid," Noah said. "I don't need a babysitter."

"Leanne's not a babysitter," his mum said. "You know that."

"Why is she here then?'

A smile came over his mum's face and she leaned forward to tousle her son's hair.

"Don't, Mum," he said, pulling away.

"You know full well why she's here, Noah. Josh is out at a business meeting and she's cooking their meal."

"Is she staying the night?"

"I expect so." She paused. "Be nice to her."

"I will."

She grabbed her handbag and car keys. "I'll be back by nine," she said. "See you later."

"Bye, Mum."

Noah went back into the kitchen where Leanne was emptying sliced onion into a frying pan on the hob.

"Has your Mum gone?" she asked.

"Yes. What are you making?"

"Spaghetti Bolognese."

"Cool," he said and decided he'd been nice to her so that was his work done. "I'm going upstairs to fly to Norway," he added as he stepped back into the hall.

"What?" she asked absent-mindedly, suddenly remembering that she should have added garlic.

Noah headed upstairs, sat in his swivel chair and turned his PS5 on. Once the game was up and running he put his headphones on and turned the volume up. This evening, he decided, he was going to move up a notch and pilot an Airbus A380.

*

Leanne added a spoonful of lazy garlic to the frying pan and stirred it in. Once the onion had softened a little she added a tin of tomatoes, a tablespoon of Worcestershire sauce and salt and pepper. That was it, wasn't it? Or was it? She decided to check the recipe and picked her phone up while still stirring only for it to slide through her fingers and into the pan.

"Shit!" she exclaimed, then fumbled for it saying, "Ow," as she dipped her fingers into the bubbling liquid. She pulled her hand out, reached for a fish slice and lifted the phone onto the countertop. She wiped it with some kitchen towel but the screen was blank.

"Shit!" she said again. She pressed the power button, but the phone remained obstinately inactive.

Leanne was debating what to try next when the doorbell rang. She ran her hands under the tap, grabbed a tea towel and walked to the front door, still drying her hands as she pulled it open.

'Sorry," she started to say, "I was…"

Before she could finish the sentence a large hand shoved her in the chest and pushed hard. She staggered backwards, grabbing the handrail of the stairs to retain her balance.

"Where's Josh?" the man at the door shouted. He moved towards her and slammed the door closed behind him.

"Who's Josh?" she said.

He slapped her across the face and her head was thrown back. She felt an immediate burning sensation on her cheek.

"Where the fuck is he?"

She looked at him blankly and couldn't stop herself from glancing at the ceiling.

"Is the little faggot upstairs?" he demanded.

"No!" she exclaimed. "I don't know anyone called Josh. You must have got the wrong house."

He growled, grabbed her left arm and pulled her to him. "Come on. We're going to find him."

He dragged her to the stairs and shoved her up. Once at the top, he was faced with four doors.

"Which one's he in?" he shouted.

"He's not," she said.

Still holding her by the arm, he pressed the handle of the nearest door, pushed it open and shoved her in ahead of him. The room was empty.

He pushed the next door open and she gulped.

"No," she screamed. "Leave him alone."

He grinned as he opened the door and marched her in. To his surprise, this room was also empty. It was clearly the room of a teenage boy though. Discarded school clothes lay on the floor next to the single bed, and a games console and monitor stood on a desk by the far wall.

"Has the little fucker gone out?" he asked.

Leanne was too frightened to respond.

He hit her again, the other cheek this time. She fell to the floor and put her hand to her face.

"Where is he?" he shouted.

"I don't know."

"Has he been back this evening?"

"Who?"

"Fucking Josh. Who do you think?" He paused., and then added, almost to himself. "He hasn't got back yet, has he?"

He bent down, grabbed her arm and jerked her up. "Come on," he said. "We're going to sit downstairs and wait for him."

He manhandled her back down the stairs and into the room at the front. Once there he pushed her backwards onto the sofa.

"Actually," he said as an idea occurred to him, "I think

you ought to ask him when he'll be home. Are you his older sister?" She didn't answer. "Where's your phone?"

"It's broken."

He leaned over her and swung his arm back, his hand forming a fist this time.

"It's the truth," she said hastily. "I was cooking and I dropped it in the pan."

He grabbed her again and marched her to the kitchen.

"There," she said, pointing to the worktop.

He grunted, let go of her and reached for the phone. She watched as he pressed the power button, stared at the screen and then pressed it again.

Leanne grabbed the handle of the frying pan and swung with all her might. He tried to dodge out of the way, but she caught him with a glancing blow to the right temple causing him to stagger back.

He let out a roar and reached forward again. She tried to pull away but he was too quick and wrenched the pan from her grasp before throwing it to the floor, sending bolognese everywhere.

Leanne's eyes lit on the knife rack. She reached out, grabbed the handle of the middle knife and pulled it out. It was a carving knife with a ten-inch blade and she pointed it shakily at her assailant's face.

"Stay there!" she screamed.

He grinned and threw the phone at her. It connected with her face and he took advantage of her momentary distraction to grab and twist her wrist.

"You're going to suffer for that," he said as the knife clattered harmlessly to the floor.

Chapter 61

"She's not answering," Josh said, as Leanne's phone went straight to voicemail. He waited for the beep and then said, "My car broke down but Luke is bringing me home. Back in five." He turned his head away before adding in a whisper, "Love you."

"How are you feeling?" Luke asked once he'd hung up.

"Still a bit shaken, guv," Josh admitted. "Not so much by him trying to grab me, more by what he's done to Callum and Dylan. Any idea why he's doing this?"

"Serial killers can be motivated by almost anything," Luke said. "It can be revenge, or sexual gratification, or because he wants to punish a group of people he regards with contempt. That was the case with Peter Sutcliffe, who the press dubbed the Yorkshire Ripper. He mainly targeted prostitutes."

Luke reflected for a moment.

"It could be any or a combination of those in this case," he went on. "I remember more about Kieran Leonard's sacking now. He was found to be a member of a banned far-right party called 'National Action' after that incident at Bristol Pride and was lucky to escape prison. His motive is probably linked to his beliefs."

"What do people on the far-right believe?" Josh asked.

Luke gave a dry laugh. "In hating almost everyone," he said. "They're ultra-nationalist, racist and intolerant of anyone who's different from their vision of the ideal man."

"Not nice people."

"No. They're not. Where's your house?"

"Just up there, guv. It's opposite the cricket ground."

Luke indicated and pulled up..

"Thanks for the lift," Josh said as he undid his seat belt

and started to get out.

"Hang on," Luke said and pointed out of the window. "Who's that?"

Josh followed his gaze and saw Noah leaning against the gatepost outside the house feeling his pockets.

"It's my brother," Josh said. He climbed out and called across. "You all right, half-pint?"

Noah lifted his head and both Luke and Josh could immediately see that something was wrong. Luke ran across the road after Josh, who was pointing at a pickup parked a few yards along the street.

"That's his car, guv," he said, panic evident in his voice.

Luke didn't need to ask whose car. "What happened, Noah?" he asked.

"I was upstairs," Noah said and swallowed. "I was in the loo and the doorbell rang. Then I heard a man shout 'Where's Josh?' and Leanne screamed." He looked at Josh. "I think he hit her then dragged her upstairs. I thought he was going to come into the bathroom but he took her down again. I gave it a couple of minutes before creeping out and escaping through the front door."

Josh turned and Luke could see he was about to run to the house. He grabbed his arm. "No, Josh," he said. "Wait." He turned back to Noah. "Where are they now?"

"I think they're in the kitchen."

"Have you got your phone?"

"No. I thought I had it, but it must still be in my bedroom."

"Here." Luke extracted his phone from his pocket, entered his PIN code and called up Pete Gilmore's number. He handed it to Noah. "Go to my car, call this man and tell him what's happened and where we are. Okay?"

Noah nodded and ran over to the car.

"What are we going to do, guv?" Josh pleaded. "He's got Leanne. What if…"

"It's you he's after," Luke said. "She'll be fine," he

added, hoping he was right. "But we need to act. We can't afford to wait for the police to get here. What's the layout of the ground floor?"

"There are four rooms." Josh pointed to the bow window at the front of the house. "That's the lounge. Behind it is the dining room and next to that the kitchen. There's also a loo on the other side of the hall."

"So there are four doors off the hall?"

"Yes, but the door to the kitchen is always left open."

"And at the back?"

"There are patio doors from the dining room to the garden, and the kitchen's got a door to the garden too."

"Will those doors be locked?"

"The patio doors will be, but I doubt the kitchen door is."

Luke glanced at the building and came to a decision. "Count to one hundred and then ring the doorbell. I'm going around the back."

Chapter 62

"You stupid bitch!" Kieran hissed.

He stood over Leanne, one leg on either side of her hips as she lay on her back looking up at him. Those staring eyes were driving him up the fucking wall.

The knife he'd torn from her grasp was in his hand now and he pointed it down at her face.

"Lie still," he said, "and don't move a muscle."

He'd been stupid ringing the doorbell and barging in. It would have been far more sensible to wait outside for Josh to come home.

Now he was saddled with another problem, another body to dispose of.

He glared down, wondering whether he should finish her now, make sure she didn't try anything.

The doorbell rang, making him jump.

Fuck!

He hesitated. If it was Josh, why would he ring the bell? Surely he'd have a key.

He looked back down at Leanne. "Are you expecting a visitor?" he barked.

"No," she said, shaking her head.

"What about your parents? Where the fuck are they?"

"They're…" She swallowed. "They're away."

The bell rang again.

He decided to ignore it. Probably the fucking Jehovah's Witnesses, or someone selling something. He looked down at Leanne and put a finger to his lips.

"Keep quiet," he hissed.

He heard footsteps and heaved a sigh of relief. Whoever it was had gone.

Then he heard a creak and the letterbox cover slowly

lifted up. He sighed. Probably leaving one of their pamphlets inviting him to learn about scriptures or some such crap, he thought. What a fucking time to choose.

He raised an eyebrow and tilted his head to one side as two fingers pushed a small oval device to the inner edge of the letterbox and let it drop to the ground.

As it fell an almighty caterwaul filled the hall and 120 decibels of deafening shrieking issued from its tiny speaker.

"What the fuck!" Kieran exclaimed.

The noise kept coming.

He looked down at Leanne and shouted, "Don't move." He wasn't sure she could hear him above the cacophony of noise, but her face told him she'd got the message.

He stepped past her to the front door and slammed his foot down on the object as hard as he could. Dozens of fragments of plastic shot away from under his shoe and the silence was immediate.

He turned back to see Leanne clambering to her feet.

"I told you…" he started to say, then realised a man stood in the kitchen doorway, beckoning her to him. Not just any man, either. This was a giant, his head bent down to enable him to duck under the lintel. The bastard had to be seven feet tall.

It was Kieran who had the advantage though.

He raised the knife and charged.

Chapter 63

Muscle memory was a wonderful thing.

Luke had been a winger in his rugby-playing days, but he'd also been able to kick a ball one hell of a long way. If his team got a penalty fifty-five or even sixty yards from the posts he'd be asked to take it. Nine times out of ten he'd make the distance.

In rugby, you were allowed up to a minute.

In the hall of Josh's house, he had a fraction of a second.

He swung as Kieran dashed at him, straightening his leg to deliver a size 14 metal toecap to the other man's wrist with maximum force. There was a satisfying crack of bones breaking, and the knife flew upwards before falling to the floor.

Kieran was thrown back against the wall. He was panting as he grabbed his injured arm with his other hand, but there was defiance in his eyes.

"Stay there, Josh," Luke said as the front door opened and Josh walked through. "Leanne's fine," he added.

"Thank goodness," Josh said.

"It's over, Kieran," Luke said. "The police will be here at any moment."

The edges of Kieran's lips curled upwards. "Callum will die if you don't let me go," he said. "Do you remember that phrase from 'Alien': 'In space no one can hear you scream'? Well, he's not in space but no one can hear him." He gave a dry chuckle. "Without water, I'd give him forty-eight hours tops."

"And if we let you go?" Luke asked.

"I'll drive a safe distance and ring to tell you where he is."

"You're asking us to trust that you'll keep to your word?"

"No choice as I see it. Can't torture it out of me in this country, can you? Fucking Geneva Convention or something." He paused. "And if you don't let me go I stay schtum and the little faggot meets his maker."

They all heard the distant sound of a police siren.

Luke focused his full attention on Kieran. "Did you ever make models with plasticine when you were younger, Kieran?" he asked.

Kieran's pupils widened and the muscles in his cheeks tightened slightly. It told Luke all he needed to know.

"What are we going to do, guv?" Josh asked anxiously.

"We're going to wait for the police," Luke said, "and then this murdering bastard is going to prison for a very long time."

Kieran's smile had faded. "There's still time," he said, panic evident in his voice now. "I'll ring you. I promise I will. He'll die if I don't tell you where he is."

The sound of sirens grew louder.

"What if he's telling the truth?" Josh asked.

"Don't worry," Luke said. "We'll go and fetch Callum as soon as the police get here."

"Where from, guv?"

Luke smiled. "Bathampton," he said.

Chapter 64

The sirens were becoming even louder. Josh opened the door and looked out to see blue and white flashing lights as two police cars pulled up.

"They're here," he said.

Kieran started to get up but Luke walked over and glared down at him. "Do you want me to break your other arm?" he asked.

Kieran dropped back to the floor. "They deserved to die," he said defiantly.

Luke ignored him and looked up as Pete, Jill and two uniformed officers entered the hall.

"Cuff him," Pete said to the nearest constable.

"No way," Kieran said. He gestured up at Luke. "That fucking monster broke my wrist."

"What should I do?" the constable asked.

"Use his belt," Pete said.

The constable pulled Kieran up and cuffed his left wrist to his belt.

"Can you give me his car keys?" Luke said, holding his hand out.

The constable extracted them from Kieran's trouser pocket and passed them over.

Luke turned to Pete. "I know where he's keeping Callum," he said. "He's in a container in Bathampton where the Harbutt's plasticine factory used to be." He turned to Josh. "Are you okay to come with me?"

"Leanne?" Josh called.

"Go, Joshy," she said from the kitchen doorway. "I'm fine."

"We'll call an ambulance on the way," Luke said as he started to walk around the officers to the front door.

"Wait," Jill said. "You've done very well, but…"

"That's enough, Jill," Pete said, loud enough to stop her in her tracks. "You carry on, Luke," he added. "I'll deal with DI North."

Luke and Josh ran to Kieran's car.

"What are we looking for, guv?" Josh asked.

"A key. He'll have padlocked the container." He unlocked the 4x4 and gestured to the passenger door. "You look over there. I'll search the driver's side."

Josh looked under the empty sandwich packet and on the floor, then clicked open the glove compartment. "Got it, guv," he said holding a key in the air.

They ran back to the beemer. Once they were underway, Luke told Josh to call 999. "Tell them to send an ambulance to the site of the old Harbutt's Factory in Bathampton. We'll meet them there."

Ten minutes later Luke slowed as they reached Bathampton High Street.

"There," Josh said and pointed to the left. "That road's called Harbutts."

"Must be it," Luke said and as he spoke there was the sound of more sirens and he looked in the mirror to see an ambulance approaching.

"Tell them to follow us," Luke said.

Josh got out and waved the ambulance down then spoke to the paramedic through the window. He climbed back into the BMW and Luke turned into Harbutts where they were faced with a development of townhouses.

"This must be where the old factory was," he said, still driving slowly. After forty yards or so he pulled up next to a small alley leading off to the left.

"This is it," Josh said. "I can see the edge of a container right down at the end."

Luke drove to the end of the alley, and the ambulance pulled up behind them. There were five containers, but it only took him a second to see that the burgundy one at the far end was the only one with a padlocked door.

"That one," he said and ran to it. He unlocked and removed the padlock, lifted the handle and swung the door open.

He and Josh walked in to see Callum tied to a chair in the middle of the container. He was looking in their direction, but his eyes were almost closed as they struggled to adjust to the sunlight that was bursting in.

"Are you okay?" Josh asked as he approached.

"Josh," Callum said, his voice weak. "Is that you?"

"Yes, Callum. It's me. You're safe now."

Chapter 65

Luke shut the crate door and fed the cocker a biscuit through one of the gaps in the top.

"Ben will see to you in an hour or so, boy," he said, then glanced to the ceiling before adding with a smile, "or maybe two or three."

Despite the tension and excitement of the day before, Luke had woken at his usual time. The walk through the fields with Wilkins had freshened him up and he decided to pay a visit to Lacock before venturing into the office.

Thirty minutes later he pulled up outside Upper Lodge, a Victorian house in large grounds just outside the village. He walked to the front door and was about to ring the bell when someone called.

"Can I help you?"

It was a woman's voice and he stepped back to see her kneeling in a patch of earth next to a long hedge.

"Hi," he said. "I'm looking for Bertie Fotheringay." As he said this he realised he recognised her. "Are you Fiona?"

She climbed to her feet, wiping her hands on her gardening trousers as she did so. A weatherblown and sturdy woman in her mid-fifties, she smiled and held her hand out. "That's me," she said. "Have we met?"

He nodded and shook her hand. "I'm Luke Sackville, Hugo's son."

"Oh yes, I remember. I'm sorry but Bertie's in London. Can I help?"

"No, it's okay. Sorry to interrupt your gardening." As he said this he saw something white in a willow trug on the ground where she had been kneeling.

She followed his glance. "I'm picking some field mushrooms for dinner," she said. "We're really lucky, we get loads of them under this hedgerow. Unfortunately, I'm allergic but Bertie loves them."

"Do you mind if I have a look?"

"Of course."

He bent down, pulled one out and brushed his finger across the top. The flesh immediately turned yellow.

"These aren't field mushrooms," he said. "These are Yellow Stainers and they're poisonous."

"No!"

"I'm afraid so." He showed her the yellow staining.

"Oh dear. I saw them go yellow when I put them in the pot, but I thought it was because of the turmeric. Lucky you spotted it." She gave a little laugh. "Maybe I should stick to Sainsbury's in future, rather than doing my own foraging."

"Yes. I think that's probably a good idea."

"Give my best to your mother and father."

"I will."

"Shall I tell Bertie you want to speak to him?"

"No, it's fine." Luke smiled. "It wasn't anything important."

After another thirty minutes of driving, he pulled up in Filchers car park and went straight up to his boss's office.

"You can go in," Gloria said. "He's practising," she added with a smile.

Luke went into the office to find the conference table and chairs had been put to one side. Filcher was bent over a putter and staring fixedly at a mug which had been placed on its side about fifteen feet away.

"Yips," he said without looking up. "Ruddy nuisance." He sent the ball towards the cup and it hit the right edge. "Mmm. Pass it back will you?"

Luke retrieved the ball and Filcher indicated for him to put it back at the base of his putter.

"I've solved Bertie Fotheringay's issue," Luke said as he put the ball down.

"Not before time."

Filcher hit the ball again and this time it hit the left edge. He waved his hand to indicate that he wanted the ball back. This time Luke ignored him and Filcher gave a loud harrumph before walking over and dragging the ball back with his putter.

"I sorted out some problems for GNE too," Luke said.

"Well done."

Filcher hit the ball and again it hit the left edge. He raised the putter and inspected the toe as if it was the culprit and then retrieved his ball again.

"Some of their staff were grooming underage boys," Luke said.

"Excellent, excellent."

"And Josh and I caught a double murderer yesterday evening."

"Good, good."

Filcher hit the ball again and this time it missed the cup completely. "Ruddy hell," he said and looked at Luke for the first time. "Tell Gloria to bring me a different golf ball on your way out, will you? This one's not working."

Luke was still smiling when he reached the Ethics Room. To his surprise, all four members of his team were already there.

"Have you seen the papers?" Helen asked, gesturing to the table in the centre of the room

"No. Why?"

"Have a look."

Luke walked to the table and it was the Independent that caught his eye. He read the headline article, next to which were photos of Damon Prendergast and Ozzy Vaughan.

Shame of Star Presenters

Damon Prendergast and Ozzy Vaughan, co-presenters of 'Rock-n-Roll-n-Rap', were sacked today by GNE after a three-month investigation. Both men had been using their celebrity status to groom and abuse boys, some as young as fourteen.

John Steadman, Head of Light Entertainment at GNE, said, "I instigated the investigation as soon as I heard rumours. These people are role models and for them to behave in this way is reprehensible and something GNE just will not tolerate."

Reggie Dowden and Marvin Winespottle, contestants on 'Hall of Flame', were also dismissed.

Luke recognised his own words in the quote attributed to John Steadman.

"Three months!" Josh exclaimed, pointing at the article. "Three hours more like."

"There's a lot worse to come for the four of them," Luke said. "The police are going to be asking them a lot of questions, and it's only a matter of time before they face charges."

His phone rang and his heart started thumping as he saw who was calling.

"Is there news?" he asked when he answered.

"Rach has come out of the coma," Wendy said. "She recognised me and said 'Hello, Mum'." He could tell she was crying, but these were tears of happiness this time. "She's going to recover, Luke," she went on. "The doctors say there's no evidence of brain damage and she might be able to come home as early as next week."

"That's fantastic, Wendy. Please give her my best."

When he'd hung up he told the rest of the team the news.

"That's terrific," Sam said, and she meant it.

Luke looked at Josh. "Any news on Callum?"

"I spoke to him this morning, guv," Josh said. "They

kept him in overnight as a precaution but he'll be going home today. I'm going to pop in on him this evening and take him two pieces of lemon drizzle cake."

"Why two pieces?" Helen asked.

Josh raised an eyebrow and smiled. "Because sharing is caring, Helen," he said. "Sharing is caring."

Thanks for reading Fog of Silence. I would really appreciate it if you could leave a review on Goodreads and Amazon.

Want to read more about Luke Sackville and what shaped his career choices? 'Change of Direction', the prequel to the series, can be downloaded as an ebook or audiobook free of charge by subscribing to my newsletter at:

sjrichardsauthor.com

Acknowledgements

Thanks as always to my wife Penny for her continuing support and encouragement. Her feedback after my first draft was incredibly useful.

After editing for Penny's comments, I had tremendous input from my beta readers: Denise Goodhand, Sarah Mackenzie, Irene Paterson and Marcie Whitecotton-Carroll.

Thanks also to the advance copy readers, who put faith in the book being worth reading.

Samuel James has done another fantastic job narrating the audiobook and Olly Bennett came up trumps again with the cover design and incorporated a suitably spooky image of GNE's Head Office.

Last but not least, thanks to you the reader. I love your feedback and reading your reviews, and I'm always delighted to hear from you so please feel free to get in touch.

THE CORRUPTION CODE

Ex-DCI Luke Sackville investigates nefarious activities at Wessex Police at the request of the Chief Constable. He and his Ethics Team put their own lives at risk as they seek to unveil the guilty.

Luke is horrified when he discovers that a long-established secret society is behind the corruption and is planning a series of attacks on the public. He finds himself in a race against time to identify and capture the guilty before innocent people are murdered on an unprecedented scale.

The Corruption Code is the fourth nail-biting book in the Luke Sackville Crime Series.

Released May 2024 - Order your copy now

www.amazon.co.uk/gp/product/B0CQG2ST7B

ABOUT THE AUTHOR

My name's Steve. I've never been called 'SJ', but there's another Steve Richards who's a political writer hence the pen name.

I was born in Bath and have lived at various times on an irregular clockwise circle around England. After university in Manchester, my wife and I settled in Macclesfield before moving to Bedfordshire then a few years ago back to Somerset. We now live in Croscombe, a lovely village just outside Wells, with our 2 sprightly cocker spaniels.

I've always loved writing but have only really had the time to indulge myself since taking early retirement. My daughter is a brilliant author (I'm not biased of course) which is both an inspiration and - because she's so good - a challenge. After a few experiments, and a couple of completed but unsatisfactory and never published novels, I decided to write a crime fiction series as it's one of the genres I most enjoy.

You can find out more about me and my books at my website:
sjrichardsauthor.com